Breezy in Bandera

Book One: Love in the Texas Hill Country

C. S. Wilkins

The characters and events portrayed in this book are fictitious. Any similarity to real persons, living or dead, is coincidental and not intended by the author.

ISBN-13: 9798550482056
ISBN-10: 1477123456

Cover design by: Art Painter
Library of Congress Control Number: 2018675309
Printed in the United States of America

Dedication

Writing has been a daily part of my life since grade school. Dozens and dozens of notebooks and journals with half-finished stories fill the bookcases in my office. While the desire to create has been strong, so many of my great friends and family have encouraged and pushed me across the finish line to complete this one. The greatest gift has been surrounded by those who have believed in me far more than I have believed in myself. I am so grateful.

Contents

Chapter 1

Early February was schizophrenic in South Texas.

As winters went, January was particularly balmy, but an Arctic blast blew in a hard freeze for several days. There had even been ice on the bridges and overpasses, which brought a halt to all traffic.

However, all that had been the prior week.

The last few days brought an abundance of sunshine and warm winds with a high of 75 degrees.

Bree was anxious as she headed south on I-35 from Austin.

She had a court appearance in San Antonio, which she anticipated would be brief. That was enough to give her butterflies, but by noon, she was to be in a small-town northwest of San Antonio, at the place she hoped would be her new home.

He checked his watch, Jed was late, which was not a surprise. His little brother was an optimist, forever convinced he had plenty of time to get everything done. Between overpromising and being naturally distractible, lacking punctuality was the essence of who he was.

Essence or no, he thought, it was a lousy way to run a business.

Zeke parked his truck across the street from the gas station where they were to meet a new client. It was unusually warm for winter, but he was well accustomed to the fickle South Texas weather. His windows rolled down to catch the breeze, he glanced to his left as he heard a truck approach. Instead of

Jed's three-quarter ton pickup, it was a sleek, black SUV with tinted windows.

It pulled up to a pump directly across from him. The door opened to reveal a pair of shapely calves, slim ankles, and black heels.

Reflexively, his left eyebrow raised in appreciation. The legs were quickly followed by the rest of her. A grin tugged at the corners of his mouth as he watched her ignore the running boards and slide gracefully onto the concrete.

She was prepared with card in hand, as she slid it into and out of the slot before opening her tank and fueling. Her dark hair was pulled into a loose bun, high on the back of her head. Shades covered her eyes. Her top was deep *aubergine* and tucked into a slim black skirt, which skimmed the top of her knees.

As her tank filled, she returned to the driver's side to secure her card and pulled out what appeared to be a well-worn, leather backpack in dark, rich brown.

When the pump stopped, she returned the handle and headed toward the store.

While slim and attractive, he dismissed her, his preference was a woman in jeans with her hair long, loose, and casual.

He checked his phone, itching to call or text his errant baby brother.

Motion ahead of him drew his gaze back toward the store, as a woman exited.

Long, dark, and wavy hair hung well past her shoulders. She wore a loose, long-sleeved shirt over a black form fitting top, jeans, and heeled boots. Had she not been carrying the leather backpack in her left hand; he would not have immediately recognized her as the lady in the SUV.

Content to drinking in the sight of her, he failed to notice his brother had arrived, until he pulled in opposite him, their windows within two feet of one another.

Turning his head, Zeke acknowledged him with a slight nod.

"Morning, Zee!" Jed looked behind him to follow his

brother's gaze. "Looks like our prospective client has arrived."

Dropping his attention away from the woman now ensconced in her vehicle, Zeke knotted his brows. "Her?"

"Yep," Jed put his truck in reverse. "Why don't you head over to the warehouse and open things up? I'll get her to follow me."

∞∞∞

Bree had no difficulty navigating the streets of the tiny town. Her research had yielded a bit of information, but not much. She knew there used to be a mill. The building she had recently acquired was once a warehouse and something of a mercantile, built in the late 1800s. The township was currently home to about twelve hundred people with a handful of businesses remaining.

In addition to the gas station, there was a diner and a Mexican restaurant, which had been described as little more than a hole-in-the-wall taco stand, but she knew those were often the best places. There was a hardware store and small market. Situated between Bandera and Helotes, major purchases were typically made in San Antonio, about 45 miles away.

She was aware the location was considered remote, but she was surprised to find how rural the actual town looked. As she parked alongside Jed's truck, only the street running in front of the building had been paved.

There were three other buildings, obviously abandoned, along that front street, three on one side with one across from them.

They were parked on a side street. Behind the building and to her left was a row of bungalow-type houses, perhaps, six or eight, but scarcely half of those revealed any evidence of habitation.

Her heart sank a little, although she was unsure what she had been expecting. Her only other exposure to the area had been a quick drive down when she realized her ex had listed it as community property. Upon arrival, it had been dark, and she had not known exactly which building it was, but on that full moonlit night, the front of the buildings manifested a charming, even welcoming façade.

In the harsh noon light, it was obviously far more decrepit than charming or inviting.

The lot was overgrown. The structures appeared to be sadly neglected, probably for decades. However, there were several mature trees along the sides and back of the buildings.

As she studied them, Jed approached and identified a few of them.

"The one closest to you is a live oak. The two at the back are pecan."

She liked the way he pronounced pecan. It was not pee-can, as she was familiar with from the Midwest, but a softer and far gentler *puh-kaan*.

She nodded; a smile covered her apprehension. Mimicking him, she said "I love pecans."

"At the far end is an elm and a few more oaks."

Redirecting her attention, she turned toward him, her gaze fixed on the much taller and broader man who stood several feet behind him. The dirty blond hair was not as curly, long, or unruly as Jed's.

Her fingers tingled and itched to run through the other man's hair, but she stopped short in her ruminations when she met the cool blue of his eyes. She squashed a shiver as she stared at them.

They were the same shade as Jed's, but their frosty glare let her know he was not impressed with her in the least.

The pang of disappointment was all too familiar. She attempted to dismiss it by focusing on the friendly Jed.

"I appreciate you meeting me here on such short notice. Thank you."

Jed grinned. "Our pleasure, ma'am."

"As I know you have an appointment this afternoon, shall we begin?"

He brought his hands together, as though he had just been reminded of something important. "Yes," he agreed, "Let's get started."

Turning around, he saw his brother. "Let me introduce you to the brains behind this operation, my oldest brother Zeke."

She stepped past Jed and extended a firm hand to Zeke. She did not bother to share a smile; certain it would not be returned.

She did; however, offer him a clipped "Bree" and nod.

He shook her hand firmly, but refrained from crushing it, as she had half-expected.

He remained without expression but gifted her a slight movement of his head.

His firm and warm hand sent heat shooting through her arm and left her fingers tingling. She quietly hoped her hand was ice cold.

In overdrive, her defenses were intent on erecting walls not even this behemoth of a man could scale.

Jed reached for a clipboard from the dash of his truck.

She stepped over and grabbed her pack, as well as a bundle of rolled paper from the passenger seat of her ride.

Jed motioned she should follow Zeke to the front of the building.

Double wooden doors, fourteen to fifteen feet tall and wide enough to drive a truck through with room to spare, greeted them, but only one was cracked a few inches open. When she was close enough to inspect, she marveled at the heavy iron hinges, which bore the weight of the doors. The thick pins were almost three-quarters of an inch in diameter and eight inches long. There were three sets of them on each door. She found it odd the hinges were on the outside, but she surmised the doors must swing out, rather than in.

Zeke waited for her to finish her inspection and step aside before he opened one door wide enough for them to enter.

Bree was surprised to find the doors themselves were at least three inches thick. Although they were bleached by the sun and years on the outside, she wondered if they could or should be refinished. She reached out to rest a hand on the inside of the one he had just opened. She liked the feel of it, solid, warm, and beautiful.

"Old world hard wood with plenty of life left in them," came the low and deep voice behind her. She was struck with the force and timbre of his voice, even though she was well aware he had whispered. The words were spoken slowly with clear enunciation and articulation. Unlike Jed, there was no drawl or accent. While uniquely American, there was no hint of anything which would place him geographically.

Despite her ramped defenses, she warmed to his gently positive words and graced him with a smile that reached all the way to her eyes.

As soon as she did, she noticed his jaw tightened and a muscle above his jaw twitch.

Her smile vanished and she tried to brush off the rejection, looking to the left of him as she took in the room before her.

Zeke watched as her eyes widened and she raised a hand to cover her mouth.

He knew the thick exterior stone walls were impressive. While more guarded in expression, he was sure his first impression was probably much like what she was experiencing.

She stepped over to one of the side windows and ran her fingers over the edge of the stones. They were well over a foot thick and created a lovely ledge on which to perch to look out.

Without changing the focus of her gaze, she asked: "How much insulation do stone walls provide?"

"It depends on how thick they are. Due to stone's density, heat will seep through a wall very slowly. With these walls, by the time the sun sets, heat is just starting to reach the cool interior. That is good for the hot summer months..."

She finished Zeke's sentence for him, "but not good for the colder months."

"Correct."

Shifting her attention from the minute to that of the whole

room, she realized it was only a front room, probably the store front. It was the width of the building, which she understood was at least fifty feet, but it was not more than thirty feet deep. While an exceptionally large room in residential terms, it felt even larger, almost cavernous, as the ceiling was twenty feet tall. The rear wall was mostly brick, but someone had installed a set of large metal doors, much like what one would expect to find on the back of semi-truck trailer with accompanying hardware to open them and keep them closed. They were painted matte black. The juxtaposition between the old bricks and stone of the rest of the front and these doors brought a smile to her face.

She stepped over to them and ran an appreciative hand over the lever that had to be lifted and pushed to one side to open. "These are brilliant!"

Jed appeared and operated the mechanism to open the doors for her. "You know," he explained, "we worked with the previous owner to design and renovate this place."

She nodded.

"These were actually Zeke's idea. While off-site, he was able to remotely draft the design, along with utilities, HVAC, etc."

She held up the rolled papers in her hand and ignoring his presence, she referred to him in the third person, "I have a copy of the plans; he did a good job."

There was no electricity in the building.

Once Jed opened the metal doors the space behind the storefront faded into darkness. She stuck her head in the opening, unsure what to expect. It smelled dusty and stale, but she detected no hint of mildew or mold.

Stepping through, her eyes slowly adjusted from the bright room she left behind to the dimmer space before her. There were windows, as she could see light coming through in slits, but they appeared to have been boarded.

"We did a lot of renovations to this place. In fact, we were not that far from being finished when the previous owner pulled the plug. To preserve the improvements and keep pry-ing eyes out, we boarded up the place before we locked up." Jed explained. "Once those boards come down, this place will be lit up, almost as bright as the front."

She heard his every word, but only nodded absently.

The space before her was L-shaped. To her right was a set of wide, open stairs leading to what she knew from the plans was a mezzanine level, not quite a true second story, but there was space for two offices and a restroom. One of the office spaces looked down onto the area in which she was presently standing, the other office was actually above her with a view into the warehouse portion of the building or the short part of the L, assuming she was standing at the junction where the two parts met. The long part of the L extended to her right.

A wall separated her from the warehouse portion. According to the plans, she knew a large utility room was beyond the door in front of and to the left of her. Beyond the utility room was a second door, which opened into the warehouse. At the far end of the warehouse were large doors to the back of the property. They had actually parked along that side of the building.

Walking over to the right, she was delighted at the expanse of the space. It was completely open, but for a kitchen area fifteen feet from the stairs and set towards the back third of this part of the building. The back wall of the kitchen was directly under the mezzanine level, but the island in front of it was open twenty-five feet to the ceiling.

"Does the roof back here have a different height than it does for the storefront?"

This time, it was Zeke who responded, his low voice traveled smoothly from the open metal doors to her, eighteen feet away. "This space appears to have been the original building and was a textile mill. The store front was added later. The warehouse was the last to have been erected. But to answer your question, there are different rooflines."

"That sounds like plenty of opportunities for leaks."

"You're not kidding." Jed interjected, "This place was a mess when we first got here."

She turned to him, inhaling deeply. "I do not detect any mildew or mold in the air."

"No, ma'am," he assured her, "that was the first order of business. Well, that and taking out all the ruined lath and plaster, rotted wood, and such."

She walked over to the back wall. She noted a heavy door leading to the back a few feet from the common wall with the warehouse, which she actually thought of a massive garage. Unlike the storefront, the walls here were brick. There were three large windows covering most of the back wall. Beginning at about knee height, they extended up eight or ten feet. Each was easily twelve to fifteen feet wide. She knew once the boards were removed, light would flood this space.

Turning around to face the brothers, her eyes narrowed on Jed. "You said this place was nearly finished when the plug was pulled. How many weeks until it is habitable?"

Jed immediately turned to Zeke.

"We were three weeks from completion when work was halted." Zeke supplied. "However, at that time, all subcontractors were lined out and secured."

Bree squared to face him across the space. Looking at her watch, she directed her words to Jed, without otherwise acknowledging him: "Don't you have an appointment?"

Jed jumped. "Oh, gosh. Yes! Thanks for the reminder."

He clapped Zeke's shoulder as he hustled by. "You got this. Thanks."

She sensed Zeke's irritation and found herself explaining on Jed's behalf. "When I made this appointment, his wife made me promise he would not be late for their ultrasound appointment with the obstetrician."

His expression remained unmoved, but Zeke appreciated the information. He knew his sister-in-law was having issues and her pregnancy was considered high-risk.

"With a few modifications to the original plans, how soon would you anticipate I could move in?"

"What kind of modifications?"

She unfurled the papers in her hand and proffered several pages to him.

In the dim light, he glanced at them. Unlike the computer-generated ones he had produced, these were hand drawn, but appeared to be to scale. She had obviously traced the exterior walls, windows, and doors from his plans. She used green to denote the creation of new walls, red for electrical outlets, and blue for water supply.

She watched him as he studied the plans. She had expected annoyance, but he had an amused twist to his lips, as his eyes scanned her changes. She was surprised when he lifted his head to glance at her and offer his assessment: "Nice."

She looked to the mezzanine and voiced the changes: "Office to the left converted to a bedroom. The restroom outfitted for a full bath with separate shower and tub. I believe there are already two sinks…"

He watched her look around the space. Deep in thought, she chewed on the inside of her cheek and bottom lip.

"I believe there is a full bath under the stairs."

"There is, but shower only."

"Okay, good." She nodded, still deep in thought. "Is there room for a double sink in the utility room?"

"There is plenty of counter space in there. It is plumbed for a sink, as well as a washer and dryer."

"Stackable?"

"I believe so."

She stepped over to the kitchen wall. There were no appliances, cabinets, or other finishes.

"No plumbing fixtures upstairs or down?"

"No."

"Heating and air?"

"Central on both. The ductwork and vents are installed, but no units."

"Different units for each zone: front room, upstairs, downstairs, garage?"

"No vents or units for garage, as you call it. Due to the area in here, there are two units to work in tandem with two temperature-controlled zones, one up and one down. The storefront will have to have its own unit, as well."

"In addition to the fixtures and cabinets," she bent to run her hand over the wood floors, "other than the floors, what needs to be done?"

"Cabinets, as you mentioned, light fixtures, plumbing fixtures, the floors upstairs and down, the stairs need risers and treads replaced, appliances, heating and cooling units, and if you decide to finish out the walls, then insulation, drywall, floating, taping, and mudding, then painting. Depending on the sub-contractors, you are looking at 2 to 3 months."

"The difference from being three weeks out is having every one under contract and lined up, supplies already on hand or ordered, same with appliances, etc."

He nodded.

"Have you agreed to take the job?"

"It's Jed's company, he has the final word."

She had a hundred more questions. While she knew Zeke would be able to answer them, she did not want to continue pulling teeth to get them. She had no idea why he was completely indifferent to her, but she consoled herself, at least he was not hostile. Plus, he seemed entirely competent. Despite his demeanor, she trusted he would do a good job for her. That is, if they agreed to do it.

Stepping over to the back door, she fumbled with the dead bolt to no avail, the door would not give.

Without a word, she felt Zeke behind her. Without touching her, he reached up and slid a bolt down and did the same at the bottom of the door.

Her hand remained on the doorknob. Covering her hand with his own, he turned the knob, the door opened freely, and he released her.

Trembling, she moved to step outside, but tripped over the threshold.

She would have planted her face in the gravel, had he not reached out and grabbed her by the waist from behind and lifted her quickly to him, her back pinned to the hard muscles of his stomach, his hand splayed just below her chest.

She leaned against him and caught her breath.

Once steady, he released her and stepped back. She turned slightly toward him and saw he had bent over to retrieve the rolled plans she had dropped, along with her backpack. He offered both to her.

Head bowed and shaken, she reached for them and whispered, "Thank you."

Silently, he watched as she walked down the side of the garage, as she had called it, turned left, and disappeared behind it. Moments later, he heard the engine of her SUV start and the crunch of the tires on the gravel, as she put it reverse before driving away.

∞∞∞

Still trembling ten minutes later, Bree realized she had no idea where she was or in what direction she should be traveling.

Checking the compass on her review mirror, she realized she was headed west instead of east. Slowing, she pulled onto the shoulder and came to a stop. Retrieving her phone from her pack, she looked at her location and saw if she turned around, a few miles in the other direction, she would drive right by Lupita's, the restaurant she had read about online.

She had not eaten since before dawn. It was almost three in the afternoon. She hoped the place would still be open, as she turned around.

Chapter 2

It was late afternoon a day later before Jed returned her call. "This is Bree," she answered.

"Hello, Bree, this is Jed."

"Thank you for returning my call."

"Of course. I understand you and your husband wish to complete the warehouse."

"Ex-husband." She corrected.

"Excuse me?" Jed was confused.

She had no desire to share how she gained the property, but she found herself explaining anyway. "My ex-husband acquired this place to settle a debt over legal fees. I got it from him in the divorce. I am the sole owner now."

Jed was unfazed. "Okay. That works. Well, as I told him last year, we did a lot of work on this property and nearly had it finished. The other guy, the one your husband got it from, poured so much money into this. We, me, and some of the subs, you know, weren't sure if he would ever be able to get his money out of it, if he sold it. The market being what it is and all. But that guy had big plans. He thought once this building was up and running, it would attract other businesses to do the same."

Bree was not interested in the prior owner, she just wanted to redirect Jed to doing the job and telling her when she could expect to move in, but he persisted.

"You know, the unofficial word was that the previous owner was laundering money and using this place, among others, as a front."

Chuckling, she decided she really liked Jed despite his lack of filter and absence of impulse control. "I think the Feds sent him to the pen, so you may well be correct."

"Really?" he made no attempt to hide his surprise, and she was spurred to tease him a little.

"If I were you, I would tread lightly and share nothing with those sources of yours, especially if someone decides you know too much."

She thought she heard him gulp and had no doubt the color drained from his face. She was almost ashamed of herself; however, he must have had her on the speaker because the deep throated laugh certainly came from Zeke.

His low voice resonated clearly over the phone, "She's pulling your leg, little bro."

"My apologies, Jed, I could not resist." She explained, "all I know for certain is that the man from whom my ex-husband acquired the property was convicted of racketeering and has been sentenced to up to ten years in the federal penitentiary. I would expect with good behavior he may be out in three."

"Oh, that's fine, Bree," Jed assured her. "I do need to be more careful. There are all sorts of people out there."

"Can I rely on you to help me make this place a home, please?"

"Yes, Ma'am." He agreed. "Zeke has the contract and the change orders. He has been reaching out to subs to put a schedule together for you."

"That is wonderful!" She almost squealed. "Please let me know when to come down, and I will bring a check."

He assured her Zeke would contact her to schedule a meeting.

By the time they rang off, she was elated and could not stop smiling.

Chapter 3

Three days later, Bree was once again at Lupita's. This time; however, it was lunch time, and the tiny restaurant was bustling. A brief survey from the doorway revealed the five booths running down the middle of establishment were full, as were those lining the wall on either side. There were a handful of small tables scattered to one side in the back, but those were occupied as well. Gesturing toward the larger picnic tables in the front, she followed the hostess to one. As soon as she sat down, two water glasses and bowl of chips with salsa appeared, along with a pair of laminated menus.

While the sun was out, it was not nearly as warm as it had been when she was last there. Checking the time, she was a full half hour early for her appointment. She decided she had plenty of time to retrieve a jacket from her vehicle. Donning it, she sat down and crossed her legs, tucking her hands between her jean clad thighs to warm them, as she perused the menu. Friday featured two specials: *chili relleno*, which she knew to be a Tex-Mex version of stuffed peppers or fish tacos, grilled or fried. The former promised to be amazing; however, she knew if she had it, she would eat it and certainly require a nap, which would not be conducive to conducting any type of business. She would save that choice for another time.

Satisfied with her selection, she pulled her notebook from her backpack and scanned her notes. She had a list of things to review with the brothers Buchanan.

∞∞∞

He knew the restaurant would be crowded, as it was one of the few places available for lunch. It was also small and could only accommodate a couple dozen patrons at a time, at least inside. He spotted her SUV before he saw her sitting alone at a large table in front. Despite parking behind her vehicle, his line of vision remained unobstructed.

Her thick mane was again untethered and free to flow around her shoulders and down her back, a slight breeze teased a few ends and threatened to carry them away. She seemed chilled, despite the jacket, as her legs were tightly crossed, one hand between her thighs, the other making notes. Her face was unlined and calm, as she concentrated on the list before her.

The tension in his neck and arms returned, as did the flurry of an ache in his stomach, just as it had when he had first seen her and every time, he had thought of her since. He resented the feeling of uncertainty that she seemed to trigger in him. It reminded him of the unsettling experience of being knocked sideways; however, he knew it would pass. This job promised to be short, fortunately, and his life here was temporary.

∞∞∞

The waitress returned, just as Bree looked up and as he sat down. She smiled at him with pencil poised above her pad. "The usual, Zeke?" she asked. He nodded politely and looked toward Bree.

When the waitress glanced at her, Bree offered "Fish tacos, please."

Smiling again at the man, she promised; "They'll be right out," and disappeared back into the building.

"Any trouble finding the place?"

She mouthed a "no" and shook her head slightly.

As Jed had stated his brother would be the one to draft the contract and set up the schedule, Bree was not surprised he was the one to meet with her. What caught her off-guard was the conflict, which raged within her, at his presence.

He appeared to have cut his already tightly cropped hair. Once again, her fingers tingled and itched to run through the thickness of it.

She avoided his eyes. She knew they were trained directly on her. Instead, she allowed her mask to emerge. She held it firmly in place as her focus settled on his hands, casually placed on the table between them. His hands were much larger than hers with long fingers. His nails were neatly trimmed. She knew they were strong, as she remembered how easily he had caught and lifted her with only one of them when she tripped and most certainly would have fallen without his quick reflexes.

Realizing her mistake at looking at him, she straightened and planted both feet on the ground, dropped her pen on the table and wiped her hands on her jeans as she surveyed the parking lot just beyond them.

Like most everything else in town, the restaurant was surrounded on three sides by unkept rural land. The highway which ran in front of it, along with the vehicles and building itself, the only sign of human activity.

He was keenly aware she seemed as uncomfortable as he felt.

Were he a younger man, he would have assumed the discomfort arose from bad chemistry like the mixing of oil and water, but the years and experience had taught him otherwise. He knew it was raw attraction that simmered between them.

Another time, and, perhaps, a different place, he would have been inclined to accept the challenge and explore that chemistry, but at the moment, he viewed it as a distraction and unnecessary complication in his life.

He also knew he could ease the tension between them with a smile and a bit of charm, after all, both came naturally to him, but he was concerned dropping the chill between them would make him more susceptible to mischief.

"I understand you have a contract for me."

Distracted by his own thoughts, he had missed her transformation. Her soft brown eyes had become piercing and direct. She sat board straight in her chair, her shoulders turned square to him. Her chin had a defiant lift to it. Her full lips were pursed into a tight line. He knew she wore her attorney hat and was fully prepared to take him on. He smiled with satisfaction.

Extracting papers from the portfolio in front of him, he laid them in front of her in three neat stacks.

Tapping the one to her far left, he identified them: "This is the contract, including Terms and Conditions."

Moving to the right, he tapped the middle stack: "This is the schedule."

His finger rested on the third pile: "These are the essential items we will need you to select to complete the project. I have identified vendors with whom we do business and who will give you discounts if you use them. These include plumbing and light fixtures, appliances, and finishes. Be aware, the schedule depends on making these selections in a timely manner to ensure availability, delivery, and installation."

"I understand."

"Also," he continued, "as most of these places are wholesale, either Jed or I will have to accompany you when you make your selections."

In response, she raised a skeptical eyebrow. Instinctively, she chafed at the thought of an unnecessary minder.

"Experience has taught us that our measurements are the most reliable. If one of us is with you, we can ensure what you select will work when it comes to installation."

Ignoring him, she pulled the contract to her, picked up her pen, and opened her notebook to a fresh page. As she read it line by line, she occasionally jotted a note.

She was only half-way through the document when their meals appeared.

Bree looked up momentarily to offer a smile to their server and indicate where she wanted her plate. Its placement clearly relayed her intent to continue with the document before indulging.

While content to study her uninterrupted, Zeke slowly consumed his lunch, only vaguely aware of what he was eating.

He was completely done with his plate removed by the time she turned to the final page of the document.

To his surprise, once she checked the few notes she had made, re-read the portions she had noted, she signed the contract, turned it around, and placed it before him. Reaching into her bag, she produced an envelope, which she opened slightly to reveal a cashier's check made payable to Buchanan Construction.

They both knew a simple check would have sufficed, but he suspected she went the extra mile to ensure there would be no lag time in the availability of funds. She was obviously motivated to move things along as quickly as possible.

She slid the middle stack to her and used the tip of her pen to go through that document line-by-line. This time, she produced a planner and wrote down the schedule on the double page monthly calendar contained therein.

Only after she had likewise perused the third stack did she reach over, pick up one of the two tacos on her plate, and take a bite; however, she continued to ignore him.

He watched her face as she chewed, her eyes trained on nothing in the distance, but on the dates and images circling her mind. He suspected she was calculating how to alter her work schedule to meet the selection demands he had outlined for her. She consumed her food as absently, as he had; however, she made no move to touch the second taco.

Instead, she picked up her phone and began searching the suppliers he had provided. In the margin, next to each name and address, she carefully added their business and showroom hours. Those proprietors with truncated or special showroom hours were graced with a red checkmark.

By the time she had completed the list, the lunch crowd had mostly cleared, and she finally acknowledged his existence again.

"According to this, most of these selections must be made within the next ten days."

He agreed, "To ensure the warehouse is move-in ready within six weeks, yes."

"I assume you and I will be attached at the hip until everything has been selected, ordered, and paid for?"

He pushed the mental image her choice of words conjured aside and answered: "Jed is covered up at the moment."

"And there is no one else?"

"I am it."

"Of course, you are."

Her words had been clipped and authoritative, to which he had responded in kind; however, he had initially taken her last comment as a bit salty, until she graced him with a slow, radiant smile that warmed him from the inside out.

Despite the alarms ringing in his head alerting him to danger, he found himself returning a smile every bit as warm and delightful as hers.

Bree was unsure of what had just transpired, but the chill, which had taken hold since she had first arrived, had lifted, replaced with a sunny sense of excitement.

Looking at her calendar, in six weeks, she thought, she would finally have a new life and a place of her own.

Her reverie was interrupted by Zeke's low warning: "Whatever you do, do not move."

Her eyes darted to his inscrutable face.

Images of hairy, plate-sized spiders danced in her head.

"Dear God, if it's a tarantula, just shoot me now." She whispered, closing her eyes tightly.

"Not a spider, but it's black and just inches from your left elbow."

She involuntarily shuddered, but otherwise refused to move.

He smiled at her stricken face.

"Open your eyes and move very slowly. I think he wants to be friends."

Confused, she did as he instructed. When she turned, on the cinderblock half wall, less than a foot behind her chair was a small black dog, thin, matted, and watching her in fear and hunger.

"OH," she breathed. Regaining her composure, she smiled and comforted him with her voice, "Well, hello, handsome. Aren't you a cutie? Would you like something to eat?"

She noted his tail twitched slightly and he almost pranced with his feet, but he remained ready to bolt any second.

"Okay," she cooed. "I know you are scared." She reached back toward her plate for the remaining taco. Pulling some of the grilled fish from it, she gently offered it.

The dog tried to keep his eyes on her, but the smell of food overcame him, and his focus shifted to what she offered.

Bree continued to quietly soothe him with her voice as she inched the offering closer to him. She watched his tongue flick up toward his nose. He shifted his weight between his front paws, as though he were dancing.

Zeke was concerned the animal may bite her, but she concentrated on willing him to eat.

"You're a good boy," she whispered. "It's okay, love, take it. It's good."

Glancing at her eyes once more, the little dog leaned forward and gingerly removed the food from her fingertips and scarfed it down.

"Good boy," Bree cheered and quickly supplied him another piece.

By the third serving, she was able to move close enough to offer a handful to him. Despite his fear, he placed one paw on her hand, as he gently ate everything she offered. Once he had consumed all the fish she had, she broke off a piece of the soft tortilla of the taco and offered it as well.

He ate that, too.

Scanning her plate for something else, she dipped the edge of another piece of tortilla into her beans and gave that to the dog.

She was surprised he allowed her to touch him as he ate.

With the next piece she offered him, she moved even closer. As he ate out of one of her hands, she reached over and picked him up with the other.

He was momentarily startled, but when she placed him in her lap and offered him more tortilla and beans, he wagged his tail as he ate.

She kept one hand on him as she looked up at Zeke. "He's so skinny."

"He's a stray."

Intent on watching the dog, they did not notice their server had returned. "Oh, that dog!" She exclaimed.

Both the dog and Bree flinched at her words. Holding him with both hands, she noted he was shaking. Anger rose within her, but she checked it before she spoke "Does he have an owner?"

"No, someone dumped several of them out here a few weeks ago. He's the only one left."

"Someone picked up the others?"

The waitress looked at her incredulously. "I don't think so. They probably starved to death or something ate them, I don't know."

Noting Bree's eyes had narrowed to daggers, Zeke diffused the tension by offering cash to settle the bill. "Keep the change. Thanks."

Turning to Bree, his voice softened. "I guess he's yours now."

Bree's eyes were wide and bright as she looked at him, a slow smile creeping across her face. "I have never had a pet," she confessed.

"Well, the best pets are the ones who choose you."

She beamed.

"Will you hold him for a quick second, please?"

He reached for the dog, and she promptly removed her jacket and the long-sleeved flannel overshirt she wore, leaving her with a form fitting, long-sleeved black tee, which accentuated her curves. She put the jacket back on, folded the flannel and carefully wrapped the dog in it and tucked him under one arm. “He’s freezing.”

“He’s probably more scared than anything else.”

“Is there a vet nearby?”

Zeke considered the question momentarily. “Yes, there is. Let me see if he is available. He is a large animal vet, which means he typically goes to where the patients are.”

He picked up his phone and made a call.

“You are in luck. His office is at his house, about ten minutes away. You will have to follow me.”

She nodded, as he gathered the documents and collected her bag. He scanned the table to ensure they had not left anything behind, then helped her to her vehicle, dog in her lap, before getting into his truck.

∞∞∞

True to his word, within ten minutes of mostly dirt roads, they pulled up to a farmhouse surrounded by nothing but pasture and a few trees. An older gentleman, probably in his early seventies, was sitting in a rocker on the front porch when they arrived.

Zeke was opening her door the moment she put the vehicle in park and killed the engine. Reaching in, he retrieved the dog with one hand, while offering the other. As soon as she had two feet on the ground, he passed the flannel clad bundle back to her. He followed her to the porch, where the man extended a hand and offered her a smile, as he introduced himself. “David Kelty, how do you do?”

“Bree Lancaster, so nice to meet you.”

“Zeke.”

“Mr. David.”

Looking down at her charge, the vet asked: “Who do we have here?”

“I just collected him at Lupita’s. I am afraid he is in sad

shape."

"People are forever dumping dogs and cats there. It is a shame. Come on in."

He opened the screen door and ushered them in. "My office is to the left, straight down that hall, last door on the right."

With Zeke on her heels, Bree led the way. She paused at the door and felt Zeke reach around her to open it.

They stepped into a brightly lit exam room in what she presumed was once a garage. There were high windows along one wall, which filled the space with sunlight. Cabinets lined two walls and were topped in stainless, as was a small island.

"Here, hon," Dr. Kelty patted the shiny surface of the island, "Let's see what you have."

She carefully put the dog down, and they unwrapped him. He trembled violently, his eyes pleading and fixed on Bree, who continued to pet him as the vet ran his hands over him.

"He's a young one." He checked his teeth. "He still has a few of his baby teeth. He is probably not quite four months old yet. Let me weigh him."

Taking the dog, he stepped over to the counter and placed him on what resembled to Bree as a baby scale, one with cupped edges to prevent an infant from sliding off.

"Six pounds, three ounces, mostly skin and bones." He announced.

Eyeing Bree, he asked: "Are you keeping him?"

"Yes, please."

"Okay, we need to worm him, start his vaccinations, and dip him for fleas. He's covered."

She nodded.

"I am semi-retired and no longer hire techs. You get a discount, if you help me, young lady."

She grinned at him. "Of course."

"Zeke," he chatted, as he filled vials and administered shots, "How are the folks?"

"They are fine, Sir. They returned from Montana in September, but my middle brother is on mission in Africa. They left two weeks ago to offer assistance there."

He looked at Bree, "Fine people, those Buchanans."

She cast a sideways glance at Zeke, reassessing him. She was not surprised to learn he had parents or two brothers or that his family was well regarded in the area.

Likewise, she dominated Zeke's attention. He watched her calm and soothe her new charge and amiably chat with the vet. She seemed completely at ease, no hint of a mask in view.

By the time they moved to the sink at the counter, she ran the water until it was warm before placing the dog in it. She had been instructed to wash him in the medicated shampoo before they applied the dip.

To his credit the young dog did not whimper, whine, or struggle in any way.

His long, stringy fur was badly matted, and the vet handed her a pair of scissors.

Zeke moved next to her and held the dog still, while she cut off the worst parts.

"He's coal black." Zeke observed.

"Except for this small white area on his chin and spot on his chest." She laughed. "He looks like he has a soul patch while wearing a tuxedo."

Dr. Kelty returned with a clip board and pen. "Does he have a name?"

She looked at Zeke who shrugged.

She scrubbed the little dog, his eyes big and gentle brown, as she mulled a name. Zeke's use of the word coal stuck out in her mind. "CoalBear," she said and spelled it "C-O-A-L-B-E-A-R."

"Colby," Zeke teased.

She rewarded him with an elbow to the ribs. "Don't confuse him."

He chuckled.

Once they rinsed the shampoo from him, David applied the flea dip with instructions to keep him still for 15 minutes and not to rinse. In the event of ear mites, he lightly sponged the inside of CoalBear's ears.

The dip had a potent smell and Bree's eyes watered.

"You okay?" Zeke asked.

She nodded.

"Wash your hands and step away, I have him."

She looked up at him, unsure who he was. She searched his face for the man with the frosty glare and stern disposition. She could not find him. In his stead was a kind face with gentle mischief in his eyes and an easy, relaxed smile on his lips.

A timer dinged and David reappeared with an old towel, as well as her flannel shirt secured in a sealed plastic bag. "Your shirt probably had fleas on it. I doused it with a bit of the dip. Leave it in here until you can wash it in hot water." He looked her up and down. "I would recommend you add the clothes you are wearing, too. Wash them together, sooner rather than later."

She resisted the sudden urge to scratch, knowing it was probably prompted by the power of suggestion rather than fleas.

Together, they toweled CoalBear dry.

Once the pup was out of the sink and standing in the towel on the exam table island, the veterinarian handed him a treat and scratched his ears gently. "He's probably a mutt, but with his size, coloring, and the shape of his tail...see how it curves over his back, he may have some Havanese in him."

"Is that good or bad?"

David chuckled, "It depends. He is obviously intelligent; you can see it in his eyes. As you mentioned, he sought you out; that is almost unheard of in strays. He must have noticed something about you, or hunger gave him courage. Either way, I bet he will entertain and challenge you for years to come."

She smiled at the dog and picked him up in her arms.

"He will need additional shots in a few weeks." He handed her his vaccination record.

"Oh," Bree looked for her bag, realizing she had left it in her truck, "I need to pay you."

Zeke pulled his wallet and settled up with the vet.

As soon as they were outside, she told him she would pay him back. He shook his head no.

When she began to argue, he cut her off, “My gift to you, a peace offering, if you will.”

“Were we at war?” was her solemn inquiry.

“Let us just say ‘To new beginnings.’”

Hugging the dog to her chest, she met and held his gaze. “Thank you.”

He smiled.

“Where to?”

“Austin for me; however, if you will let me know when you are available, I would like to knock out that list of vendors, if you do not mind.”

“When are you free?”

“I am at your disposal.”

“Okay, I will text you my number and email. If you could email me, I will send you my schedule for the next week and we will make it happen.”

“Thank you, again.”

“Follow me to the highway, take a left and it will lead you back into town. Do you know your way from there?”

“GPS can take it from there. These dirt roads do not show up.”

He reached over and rubbed CoalBear’s ear.

“Dogs are good luck.”

“He better be,” she chuckled, “I have been staying in my boss’s guest house. I am not sure pets are allowed.”

“Did he specifically tell you no dogs?”

“Are you a lawyer in your spare time?”

“No, ma’am.”

“You certainly sound like one.”

“Ouch.”

“Hey!”

Sobering for a moment, he put a hand on her shoulder with a gentle squeeze. “We will get you moved into your new place soon, I promise.”

Moved by the change in his disposition, she was awash in gratitude and hoped he could see it in her eyes because she did not trust herself to speak.

He released her shoulder and moved his hand to the middle of her back, urging her toward her vehicle.

She was surprised at how quickly she had adapted to having him open her door and help her into and out of her truck. It made her feel secure and looked after. She liked it.

He waited until she had buckled up and started the engine before he closed the door and walked over to his truck. Nodding at her, he put it in gear and led her to the highway.

For the two-and-a-half-hour drive back to Austin, CoalBear slept soundly in her lap and her mind drifted over all the events of the day.

Chapter 4

Bree need not have worried about how to tell Donovan about the dog. She made it back to the guest house before dark, even after a quick stop at a pet store for a host of dog related accessories. The kids ran over to greet her before she had a chance to park.

Donovan and his wife had three children, the nine-year-old Millicent and seven-year-old twins Brandon and Joshua, Brando and Josh for short. He often referred to his daughter as MIT, Management-in-Training.

CoalBear was terrified of the rambunctious twins but instantly bonded to the quiet Millie. Bree had to warn the boys not to scare the puppy with loud noises or rough play. They tried their best to remain calm around him, but it was not their nature. They quickly became bored and ran off.

Millie outfitted him in his new harness and took him for a brief walk to relieve himself, as Bree unloaded the SUV.

Within minutes, Donovan appeared.

"A Hell Hound, Bree, really?" he greeted her.

While he was not smiling, she detected a bit of humor in his tone.

"He was starving, Donovan, I didn't know what else to do." She shrugged with a hopeful smile. "Besides, he chose me, and I love him already."

Watching his daughter carefully petting the puppy in her lap, he sighed "You don't appear to be the only one smitten."

He bent down and scratched him behind the ears. CoalBear gently licked his fingers once.

Millie looked up at her father with her liquid brown eyes: "Papa, he is so sweet."

He rose and looked at Bree, "I can see where this is headed... I am going to have to deal with Management about this, I can feel it."

"I thought you were the one opposed to pets, not Evangeline."

"Exactly."

"I am sorry, Donovan," she smiled. "My place should be ready to go in six weeks."

He nodded, his gaze returned to his first born and her furry charge.

Millie was happily chatting to the dog who appeared to understand every word she said and responded by wagging his tail as he looked up at her face.

Bree could almost read his mind. She knew the shy child rarely spoke and in the few minutes she had been with the dog, she had not stopped chattering with him.

While his focus remained on the child, he spoke to Bree, "I guess things happen for a reason."

"I am told dogs are good luck."

"We shall see how this goes over the next few weeks."

Bree smiled at him. "Thank you."

When he finally faced her again, he offered a wry grin. "It's all good, Sweetheart. We have enjoyed having you here. Is there anything you need?"

She shook her head. "I am great."

Donovan checked his watch. "Supper should be ready in half an hour or so; you are welcome to join us."

"Thank you, no. I have some things to take care of, if you don't mind."

"No problem." Donovan assured her, as he took his leave. "Send her up in a few, please."

Millicent waited until her father was several yards away before she reluctantly released the dog, gained her feet, and handed the leash to Bree. "May I help you train him, please?"

Bree blinked. "Train?" She had not given a thought to it.

"Yes, my friend Sarah has a dog, Bentley. He's a goldendoodle. They take him to classes to learn how to sit, stay, down, and walk on a leash. When I go over there, I help her practice with him."

"That's an excellent idea. I know nothing about training a dog. I could use the help."

The child's smile was splendid and bright. "I will text her and ask her where they take classes and look them up online for you. I will email you what I find."

Impressed with her knowledge and resourcefulness, Bree grinned back. "Wonderful, Millie. Thank you."

Despite no one else around, she leaned in conspiratorially and whispered to Bree "If Papa sees how responsible I am and how well we can train CoalBear, maybe, just maybe, he will allow me to have a dog, too."

"I think you may be right, and I am grateful for your help."

She could not contain her excitement and spontaneously wrapped her arms around Bree's middle for a quick hug.

Bree hugged her back, grateful for the warm contact.

Millie reached down to pet CoalBear again and told him she would return soon to play with him.

Bree watched her run up the hill toward the main house before she bent down to pick up the dog and cradle him in her arms. "You, my little friend, are very special, indeed."

∞∞∞

With her clothes safely in the wash, food and water bowls set out for CoalBear, Bree showered before sitting down in front of her laptop. She zipped out a quick email to Zeke with her contact information and schedule.

True to her word, Millie had obtained the information and provided a link to a pet resort in town with puppy training and basic obedience classes. The puppy training was for dogs six months or younger and consisted of one-hour classes, once a week, for six weeks. There were spots open on Tuesday evenings from 7:00 to 8:00 pm.

Bree occasionally helped Evangeline pick up or ferry one or more of the children during the week, when there were conflicts. She did not think Millie had dance on Tuesday nights, but she would ask if she could accompany her before signing up. She sent a joint email to the child's parents before replying to Millie and thanking her for the information.

The washer beeped. As she began to move, her email dinged. Zeke had responded.

She opened it to find a brief outline of his schedule for the next week.

Comparing his schedule to hers and against the list of vendors, she surmised Wednesday and Thursday would be the best days to knock out most all of the selections. As it was Friday, that would give her the weekend and two days to square away her day-job responsibilities, as well as create some sort of design and color scheme for the warehouse.

She immediately replied to Zeke to pin him down for those days. She then crafted an email to Donovan to let him know she was taking a couple of days off, as well as give him a brief rundown on the status of her current cases.

Once those were done, she pulled out her notebook and jotted down a personal To-Do list.

She felt a pair of paws on her calf and looked down to find CoalBear looking up at her. She scooped him up and into her lap, talking to him as she made her list.

Surveying the immediate tasks, Bree knew there was a great deal of work ahead of her, but for the first time in recent memory, she felt hopeful and excited about the future.

Chapter 5

Zeke's suggestion they meet in San Antonio had been the prudent one, rather than Bree driving past the city to the warehouse, then turning around and driving back, but Bree knew they had been working on the warehouse, and she was anxious to see the space with all the boards removed from the windows. She had an idea of what colors and finishes she liked but needed to see the space in natural light to make sure they were what she wanted.

She did not expect Zeke to understand, as it sounded a bit fickle to her own ears, but he had agreed without argument or further discussion.

When her alarm buzzed at 4:30 in the morning, she doubted the wisdom of her decision, but once her feet were on the floor and she was vertical, she knew she would be okay.

CoalBear was less enthusiastic.

She had purchased the crate with the specific thought it was where he would sleep at night.

The first night, she had even put him in there with a nice plush mat. While he had not complained or whimpered when she closed the door, his soulful eyes had been her undoing.

Within five minutes, she had him out of the box and in bed with her.

She had heard of pets and children becoming Velcro, not CoalBear, though. He was more like a suction cup. As soon as she settled into bed, he attached himself to her stomach, molded himself against her, and became dead weight. He did not move an inch all night long; however, she found it comforting.

Bree had always found sleep more foe than friend, but now

when she woke at various times throughout the night, she found herself reaching down and stroking his soft fur before drifting off again.

In addition to her, the dog was attached to the bed. He was not an early riser, and he often encouraged her to lounge far longer than she ever had. Even after she rose, he was reluctant to leave the bed. She had to use two hands to lift him because he refused to stand or move on his own.

He was still small and under ten pounds, but he had been gaining weight with the regular meals. She knew he was already rotten and spoiled, as she had to carry him outside and place him on the ground to take care of business, otherwise, he would not budge until mid-mornings.

Otherwise, he was a lovely companion. He did not chew on anything but the toys and treats she provided. He had not had an accident inside. He was good about letting her know when he needed to go outside. He was so well behaved; he accompanied her most places in a leather tote she had purchased specifically to carry him.

Only after she had carried him outside in the dark and brought him back inside, did he liven up a bit. His days of hunger were not that far behind him, and he continued to be enthusiastic about food. He enjoyed his breakfast, as she showered and dressed.

They were on the road by 5. She pulled up to the warehouse and parked next to Zeke's truck before 7:30.

Fetching the tote from the back seat, she set it on the floorboard of the front passenger seat, folded the sides down, and offered it to the dog. She laughed as he jumped right in it. She had a small towel folded in the bottom of it as a cushion for him. As long as she had the bag between her body and her arm, hanging on straps from her shoulder, he was content to nap quietly. Unbeknownst to anyone around her, she had been able to take him to the office and grocery store without detection.

Millie's parents had agreed to allow her to accompany them to puppy classes. They had gone to their first one the night before.

Bree was amazed at how quickly CoalBear learned his reward marker word "Boom" and within minutes was sitting on command. Millie, of course, was better versed with all of it, but Bree and CoalBear soon caught on, as well.

She had hoped the classes would give the little dog a bit of confidence; however, he had shown no fear of the other dogs in the class and actually walked with a bit of a swagger in front of them.

There were only five dogs in the class, and the instructor had taken a few minutes with each of them to get to know them and their owners.

When Bree had expressed her concern and shared her little dog's background, the instructor laughed and told her most small dogs were unaware of their size and this one had an alpha mentality, which had surprised her, but she knew scant about dogs.

In addition to her tote with the dog, Bree grabbed her backpack and the breakfast tacos she had picked up in New Braunfels.

She found the back door open and Zeke with a measuring tape in hand making notes. He wore jeans and hiking type boots with a simple, buttoned chambray blue shirt with the cuffs of the long sleeves rolled mid-way up his muscular forearms. Bree found everything about him to be powerful and virile.

She had intended a bright greeting, but her "Good Morning!" came out breathless and quiet.

He heard her anyway, looked up, and graced her with a smile.

"I didn't expect you until 8."

"Very little traffic."

He nodded and studied her. She wore jeans and a teal-colored blouse, probably silk, buttoned up the front with sleeves rolled just past her wrists. He noted she again had a gold bangle on the left arm and simple gold hoops in her ears. Her long hair was pulled back in a loose bun. On her face was just a hint of mascara and lip gloss. He found her naturally beautiful with her high cheek bones, dark eyes, and full lips, especially when she smiled, as it reached all the way to her eyes and made them sparkle. She placed a paper bag on the counter, followed by her pack. He watched her bend down with her other bag and gently place it on the floor before holding down one edge.

He laughed when he saw CoalBear's head pop up the second before he alighted from the bag and ran over to him.

"Hey, little buddy!" Zeke scooped him up. "He's a cow! What have you been feeding him?"

Bree joined his levity. "He's not fat! He's just not quite so skin and bones as he was last time you saw him."

"He looks great!" Zeke grinned at him. "Have you been a good boy, Colby?"

CoalBear wiggled in delight, his tail beating furiously.

Zeke put him down and watched him dart around the room happily.

"It's hard to believe that's the same dog from last week."

"I can hardly believe I have not had him a week yet, but I do not know how I have managed to live this long without him."

"Uh Oh…I bet he's sleeping with you, too."

She pulled a face. "Guilty."

"I am not surprised."

"However," she defended herself, "I have been sleeping so much better with him."

She glowed with affection as she watched the dog investigate the room and make his way over to the counter where she had left the bag. He rose up on his hind legs, sniffing.

"Ah," she laughed, "I brought breakfast."

She opened the bag and offered it to him.

Zeke leaned over and took a whiff. *"Carne guisida!"*

"Gosh," she stated with amazement, "You are good!"

"*Los Gallos* is written across the top of the bag. That's their specialty."

He helped himself and she followed suit, her eyes scanning

the space around them. The sun had risen just after seven and light had begun to fill the room. With the boards removed from the windows and the lights shining brightly, she could appreciate how large the room was.

There was plenty of space for two people to work in the kitchen together. With taco in hand, she stepped behind the kitchen and found about fourteen feet to the back wall.

Zeke followed her.

"Now," she began, "the plans show a perpendicular wall coming out from the middle of the kitchen wall all the way to the back wall, right?"

"Correct."

"As there is not one now, it would obviously not be load bearing."

"That's right."

She sent him a questioning look.

"I see change order written all over your face."

"Maybe not."

She studied it for a moment longer.

"Is four feet wide enough to allow for comfortable passage?"

"As in a hallway?"

She nodded.

"Yes."

"If we were to keep the wall, but extend it only 10 feet, instead of the entire 14 feet, could we create a U-shaped pantry on the stair side and an office alcove space on the other side?"

"Standard pantry shelves are 12" deep. Interior walls are 4.5" thick. So, two walls take up 9" of the 10 feet and two sets of shelves take up another 24", which will leave you 87" or seven and a quarter feet between shelves. A pantry will work."

"What about an L-shaped desk on the other side?"

"Closed in with a door or open?"

"Open."

"You have plenty of space if you leave it open.

"Will you write that up for me, please?"

"Yes, Ma'am."

She faced him squarely. “I do understand these kinds of changes will add time and expense, I will try to keep them to a minimum.”

“I understand this is the first time you have the benefit of light to see this space properly. If you are going to make changes, now is the time to do it, not three weeks from now.”

He had finished his taco and saved the last morsel for the dog. Holding it up for her to inspect, he raised an eyebrow in askance before offering it.

She nodded and smiled before turning to finish her breakfast.

∞∞∞

Bree walked the rooms, upstairs and down. She took a few photos with her phone camera and added a few more notes. She knew their first appointment was at 9, forty-five miles away.

Zeke followed behind and turned off lights and began closing things up.

“Do we need to take two vehicles?” she asked.

“That depends,” he responded. “Were you planning to return to Austin tonight?”

“I thought I would get a room, is Bandera or Helotes closer?”

“Bandera, but I have a better idea.”

“Okay?”

“I have a guest room at my place and Wi-Fi, you are welcome to both. Our last appointment is an hour from here. We can grab a bite on our way back.”

“First, you may be sick of me by then and second, I truly hate to put you out.”

“It is no trouble at all. Plus, the accommodations in either Bandera or Helotes may be a bit rustic to your liking. Not to mention your little buddy there.”

“You are very kind, and I would like to say yes, but on one

condition."

He raised an eyebrow.

"Dinner is on me, please?"

"You drive a hard bargain."

"Speaking of driving, do you mind if I drive?"

"Not at all, I just wonder why?"

"Even though I am off today and tomorrow, my boss will probably call. I think better when I am driving."

"That's fine. If you don't mind, I will pull my truck into the garage to secure it."

"Great."

He motioned toward CoalBear. "Let him run around outside for a few minutes, and I will lock up and meet you at your ride."

∞∞∞

Twenty minutes later, Bree's phone rang over the vehicle's Bluetooth, and she answered simply: "Hello."

"Good Morning, Sweetheart."

Zeke felt a prick of irritation at the smooth voice and endearment. Out of the corner of his eye, he saw Bree smile.

"Good Morning, Donovan."

"Nightmares?"

"No, why?"

"You emailed me at 1:45 this morning."

"Oh, that, yeah. I woke up and remembered I promised you an update on the O'Malley case."

"You have until Friday to get that to me."

"I know, but I thought I would take care of it while it was on my mind."

"Do we have anything outstanding?"

"No. That was the last one. You are now up-to-date on all my files."

"Looks like you have a full platter and then some..." He paused.

She thought about arguing that she could handle it, but she could tell her boss had something in mind.

When she did not respond, he continued: "Two of these are civil trials, one set for next month and the other for the following month."

"That's right."

"I may reassign the trials; Thompson and Murdock each have light loads at the moment. I need to find work for them."

She hated relinquishing any of her cases, especially where she had developed relationships with the clients, but she said nothing.

"Also, the appellate work seems to be picking up, I would like for you to have help with that."

"Donovan," she sighed, "what's going on?"

"When was the last time you took more than a day or two off?"

"I am taking two days off now, and I was out on Friday."

"As many hours as you work a week, that is really not time off."

"What are you saying?"

"I asked George to give me a report showing your VPN access over the last month. On average, you are logged onto the server more than 65 hours a week. Two weeks ago, you were on over 70 hours."

"Do you have a problem with my work ethic or work product?"

"No need to get defensive, but if I don't look after you, who will?"

"I am perfectly capable of taking care of myself."

"Apparently not, Sweetheart. As efficient as you are, those hours tell me I have overloaded you. The last thing we need is for you to crash and burn. Trust me, I have enough things to feel guilty about without you hitting a wall."

"Donovan..."

"Nope. I am not listening."

"This is what I do. I work weird hours and I am often at my

best in the middle of the night when there are no interruptions or distractions."

"There is nothing wrong with your work, Bree. As usual, it is exemplary, but I want to assign Mitch to work with you on appeals."

"Mitch?"

"Yeah. What's wrong with Mitch?"

She hesitated, knowing it would not be unlike Donovan to have the man sitting in on the call. She elected to proceed as though he were listening.

"Mitch is a nice man with impeccable manners. I am sure he is a decent lawyer."

"But..."

"However, I get the impression he has far more confidence in his ability to schmooze than in his intellect."

"Harsh."

"For example, after we met with the Geoplastics people, he and I had a difference of opinion. As we were discussing it, he changed the subject, literally in mid-stream, and asked me if I had cut my hair."

"I am not following you."

"He was losing the argument and rather than concede defeat, he decided to try to charm his way out of the discussion."

"You do have nice hair."

"Donovan."

"Not many people win arguments with you."

"It was not the first time. When he interacts with people, he is heavy on the charm and flattery, light on the facts and law. In my opinion, that does not make anyone a particularly effective attorney, especially at the appellate level. Three-judge panels are generally not moved by charisma."

"He is bright, and I am confident once a more experienced attorney enlightens him, he will become a more effective attorney."

"What do you have in mind?"

"Take him under your wing. Have him ride shotgun on that

case you have going up to the state supreme court in a couple of months."

"I have been working on that case for over a year."

"I know, no one knows it better than you. Next week, I need you to come in. I have a new client I want you to meet. He is unhappy with his present representation and has two cases in various stages of appeal. One is in your wheelhouse."

"Commerce clause."

"Bingo."

"In order for you take it on, we need to make room on your plate."

"Why do I feel as though I have just been played?"

"Sweetheart, you get lost in the weeds. It's my responsibility to look out for you."

"Is Mitch on board?"

"I leave that to you."

"Fine."

"Your enthusiasm is underwhelming."

"I have already agreed. What more do you want?"

"In other news, my oldest is enchanted with your Hell Hound."

"Oh, Donovan," she giggled, "You should have seen them in class last night. She took over handling him and worked with the instructor on getting him to walk on a lead. She was a non-stop chatter bug all evening."

"I know, we heard ALL about it."

"I hardly recognize our shy and quiet Millicent."

"Management and I are discussing a dog for her."

"Yes! She will be over the moon."

"Hold on, it is not a done deal, yet. We are going to continue to monitor how long this continues with yours. The shine may wear off in a week or two."

"Smart money says her interest only increases."

"You and Management." He sighed. "What kind of dog do you have?"

"The vet said he was a mutt, but probably had some Havanese in him because of his size and the way his feathered tail curls and fans over his back."

"Management thinks we would be better off going to a shelter and letting her make a connection with one there, but I would prefer to control what we get and find a breeder for something like your Havanese. Otherwise, I fear she will come home with a Great Dane sized beast who drools, and the boys think they can ride."

Bree laughed at the images he provided.

"I know next to nothing about dogs, but your daughter seems to be a wealth of information. I am quite sure if you asked her, she would present you with a thoroughly researched Power Point outlining the relative merits and detriments of both scenarios. Plus, there may be a Havanese rescue group in Austin to hedge your bet."

"She is a thinker, that one, and that is an excellent suggestion."

"I do appreciate your and Evangeline allowing her to accompany us to puppy training. I know it is on a weeknight."

"You are good to the kids, and we appreciate you. As I told you the other day, things happen for a reason."

After they rang off, Bree shot a glance at Zeke. He seemed to be lost in thought and gazing beyond the side window.

"I am sorry to bore you with office stuff."

He turned and studied her profile. He was not the least bored and learned quite a bit about her. She and her boss Donovan appeared to have a close and friendly relationship. She was a workaholic and apparently exceptionally good at what she did. Donovan seemed to have pet names for most everyone. He gleaned he referred to his wife Evangeline as Management and CoalBear as the Hell Hound. Of course, his name for Bree was Sweetheart. He was particularly interested in how smoothly and adeptly Donovan was able to persuade Bree to do something she obviously did not want to do.

"He seems fond of you."

"Donovan?" She smiled. "I have known him and his wife for

a long time. Donovan and I went to law school together. When he opened his firm several years ago, I was the first one on board, after his secretary."

"He seems like a good boss."

She sighed.

"I hate to admit it, but he really is. He has a way of instinctively knowing what motivates people and getting them to do what he thinks is best for them and what he wants them to do. It is unnerving sometimes."

"You really think he played you?"

"I think he persuaded me to do exactly what he wanted me to do."

"That is a qualified answer, if I ever heard one."

She briefly glanced his way and saw he was smiling at her. If the road and traffic had not demanded her attention, she would have liked to stare into his deep blue eyes much longer.

"I am aware I work a lot. I take pride in my work and strive to do the best I can. When I know I am going to be out, I want to make sure things are taken care of so nothing blows up or becomes a crisis for someone else to handle."

Zeke completely understood her position. When he was wing commander, he felt responsible for the squadrons under his command and spent nearly every waking moment ensuring every single person under him was accounted for a taken care of. The red tape was what kept him up at night...

"It sounds like you could use a bit of help. 70 hours a week is not sustainable for anyone long term."

"It is not that bad."

"Not if it is your entire life."

When she glanced his way, he was once again staring out the side window.

Pressing a button, she instructed the virtual assistant to call George.

A deep, gravelly voice answered. "Maskas here."

"Good morning, George."

"Bree!" the voice brightened, but it was still rough. "How are you?"

"I am well. Thank you. You?"

"I owe you an apology."

"Why?"

"Donovan asked for a report of your VPN usage for the prior month. I ran it, and he came by to pick it up before I had a chance to give you a head's up."

"No worries, George."

"You work too dang much, young lady. If you keep it up, you will look up one day and be as old and grumpy as I am."

"You are not grumpy, my friend."

"Ha!" He chuckled. "Apparently, you bring out the best in me."

She beamed.

He continued, "What can I do for you?"

"Mitch will be working with me."

"Oh?"

"We will need to give him read-only access to my research files, please."

"Revolving passwords?"

"Yes, if you do not mind."

"Not at all."

"How long will that take?"

"A few minutes."

"Okay, I will call him shortly."

"Same setup as you have?"

George had been a cryptologist for the CIA for thirty years before he retired. Donovan became acquainted with him through a friend of a friend and was responsible for talking him out of retirement and into handling the firm's computer systems, most particularly cybersecurity.

"If you think that is best."

"For now, yes…"

She could hear his keystrokes over the phone.

"*Brothers Grimm* or *Lord of the Flies*?"

"How about *The Shining*?"

He chuckled again. "*Of Mice and Men*, then."

"That is a short one, you do not expect him to be around long then?"

"I just happen to have two copies of that one at the moment. I will order *The Shining* if he lasts two weeks with you."

"I am not that bad. I have no intention of running him off."

"No, my dear, but once he realizes how many light years ahead of him you are, he may remove himself."

She knew he was joking, and they shared a laugh.

"It is done."

"You are the best, Sir. Thank you!"

"Are you okay, Bree?"

"I am fine, truly."

"You work a lot of hours."

"I have nothing better to do, George."

"You should work on that."

"I got a dog."

"I actually heard that. Donovan grumbled something about it this morning."

"I will bring him by to see you when I am next in the office."

"I look forward to it."

"George?"

"Yeah."

"Will we be able to tell if he tries to download any of my stuff?"

"In read-only, he can cut and paste into a new document. I cannot track that, but I can tell if he downloads large files. I can even pinpoint which files. With the network and VPN, even if he is in the office, he will only be able to download onto one of our laptops. I can monitor what is on his machine, but once downloaded, there is nothing to prevent him from sending it outside the firewall or saving to a thumb drive."

"I have years of work in those files."

"You think there is something in there to compromise any of our clients?"

"No, I have redacted identifying information. There is nothing in them that is not also part of the public record for those cases which appear in the case law."

"Well, if he takes a copy of everything, what can he do with it?"

"It is basically a manual outlining everything I know about practicing law, especially appellate work. I created a system to make what I do as efficient as humanly possible. He could take it and, in a month, beat me at my own game."

"Lady, he is not a threat to you. No one does what you do better, and you know it."

"Do you trust him?"

"I do not trust anyone; however," he paused, and she knew he was choosing his words, as he did with everything, carefully. "I like him. I think he is young and still has a great deal to learn."

Bree did not take his sentiment lightly. There were few people George felt compelled to share the time of day, much less like.

George continued: "Donovan must think well of him or he would not suggest it."

"What makes you think Donovan suggested it?"

"He asked me what I thought about him this morning, right after he looked at that report."

Zeke could feel the tension enveloping Bree following her conversation with George.

He was aware she knew where she was going, as she had plugged in the address on her navigation system. They were about fifteen minutes out from the appliance vendor.

He heard rustling from the back and turned to see CoalBear circling his bed on the second seat. Reaching back, he collected the pup and brought him to his lap.

He had always liked dogs, albeit larger ones. Scratching lightly behind one ear, CoalBear half closed his eyes in pleasure.

Bree briefly smiled at the dog before having the virtual assistant dial a number for her.

"Mitch Haynes."

"Hi Mitch, this is Bree. Do you have a moment?"

"Bree. Of course. How are you?"

Zeke noted the man had a slightly higher pitched voice than he had expected, but he also caught a hint of apprehension in it, as well.

Bree's voice was lower than normal, but she spoke clearly with careful enunciation, each consonant and vowel precisely spoken. Her words were not directed at him, but her manner made him uncomfortable.

"Actually, Mitch, I think I have bitten off more than I can chew. Would you be interested in helping me with one of my appeals cases?"

Zeke had been trying not to eavesdrop and strove to appear disinterested in her conversations, but her tact in addressing the other man was nothing short of gracious. He was surprised that it surprised him so. He turned to face her with a bit of wonder across his face.

She glanced at him and gave him a slight smile. Her eyes were clear, indicating to him she was at peace with the decision.

Clearly caught off-guard, Mitch stumbled over his words "Ummm, Bree, uhhh, yeah. I would be happy to work with you on any of your cases, appeals or otherwise."

"I have no idea what your workload is at the moment, but I have a case that is set for oral argument before the state supreme court in two months. We have a brief due in ten days."

"I have a hearing on Friday, but nothing else is pressing for the next fourteen days."

"Good."

"What do you need me to do?"

"The brief is 90% complete; however, I am concerned I may have missed something."

"Okay. I have not done any appeals work. I am not sure where to start."

"I have all of my research files on Q. They are all encrypted and password protected. George will set you up with a system he and I use to access those files."

Mitch chuckled slightly. "I have heard rumors about secret files that only you and George know about."

"Once you have access, you will see a folder tree. The top one is simply titled 'Bree.' Start there, there is a brief explanation of how things are organized, as well as a table of contents of sorts. Understand, this is more of a system, rather than a how-to course. I apply this system to everything I do. Once you have a chance to glance at it, see Monica about access to this client's file. You will not be able to override the bookmarks or comments I have made in it, but you will be able to see my notes and make additional notes of your own."

"You set up this system?"

"Yes."

"Does anyone else use it?"

"No; however, while it works well for me, it may not be your cup of tea, and I completely understand. I do not have time today or tomorrow to sit down with you and talk you through it. The best I can offer is to show you how I do what I do and why."

"This is great. I learn better by reading it for myself, rather than lecture, anyway."

"Good. So, do I. When you have a grasp on the how and why, I would like you to look through the file and pretend it is a law school exam. As you read through it, apply a scattergun approach, and identify each and every possible appealable issue. Be sure to cite by page and paragraph. Be creative and think beyond the norm. If you would, zip me a copy of those issues, no need to flesh them out."

"Will do."

"My thought is we will trade. You give me your initial thoughts, and I will send you a copy of my brief. You tell me what I have missed and why."

"Bree, I appreciate your giving me this opportunity."

"Mitch, please understand, I am completely mercenary. I

would like to take a month-long vacation and not worry about things I have left undone. If you are willing to take this on and do what it takes to get up to speed, I can take time off without guilt."

They chatted for a few more minutes and finished up, as Bree negotiated the vehicle off the road and into a parking spot.

She killed the ignition and moved to grab her pack from the back seat.

Zeke gently touched her arm. "Hang on a second."

Her face a question mark, she looked at him.

"Are you okay?"

"What do you mean?"

"You obviously did not want to do that, but you could not have been more gracious or kind in allowing him to believe he is helping you."

She glanced down at the dog in his lap, wagging his tail with excitement. She reached out and pet him gently, the motion releasing a bit of her own anxiety.

"It is not Mitch's fault I am insecure about sharing my work product or that my boss and the IT guy think I work too much and too hard."

"No, but there are hundreds of different ways you could have handled that, and I can think of no other that would set him up for success more than the one you chose."

"Perhaps, I do not trust my own judgment as much as I do Donovan's and George's."

"What do your instincts tell you?"

She frowned and drew her brows together while she chewed on her bottom lip. Quietly, she repeated the question "What do my instincts tell me?"

Returning his gaze once again, she said: "My instincts tell me Mitch is no real threat to me because if he learns everything I know, I will simply have to up my game a few more notches, and I will be just fine."

"So why are you insecure?"

"No one helped me. Certainly, no one handed me a manual

to show me what to do and how to do it when I became an attorney. I had to learn it all on my own. I am proud of my work product, but my stomach does flips when I think about handing it over to anyone else."

"If he deleted it all..."

She interrupted him with a smile. "No chance of it being gone forever; George and I both have digital copies, in addition to a hard copy."

"What would you do with a month off?"

Her smile widened and a mischievous glint adorned her eyes. "I am afraid, Mr. Buchanan, I do not know you well enough to share that."

He found her absolutely beautiful and completely beguiling in that moment.

CoalBear was far less enchanted. He was restless and ready to go. He pranced his forelegs on Zeke's lap and whined slightly.

"Okay, you little beast," Bree teased. She grabbed the tote and rolled down the sides just as the dog wormed his way into it, turned around and popped his head out of the top.

"He has you trained." Zeke chided.

"I live to serve my canine master, apparently."

Once he introduced Bree to the salesman Steve, Zeke moved to one end of the showroom and leaned against one of the kitchen displays, his arms crossed, content to observe.

Bree adopted an expression of pleasant reserve. He knew she heard every word Steve spoke, but she allowed her gaze to wander. He was not certain, but her eyes seemed to linger a second or two longer on a professional grade, cobalt blue range with far more than the standard four burners and not one, but two ovens; however, as she approached it, she inspected the stoves on either side of it by opening the oven and fiddling with the knobs, but she did not touch the blue one.

She occasionally interacted with Steve, but she was largely quiet.

She eventually made her way to stand in front of Zeke, her eyes shining with mischief.

"How's it going?" He asked.

"Propane or natural gas?"

"Propane."

"Tank or piped in?"

"There is a hookup for a tank on the west side of the building, near the back. The old tank was rusted. A new one can be buried, if you like."

"In addition to the range, are there gas fittings for a tankless water heater and dryer?"

"Those are in the utility room along the exterior wall, as they need to be vented."

"Thank you. I have made my selections."

He raised an eyebrow. "Kitchen appliances and washer/dryer?"

She nodded.

"The blue one?"

She grinned. "Did he pick up on that?"

Zeke looked past her. Steve was on the phone with his back to them. "Doubtful."

"How are we on time?"

Checking his watch, he smiled "Depending on how long it takes for him to write it up, way ahead of schedule."

"Are you aware of a place that deals in architectural salvage?"

"Yeah. Every other month there is a flea market with auction in Georgetown, just north of Austin."

He pulled out his phone for a quick search. "In fact, it's this weekend, Saturday and Sunday from 7:00 to 7:00."

"Is it open to the public?"

"The auction requires certification as a business in the industry, but the flea market is open to the public. What are you interested in?"

"I am not sure, really. But I like the idea of converting found things into useful items, using an interesting old door as a desk with a piece of glass on top. Using vintage glass transformers as pendant lights. In fact, I have a friend who takes found glass, heats them, and creates interesting shapes for lighting. He has promised to do a few pieces for me."

"It has been a while since I last went, but I usually come across something I did not know I wanted. If you would like to go, I can pick you up with a trailer for our finds."

Her eyes widened and she chewed on her bottom lip, unsure of her good fortune. "Are you serious?"

"Of course."

"I would love to go, but a part of me feels as though I am taking advantage of you."

He liked the idea of her taking advantage of him; however, he did not share that with her. "Which day works better for you?"

For the second time since they met, she asserted: "I am at your disposal."

He saw Steve making his way toward them and straightened to greet him. "We will work out the details."

"Well, Ms. Lancaster," Steve interrupted. "Do you have any questions?"

She reached into the side pocket of her tote and removed a small notepad. She opened it, removed the top sheet, and handed it to Steve. "Here are my selections."

Steve looked at the list she provided, clearly confused.

Bree's face serious, as she had the attorney mask in place. "I used the make and models provided by the manufacturer."

Steve stammered, slightly, "Umm, one, no, two of these items, we, uh, don't even have right now."

"If they are not in stock, how long will they take once you order?"

"Usually two weeks..."

She looked at Zeke, who nodded.

She redirected him. "I have an idea of what these should cost me and know exactly what I am willing to spend. Please keep that in mind when you draft the estimate."

With an open mouth, Steve looked from Bree to Zeke and back to Bree.

"I understand you need a few minutes to put that together. My number is at the bottom, along with my email. Once it is ready, please email it to me, and I will get back with you. Thank you."

She did not wait for a response and stepped between the men, as she headed for the door.

Zeke followed with a nod toward the salesman.

They were done, at least there.

From the appliance vendor, they stopped in at the cabinet maker. Just as she had done before, Bree walked the showroom, selected the style of cabinets she wanted in the kitchen, bathrooms, and utility room, as well as the finishes. She chose to have the kitchen and utility room cabinets painted a neutral taupe with matte black hardware. The cabinets in both baths were to be a slightly darker shade of the taupe.

The sales consultant took the measurements Zeke provided and promised to send them a mockup for review of placement and finished dimensions. He assured them this was something they could coordinate via email and phone.

Bree asked and was delighted to receive samples of the paint finish in the colors she wanted to select tile, which was their third stop.

At the rate at which she was making decisions, Zeke anticipated they may be able to knock out all the selections in a day, as they actually spent more time driving between businesses, than they spent at the establishments; however, he knew choosing tile and countertops tended to be overwhelming due to the sheer number of options.

For his part, CoalBear was content to nap in the tote, as long as he could ride in someone's lap while they drove. Zeke realized too late it may have been an error to have collected him from the back seat earlier that morning. He hoped it would not create a problem for Bree later.

A few minutes after she walked through the tile displays, Bree turned to him.

"You okay?"

"I think I am over my head here."

He smiled knowingly. "There are a lot of options."

"I have a good idea of the color I am looking for, but I could go crazy with those glass backsplash tiles. They are absolutely gorgeous."

He understood completely and tried to help. "Tell me what you envisioned before we walked in."

"Other than the blue range, the rest of the kitchen appliances are in the same line with the same handles, but they will be stainless steel."

This surprised Zeke. He had assumed she would have purchased them all in the same color, but now that he knew she did not, he thought having the range in a statement color alone would create more of an impact."

"I like that. Good thinking."

"The cabinets, as you know, will be neutral, as I hope will be the backsplash and counter tops; however, at four feet wide, that range needs something interesting above it, between the cook top and vent hood."

"I follow you."

"It would also be nice to have a recessed ledge on which I may place a bottle of olive oil, perhaps balsamic vinegar, and also to add interest. Is that possible?"

"Yeah. We can frame out that wall and give you a recessed focal backsplash. No problem. It might be nice with specialty tile, maybe that glass tile you are fond of..."

She squealed and almost hugged him.

Instead, she had his arm in both of her hands and squeezed in delight.

He laughed at her enthusiasm.

"Find your neutral backsplash first." He instructed her.

She released his arm and off she went.

Again, he was content to watch; however, his phone beeped, and he was compelled to step outside to answer it.

"Zeke."

"Zeke, this is Steve, do you have a minute?"

"Yes. What's up?"

"I have Ms. Lancaster's estimate."

"Okay. How bad is it?"

"Actually, I was wondering if you could tell me something, first."

"What do you mean?"

"Has she been shopping elsewhere?"

"I am not following you."

"Everything she chose is being closed out by the manufacturer. I was unaware of that before I called to see the availability of the items we do not stock."

"All I can tell you is she is one smart lady who knows how to do her homework."

"Well, she should be pleasantly surprised when she sees this estimate. She is getting high end, professional grade equipment at a deep discount."

"Outstanding."

"Also, I wanted to confirm. The only item in the signature cobalt blue is the range, everything else appears to be stainless."

"That's correct."

"Good. I will email each of you the estimate now."

"Thanks, Steve."

Stepping back inside, Zeke chuckled to himself. He had a feeling Bree would not be surprised in the least with the news.

He found her at the far end of the showroom where they stocked those items that were discontinued, no longer available for order, and offered at a discount. She had the cabinet sample with several pieces of the same porcelain tile laid out in a subway fashion with a sheet of glass tile.

As he walked up beside her, her eyes never left the array in front of her, but she acknowledged his presence with a question: "What do you think?"

The porcelain pieces were 2-inches by 4-inches and made up of mottled beige colors a shade or two lighter and creamier than the taupe of the cabinet. Instead of a slick and smooth surface, they had a gradual uneven texture to the surface, much like a rock. They had the appearance of natural stone, only glossier. Both the tiles and the cabinet color had cool undertones that worked well together. The glass tiles were much smaller, almost mosaic, and not quite 1-inch square. The background tones were in the beige family, but there were pops of jewel toned color in different greens and blues, as well as browns. Like the beige and taupe, they were cool colors, rather than warm ones.

He stepped back and studied them from several feet away before moving closer once more.

"That is amazing, Bree. You nailed it."

Surprised, she faced him. "Really?"

He looked at them again, this time reaching out to touch them. "They are beautiful. Just enough color to compliment the range, but not compete with it."

Delighted, she cast her eyes back toward the tiles as she leaned in with one arm behind his back and hugged him absently.

The contact was brief, and she seemed not to have noticed what she did, but it felt good to him. The instant she withdrew, he missed it.

"Now, I have no doubt you are far better with numbers." She counted the boxes which contained the porcelain tiles. "There are three and a half boxes, and each box covers 18 square feet."

She looked up at him with a slight apprehensive pout. "Are there enough?"

"That wall is sixteen feet long and except for the four feet where the range will go and the three feet where one cabinet extends from the floor past the countertop and up, you will have upper cabinets. Three boxes cover 54 square feet, plus whatever is in the fourth box. Sixteen times three is 48 square feet, not subtracting the area behind the range with your specialty tile. You are good."

She grinned.

Thinking out loud, she said: "Whatever savings there may be in these discounted tiles will be negated by the glass tiles, though."

"You will also need to find edging to go around the lip of the recess all the way around. There should be stone pieces to coordinate with what you have going on."

She blinked twice at him, processing the information. "Oh, I had no idea. Thank you!"

"That's what I am here for."

He moved to collect a cart for her tile.

When he returned, he checked the boxes to ensure each contained the same tile before moving them into the cart.

The glass tiles were sold by the sheet, each twelve inches square. He quizzed her, and they decided eight sheets would cover a two foot by four-foot square area, but she also needed a few more to be cut and trim out the recessed area on four sides.

With assistance, they were able to locate the trim pieces, which were in stone.

Bree knew she still had to select tile for the bathrooms and utility room, but she needed a break.

Reaching for his arm, she sought his attention, "Zeke," she spoke his name quietly, and he realized it was the first time she had said it.

He looked down on her flushed face and drew his brows together.

"Would you mind if we took a break once we take care of these?"

He glanced at his watch. It was well past noon and they had covered three of the four places on their list for the day.

"Absolutely."

Grateful, she smiled her appreciation.

As there was nothing to order, Bree purchased the tile, and she watched as he loaded it into the back of her SUV.

After he closed the back, he held his hand out to her.

Instinctively, she handed him the keys. He took them in one hand and placed another on the middle of her back and guided her to the passenger side of the vehicle, opening the door for her, as he took the tote and the dog from her. Once she was buckled in, he handed her both and shut the door.

Before he got in, he adjusted the electric seat to allow him room.

He started the engine and turned toward Bree. He found her leaned back into the seat, CoalBear in her arms. Her eyes were closed, and she had a dreamy, relaxed smile on her face.

He was enchanted with her.

His voice low and smooth, he asked "What are hungry for?"

She shrugged and half opened her eyes, gazing into his dark blue ones, eminently pleased with life at that very moment.

When she spoke, her voice was a soft whisper. "Surprise me."

Zeke drove them to a small Italian restaurant he was familiar with that had patio seating. Once harnessed to a lease, the dog was able to join them.

Once they were seated and their drinks arrived, Zeke looked at her intently.

"Why are you here?" he asked.

She gave him a sideways glance and a nervous smile. "Umm. I thought we were going to have a bite to eat."

"What I meant was why did you choose to move here?"

"Oh. The short answer is divorce. He wanted to keep the house, furnishings, and his 401K. He took this property as part of his fees from a client he was defending against criminal charges. As we were hammering out the community property settlement, I drove down, took a look around, and fell in love with it. My job, thanks to an amazing boss, is mostly portable with occasional oral arguments and hearings, but those are not very often. It seemed like a good fit."

"It is kind of isolated out here with not much of a social life."

"Honestly, I do not people very well. I am something of a

hermit. I have longed to live somewhere you had to go to get to, a place where people do not drop by because they happen to be in the area. They visit because I am worth the time and effort, not because I may happen to be convenient." She paused. "Gosh, that makes me sound demanding and high maintenance, and I am not either of those things."

"Are you concerned about becoming lonely?"

"I am not sure being alone bothers me, as it seems to other people. I tend to live in my head where I have an extremely rich internal life. Besides, my circle is quite small, and while I do not see my friends all that often, I am especially good at entertaining myself."

"What interests you?"

"Other than present company?" She smiled provocatively.

Her flirtation scored, and he laughed, genuinely pleased.

"I am going to ignore that comment for the moment."

"Right this second, I am tired of talking about me. I would rather know about you."

"Fair enough."

"Jed mentioned you are a pilot in the Air Force."

"Was. I retired a few months ago after twenty years. I joined at eighteen."

"Impressive."

He shrugged.

"What next?"

"Still trying to figure out what I want to be when I grow up."

"You also have a degree in aerospace engineering?"

"My little brother talks a lot."

"From what I have seen, you have skills in carpentry, construction, and electrical."

"I like to work with my hands."

She only gave a passing thought at what he could do with those hands but continued with her probing. "With your background, you could become a commercial pilot, a flight instructor, design planes or rockets, even build residences or commercial buildings. It probably would not take too much to earn an architecture degree, if you were so inclined."

"You don't miss much."

"Am I close to being warm?"

"Commercial pilot is out. I am tired of the gypsy lifestyle."

She nodded.

Any further conversation was interrupted as their server arrived with their meals.

Later, they returned to the tile place, and Bree was able to choose the flooring for both bathrooms and the utility room, as well as the tile for the built-in showers and bathroom/utility room backsplashes.

From there, they visited a business, which specialized in countertops. Bree had initially wanted quartz in the kitchen, but when Zeke advised placing hot pots on it might change the color of the resin, which would compromise it, she elected to use quartz in the utility room and granite in the kitchen. They found a creamy white granite with chocolate flecks in it that complimented her other selections handsomely.

For the bathrooms, she decided to go with a darker granite.

By two in the afternoon, the four stops they had planned were checked off the list.

Checking her phone, Bree was delighted with the email and estimate from Steve. They drove back to place her order.

Returning to the vehicle, Zeke held her door and tote with the dog while she got in. She graced him with a smile in appreciation.

Once he had assumed the driver's seat, he offered: "Are you up for plumbing fixtures?"

Feeling her oats, she teased: "Is that what the kids are calling it these days?"

He doubted she was seriously flirting, but he enjoyed the easy rapport they had established throughout the day.

"I'll take that as a yes."

Retrieving her notebook and with pen in hand, despite Coal-Bear in her lap, she went through her list making notes of the names of the granite she had ordered and added the dates on which the items were to be available for delivery. Thereafter, she flipped through the notes she had made regarding plumbing. Once she had refreshed her memory, she had a good idea of what she was looking for.

Money-wise, she was pleased to see she was well under budget, although the kitchen package was still expensive.

She turned to study Zeke's profile. She found him handsome no matter the angle. He had a strong chin and jaw line. His nose was straight. He had attractive lips, especially when he smiled.

He felt the attention and cast a quick glance her way.

"I appreciate your help and your patience with me today. Thank you."

He chuckled. "As quickly as you move and make decisions, patience has not been needed."

"Really? I feel as though you have been cooling your jets on waiting for me all day."

"Darla, Jed's wife, usually takes the clients around for selections. She has a 3-D mind and is extremely good with color and design, much like you."

"I don't know how good I am, I guess we shall see. I have never done anything like this before."

The admission surprised him, and he allowed it to show in another brief glance.

"Truly. When we bought the house at Lakeway, I looked forward to decorating it and making it our own, but my mother-in-law had different ideas. Clint lives to please his mother, which meant I was outvoted on everything."

Out of the corner of his eye, he saw her shrug and look away.

"That is too bad."

"It does not matter now. I had no qualms leaving that house and its 80s décor behind."

"Eighties?"

"Think wallpaper in every single room with matching fabric and high gloss cherry-stained Queen Anne style furniture."

He groaned.

"Wait, shiny brass fixtures, too. It was awful."

"That would actually give me nightmares."

She giggled, imagining Zeke walking through what had been her matrimonial home.

"Anyway, this is the first time I will have a place to call my own, and I am thrilled."

"It is going to be amazing, Bree. I love everything you have put together so far."

She reached out and lightly squeezed his forearm. "Thank you, Zeke. I literally could not do it without you."

There it was the second time she had actually used his name. She had also touched him again. He liked the sound of his name on her lips and especially the feel of her touch. The alarm bells were ringing in the back of his mind, but he silenced them, at least for the moment.

True to form, Bree made one lap around the showroom, asked a question about the gauge of stainless steel, and made her selections. Sinks, taps, and toilets were all crossed off the list. Next to the kitchen sink, the item on which she spent the most time was the free-standing tub for the upstairs bathroom.

Remaining on their list were light fixtures, cabinet hardware, closet and pantry organizational systems, and flooring upstairs and down; however, he could tell she was done for the day.

Her phone had rung several times, but each time she had checked it and sent it to voicemail.

His phone had rung, as well. He waited to return the calls when she was engaged in selecting items. He knew he had a number of emails to return, but they could wait.

When they were once again safely in the vehicle, she quizzed him about floors.

"The existing floors are wide plank oak?"

While the engine was running, they were still parked, and he turned his full attention to her. "Yes, they appear to be rough sawn oak, as in they were not sanded smooth as one would expect in a residence."

"Rough mill or warehouse floors?"

"Exactly."

"How thick are they?"

"I am not sure. We can certainly pull one up to measure, but probably, at least, an inch and a half to two inches. If you are thinking about sanding them down and finishing them, they should be thick enough to do that."

"I am leaning that way."

"In that case, rather than use the existing wood as subfloor, we need to go over every inch to ensure what is underneath is stable, screw down any loose or creaking boards, before we do anything else."

"The same upstairs?"

"On the mezzanine level the planks are not as wide and may not be as thick. I will check those out."

"You mentioned new risers and treads, I believe?"

"Yes, what is on them now are thin boards that are well worn."

"How well does oak take stain?"

"How dark are you thinking?"

"I respect the hardness of oak, but I am not wild about the orangey color when clear coated."

He nodded. He was not a fan, either. He preferred deep, almost chocolate stained woods.

"We can stain it just about any color you wish."

"I love really dark floors. While they show everything, I am leaning toward a rich coffee stain."

She was keeping with the cool tones, and he liked it.

"That will look great with your kitchen. Tomorrow, you can choose which stain you like best. We can pick up a tester pot. I will pull up one of the boards, flip it over, sand it down, and try it out for your inspection. I will bring it along this weekend when we go to Georgetown."

"I feel so high maintenance. I am sure you and Jed have other clients."

"Actually, Jed is working on a couple of other projects. I am responsible for this one."

His tone and demeanor had not changed. It was as warm and friendly as it had been all day; however, she reminded herself theirs was a working relationship. He was the contractor, and she was the client. He was simply doing his job.

He was unsure what had transpired, but she completely withdrew into herself before him. Her posture was no longer relaxed and comfortable, but tense and tight. She appeared to occupy half the space of the passenger seat as she had just moments before.

The dog sensed the change. Instead of excitedly looking out the window or around the cab of the vehicle trying to sucker them into attention, he stood in her lap with his paws on her chest, looking at her intently.

Bree had completely disengaged from him, as well. She absently secured him in her lap, but her thoughts and focus were miles beyond the window.

Frowning, Zeke put the vehicle in drive. They had already discussed and chosen a restaurant for dinner earlier. He headed there.

∞∞∞

Without a patio, they gave the dog a chance to relieve himself before they cracked the windows and Bree made him a bed on the front passenger seat. She produced a bully stick to occupy him until they returned. The sun had set, and it was still cool enough for them not to have to worry about him overheating in the vehicle. He seemed content with his treat, which made Bree more comfortable leaving him.

Once she knew where their table was, she excused herself to freshen up and discreetly ensure their server was aware she would cover the bill.

Zeke had waited for her return to order their drinks.

He found her polite and responsive, but something had definitely shifted in the prior hour. He wanted to ask, but he felt as though the query would push her further into her shell.

Instead, he openly studied her across the table from him. He watched as she interacted with their server. She was friendly and kind, addressing her by her name after she introduced herself. When the lady shared the specials, Bree asked which one she preferred and why. They chatted briefly about another item or two before she requested a few more minutes to consider her choices.

She finally turned to him. "What do you think? Anything tickle your fancy?"

His first thought was that she tickled his fancy, but he refrained from sharing. "I am in the mood for steak."

"The ribeye with the crabmeat sauce sounds lovely."

"And you?"

"Nothing as refined as you. That jalapeno burger with cream cheese and avocado is screaming my name."

Chuckling, she had caught him by surprise, as he was certain she would choose the grilled fish.

"Play your cards right, I may even share my onions rings."

Delighted with a flash of the woman he had come to know; he teased her back "I'll see your onions rings with a bite of prime ribeye and crabmeat."

"Done."

When their meals arrived, she cut her burger in half and took a bite. She groaned as she chewed and rolled her eyes back in pleasure before wiping her mouth.

"That is amazing." She emphasized each word.

Zeke could not look away from her, he recognized few things were as satisfying as seeing a woman comfortable enough in her own skin to enjoy a tasty meal.

Before he consumed any of his food, he sliced off a bite-size portion of meat with a generous helping of sauce on top and offered it to her. He would have liked to have fed it to her, instead he slid his plate toward her.

With a twinkle in her eye, she did not hesitate to stab it with her fork and bring it to her mouth.

"Ummmm," she shared before she chewed, licked her lips, and said: "That is divine. Good choice."

Only then, did he partake.

He nodded in agreement.

They ate in silence for several minutes before she caught the eye of their server and asked for a small plate.

She returned immediately, and Bree carefully slid the other half of her burger onto the plate with her knife, along with several onion rings and pushed the plate toward Zeke.

"A small token of my gratitude for hauling me around all day and answering each and every one of my inane questions."

"Would you like more steak, Bree?"

"Lord, no. I wish I could, but after that lunch earlier, I am struggling to finish this. Thank you."

The chill had passed, but he sensed she was still a bit off kilter.

"Are you okay?"

"What do you mean?"

"You seemed to withdraw earlier; I was concerned something had upset you."

She looked down and took a breath before taking a sip of water and blotting her mouth with the edge of the napkin.

"I am fine, actually. I have had the best day today. I could not be more pleased with everything we have accomplished thus far."

Zeke leaned forward and spoke quietly, willing her to meet his gaze. "I am happy to hear that."

When she did, she could see the concern in his face.

"Sincerely, I am elated."

He waited, watching.

She sighed.

"I am just weird."

An internal struggle played out across her face.

The server returned to inquire whether they needed anything. Zeke assured her everything was excellent, but after a brief glance at Bree, she backed away.

"Talk to me."

"I really do not play well with others, Zeke. I am the least social human you are likely to encounter. I thrive when left to my own thoughts."

His smile was as gentle as his words. "You mean you are an introvert, and socializing requires a great deal of energy. Today was a busy day with loads of interaction, and now you need to withdraw to build up your reserves again?"

She blinked and frowned at him. For a moment, he thought he may have missed the mark.

"How did you know?"

"You have that attorney mask you don for battle, but most of the time your face is unguarded and transparent. You are moving to a tiny town where you basically know no one to live indefinitely, and you seem to have no qualms or reservations about it at all. You work all hours of the day and night. Your closest friends appear to be your boss and the IT guy at work."

Her eyes grew liquid and bright. He had not intended to hurt her feelings.

"That makes me sound sad and pathetic."

"Not at all, Bree. I think you are incredibly strong and independent. It is okay to withdraw a bit and regain some of the energy you expended today."

"And you?"

"What about me?"

"You do not seem like an extrovert, although you are friendly with excellent social skills."

"I spend most of my time alone. I guess I am more introverted than extroverted, but I have never really thought about it."

The remainder of the meal continued in relative silence.

Zeke noted she made less of an attempt to mask her feelings. He also noted her energy was bottoming out, she had become almost lethargic.

He motioned to their server for the bill and learned it had already been taken care of.

Extending his hand across the table, she placed her hand in his as they rose to their feet. "Thank you for dinner, Bree. I enjoyed it."

Rather than release her entirely, he switched hands and led her to the vehicle, where again, he opened the door and helped her in by collecting the dog until she was buckled in.

Within minutes, the rolling of the vehicle lulled her to sleep, CoalBear curled in her lap.

Foregoing the collection of his truck, he drove straight to his home and debated whether he should carry her in or wake her.

The dog made the decision for him. As soon as they stopped, his head popped up, and he revealed a bundle of energy, his prancing front paws kneading Bree's lap and arms until she was awake, albeit groggy.

In moments, Zeke was at her side, door open with CoalBear in one hand, as he reached across her to release the buckle with the other.

"Let's get you inside."

"I need to walk the dog."

"I have the dog."

She reached back and pulled her pack with her as she stepped down from the vehicle, one hand on his arm.

She continued to hold on, as he led her through the dark to the front door.

He opened it in an instant and flicked on a light. Releasing him, she covered her eyes against the brightness.

With a hand on her back, he guided her through a living room to a hallway on the left. They immediately turned left and into a guest room. He switched a bedside lamp on before turning down the bed.

"The bathroom is next door. Why don't you clean up and call it a day?"

She nodded and reached for Coal. "He needs to eat."

"I have him. I will get his stuff from the truck and bring him to you after he has had a chance to eat and run around outside for a few minutes."

She leaned into him.

He hugged her.

She was not certain, and she may have imagined it, but she thought she felt him kiss the top of her head the instant before he pulled away.

"Rest."

Chapter 6

He felt her silky-smooth hair caress his cheek before she showered him with quick wet kisses. Smiling, he gently pushed her away as he enjoyed a languid stretch, but she would not be denied and peppered his shoulder with more kisses, her hair tickling his underarm.

He cracked open one eye with her name forming on his lips, when he realized CoalBear was in his bed.

He chuckled at his mistake and carefully pushed the dog away from his face before offering him scratches behind the ear.

Rolling over, the clock read 5:37.

He suspected if the dog were up and about, his mistress must be as well.

Tossing the covers back and momentarily covering the pooch, Zeke rose.

His mission a success, the dog bounced from the bed and trotted through the door triumphantly.

∞∞∞

Bree was bent over the kitchen table on her laptop, sitting cross-legged with the dog curled under chair when Zeke found her.

She was fully dressed. Her hair hung down around her shoulders and flowed across her back.

He cleared his throat to announce his presence.

She jumped slightly, unfolding her legs from her perch on the chair, and stood to face him.

Her eyes were clear. She appeared refreshed and energetic.

"Good Morning!" She greeted him warmly.

He had shaved and was freshly showered, his hair slightly damp. In his jeans and pressed shirt, he was every bit a rugged Marlboro Man.

"Did you sleep well?"

"Like the dead. Thank you. And you?"

"Very well, until your little friend there decided to rain kisses on me."

Shocked, she glanced down at the dog. "Coal!"

He remained curled but acknowledged her with a single thump of his tail.

"I apologize, Zeke." She laughed.

"It's fine. He is a good boy. It was time to rise."

Glancing at her computer, he asked: "Did you figure out the password?"

"Oh," she shook her head. "I am using my phone as a hot spot."

He gave her Wi-Fi access for her phone and computer.

"Have you been up long?"

She shrugged. "Not really. Only since about 4. I had a slew of emails, mostly from Mitch of One Thousand and One questions."

He poured a cup of coffee from the pot she had made.

"Is he in over his head?"

"I suspect he thought so at first and began sending me questions; however, as I read through them, he figured things out for himself the further into my notes he got. I think he will be fine."

"That's good, right?"

She was conflicted, he could tell, as she pursed her lips and chewed on the inside of her bottom lip.

"Yeah. I guess it is."

It was not quite daybreak when they loaded up and headed to retrieve his truck at the warehouse.

As he knew the way, Bree was content to allow him to drive.

It also gave her a few minutes to sort her thoughts.

She had resented Donovan reassigning the files in which she had upcoming trials and she had been unhappy about bringing Mitch on board to help her with appeals, but she realized a good bit of pressure had been removed from her. She had room to breathe and think about things other than her workload. She was grateful.

She had enjoyed working on making the warehouse a home stamped with her own personal taste and style. She felt she had extra time to enjoy the process, instead of rushing through it quickly to get back to her job responsibilities. She silently said a blessing for Donovan.

Zeke found Bree exceptionally quiet, but she seemed more relaxed than she had the night before. He noted she occupied more of the seat. Instead of tightly crossed arms and legs hugging the door, she was centered with upper limbs casually splayed on the center console and armrest of the door. Her legs were extended in front of her and loosely crossed at the ankles.

Surprisingly, CoalBear was quietly nestled on the second seat behind him. It was not the first time he had considered the dog a barometer for Bree's emotions.

The sun had risen by the time they arrived at the warehouse. Bree allowed the dog to roam free as Zeke opened the garage for his truck.

She had wondered as to the building's orientation and was pleased to learn the front faced due south, which meant neither the morning sun from the east, nor the withering afternoon sun from the west would shine directly into the tall and wide rear bank of windows to her home.

A dog barked, but it sounded nothing like CoalBear. Alarmed, she scanned the grounds for him and found him several yards away, ears pricked and tail high. Kicking herself for not keeping him on a leash, she shouted his name and ran toward him.

Zeke heard the high pitch of her voice calling for Coal. He stepped around the end of the garage to see her bend over to scoop him up when a golden, long-haired beast plowed into her, knocking her down and rolling her completely over.

He could hear a man's voice calling off to his left, but he ignored it, as he ran toward her.

By the time he reached her, it was apparent she was not under vicious attack. The big dog was licking her face and playfully nipping at Coal who was delightfully dancing around them and yipping back.

Rolling Bree from her side to her back, he checked her for injury, as the other man ran up and kneeled beside them.

"Are you okay?" the man breathlessly asked.

Bree looked at Zeke. "What the hell?"

Zeke helped her to her feet and dusted her off.

The dogs were running around playing chase.

"I apologize for Molly. She has no idea how big she is."

Bree had not yet found her humor. "You have a moose for a dog, Sir."

"Yes," he agreed. "Yes, I do. She's not even a year old yet. I am so sorry."

Satisfied she was fine, Zeke's face broke into a smile.

She turned on him.

"Amused, are we?"

Her hair was a mess with dried grass and long dead leaves hanging from it.

He reached to pull detritus from it.

The other man stood a lanky five foot, ten inches or so and was probably about 170 pounds. He wore wrinkled scrubs and sneakers. He appeared as though he had worked the night shift.

Extending a hand to Bree, he introduced himself, "Brett Parker."

Still annoyed, she gave him a hard look, but offered hers. "Bree Lancaster."

Zeke nodded, continuing to pull vegetable matter from Bree's hair. "Zeke Buchanan."

"Very nice to meet you both. I moved in last week." He

pointed to one of the bungalows behind the warehouse. "I work in the ER."

Zeke had heard there was a new doctor in town.

"Dr. Parker?"

"I am afraid so." He looked at Bree apologetically, "So much for the oath to do no harm..."

She finally released her irritation and laughed.

"I am fine, Brett. It simply scared me, that's all."

She bent over and called the dogs to her. They ran over immediately.

"She's beautiful," Bree smiled as she affectionately ran her hands over the dog.

"She's really a doll, a Golden Retriever, but for some reason, she is much larger than her littermates. She is usually much better behaved, but I just got off a 12-hour shift, and I guess she had quite a bit of pent-up energy."

"It's fine. No harm done."

Brett eyed the couple and surmised from their body language they might be an item. "You guys are renovating the warehouse?"

Bree nodded and glanced at Zeke for confirmation. "It should be move in ready in a month and a half or so."

Zeke winked at her, satisfied with not only her answer, but how the man's real question was lost on her. He was well aware Parker was assessing her availability. Oblivious to the male posturing, his sweet, literal Bree had missed it.

Brett observed the warm exchange between them, a twinge of disappointment added to his general feeling of exhaustion.

"It was nice to meet you both. I do apologize for the scare, Bree. I look forward to getting to know you both."

Once he and Molly were well on their way, Bree turned to Zeke and sighed. "I am fully awake now."

"Me, too!" He wiped off his hands by lightly slapping them together and added, "I definitely got my cardio in for the day."

"I am sorry." She gave him an apologetic look and placed a hand on his chest. "Thank you for checking on me and cleaning me up."

He covered her hand with his own. "My absolute pleasure."

He thought about kissing her, but the miscreant CoalBear had other thoughts. He stood at their feet with fully erect ears and tail high, watching Molly disappear into the house. He emitted a high-pitched whine.

"Uh oh," Zeke scooped him up, "He's in love."

"The vet will take care of that..."

Zeke cringed.

∞∞∞

If possible, Zeke found Bree had become even more efficient in her ability to assess options and make selections. He chaulked it up to increased confidence and a fair night's rest. They had completely blown through the entire list of vendors by early afternoon, even with a break for lunch.

While they had driven two vehicles into San Antonio, he had parked his truck at the first place they visited. All that remained was to drop him back there to collect it, and they would be done.

Bree was in the driver's seat and pulled in beside his truck and put her ride in park before turning to face him.

"Any chance we will be ahead of schedule, Mr. Buchanan?"

"No promises, Ms. Lancaster, at least not this far out. A lot can happen."

She knew he was right, but having done what she could to hurry things along, she was restless.

"I appreciate all your help and expertise."

He smiled and reached out to cup her face, lightly running his thumb over her bottom lip. He had every intention of pulling her closer to him, when her phone rang with the digital assistant announcing Donovan was calling.

They both sighed.

"I will see you in a few days."

She nodded and answered the phone, as he closed the door.

He watched her back her rig out of the spot and drive away, gracing him with a smile and a wave as she left.

Zeke sighed again.

Chapter 7

Between his GPS and Bree's directions, Zeke had no difficulty finding Donovan's lake house. His dually work truck was out of place in the gated community of well-manicured lawns and established oak trees with houses set well back from the street on expansive lots.

As he pulled into the circular drive, he noticed a man operating an edger along the sidewalk in front of a stately home. The presence of a pair of young boys close by suggested Donovan may be a man interested in doing his own yard work.

Stepping from the truck, Zeke approached him. At six foot, three, almost four inches, he estimated the other man was a good six feet tall. His dark wavy hair was greying at the temples. He guessed they were also about the same age.

The man straightened and extended a hand.

There was no battle for supremacy in the firm, but respectful handshake he offered.

"Zeke Buchanan," was his simple introduction.

"Donovan," he replied succinctly.

"A beautiful place you have here."

Donovan raised an eyebrow. "Between you and me, I would much prefer a camp way down in South Texas, but Management had other ideas."

Zeke laughed. He liked the other man instantly.

"When you are ready to hunt white tail or mule deer, let me know, I have buddies with a lease over a thousand acres."

"Seriously?"

Zeke nodded.

"I am in!"

Around the corner, the boys reappeared. "Papa! Papa!" They

came running.

Donovan rolled his eyes as they skidded to a stop, each wrapping chubby arms around his legs.

"These are the Hellions," he explained.

To his sons, he directed: "Can you gentleman introduce yourselves?"

Amused, Zeke watched as each of the boys straightened. The one on the left offered his hand and stiffly said: "Brandon Donovan, pleased to meet you."

Zeke responded in kind.

His brother followed suit with "Joshua Donovan, how do you do?"

Again, Zeke responded in kind.

Brandon spoke again, "Our mother, Miss Evangeline, asks if you and Bree will return in time to join us for supper this evening."

Zeke cast a sideways glance at Donovan who gave the briefest of nods.

"We will be back in time, thank you."

With a roar, they were in motion and off again.

"How can you tell them apart?"

"I insist Brando wear red and Josh wear anything, but red."

"Good to know."

"Air Force?"

Zeke raised an eyebrow before smiling and asking in kind: "Army?"

Donovan nodded.

"Bree is in the guest house. Around back and to the right."

"Thanks."

As he began to walk that way, Donovan's voice carried to him "Ask Bree to leave the Hell Hound to distract the kids...I need all the help I can get."

Zeke acknowledged the request with a casual salute.

He chuckled as he walked. Donovan amused him. He knew he called his wife Management, but Hellions and Hell Hound were too much. He was certain he would be anointed with a special moniker if he had not been already.

As promised, the guest house was 20 yards beyond the side of the house. To his left was an expansive patio and pool. Past the pool, 30 yards or more and down a hill was a deck and the lake, as well as a small dock with a boat lift. He admired the view, as he continued down the path.

The house was relatively small. It had a covered patio. A sliding glass door led to what appeared to be a one room efficiency. Standing at the partially open door, he saw the Hell Hound on a Queen bed to the right. There was a small kitchen along the back wall. Bree was seated on a bench with her back to him operating a machine. He watched as she threw something across the front of her with her right hand, caught it with her left hand, and pulled a horizontal bar toward her with the right.

She repeated the process but threw left to right before rocking and pulling the bar to her again with the left hand. Her feet also moved along pedals. It took him a moment because he had never actually seen anyone do it, but he surmised the machine must be a loom, and she was weaving.

He rapped gently on the door frame. She jumped at the sound and spun around. CoalBear had already recognized him and was standing on the bed, tail wagging.

She opened the door, face flushed, and smile wide.

"Hi! I apologize for keeping you waiting. I was going to meet you in the drive."

"I am early. No worries."

He looked over the top of her head. "What are you working on?"

"Nothing." She dismissed it.

He realized she seemed shy and almost embarrassed.

"I had no idea you were a weaver." He asserted gently.

When she realized he was not going to tease her about it, she stepped aside and motioned him in.

He walked over and carefully moved a finger over the handwoven fabric, completely amazed.

"This is beautiful. What does it want to be?"

"Nothing special. These are just cotton tea towels."

He inspected them more closely.

"There is almost a lace-like pattern to them. These are anything but ordinary tea towels."

He could see her face light with pleasure, as she stepped behind the loom.

"This weave structure is called Huck lace. You certainly miss nothing."

"I am impressed."

She beamed. "Thank you."

From the fabric, his attention turned to the loom itself. The wood was smooth with use and darkened with age.

"Where did you find this?"

"This is Meg. She is the smallest of my looms."

"Looms as in plural?"

"Shush."

He chuckled. "Continue, please."

"I spent four years looking for one this size. She has a twenty-four-inch weaving width and eight shafts."

"The more shafts, the more complicated the weaving pattern?"

Bree was pleased and astonished by Zeke's interest and perception.

"Yes." She studied him anew. Instead of his typical well-worn jeans and work shirt with utility belt, he sported a crisp, dark pair of jeans. He still wore boots, but these were more like hiking or walking shoes, rather than the blunt, steel-toed boots he usually wore. He was always neat and clean, but he seemed to have taken greater care with his appearance. She suspected he also had a fresh haircut, but she had grown accustomed to his close crop.

While ruggedly handsome in his work clothes, he was undeniably attractive with this bit of polish.

If she were studying his appearance, he was completely unaware because his focus was on her lovely face with her thick, dark hair cascading over her shoulders and halfway down her back. Her eye lashes were slightly darker with mascara and there was just the hint of color on her luscious lips. She had a form fitting sleeveless tee tucked into a pair of jeans that hugged her behind. Her sandals encased a fresh pedicure with rose colored nails. She was gorgeous.

Struggling to carry the conversation, he asked: "Four years?"

She mouthed the word "Oh" before a giggle escaped her and she said "Yes. I finally found this one for sale in California."

"That far?"

"I probably should not admit this, but I bought her, flew to San Francisco, rented a SUV, picked her up, and drove her back to Texas."

He grinned.

"I can actually relate."

She raised an eyebrow.

"Yeah. 1968 Ford Mustang GT."

"Steve McQueen!"

"The Bullitt car, yes."

"I bet that was a pretty penny."

"Well, it was in rough shape. I hauled a trailer from here to Pensacola and back to get it."

"Do you still have it?"

"No, a buddy of mine wanted it more than I did."

"Cool car, though."

"Speaking of trailers…"

"We should get going, I know." She grabbed a light, long-sleeved button up shirt and tied it around her waist and grabbed her pack.

"By the way, the Mafia Boss said the Hell Hound should stay to distract the Hellions."

"Oh, gosh," she cracked up, "I take it you met Donovan."

"And the boys."

"Mafia Boss," she giggled uncontrollably. "That's so appropriate."

"Let me know what he christens me…"

Chapter 8

The auction was swarming with people by the time they arrived, but Zeke had acquired a parking pass well in advance, and they had a reserved spot much closer to the auction barn than the regular parking allowed.

As he had explained, in addition to the auction, there were vendors in tents lined in rows; however, as this was an every other month event, she could not appreciate the number of tents, the amount of goods available, or the sheer number of people milling about. The auction was restricted to industry, but the tent sales were available to the public. There were also food trucks and live entertainment at one end, which created an almost carnival-like atmosphere.

She looked at Zeke as he handed her a lanyard with ID. "A band?"

He shrugged. "It's been a couple of years since I was last here. The band is new to me."

He was on his phone. "I am sending you an invite to a tracking app. Please download it. We will probably have to split up as our lists are different. You can delete it after today."

"Good thinking."

"You okay?" He sensed her anxiety about crowds.

"A little overwhelmed, but fine and kind of excited."

"If you see something you love, negotiate, and do not be afraid to walk away. On the app, you can pin a location, if you want to return to it later."

"But this place is huge. I am not likely to make my way back around."

"True; however, if we need to pick it up you will have to pin it. Just know, usually, they will transport it to the holding pen for loading. Just make sure they have your ID number attached to it."

"Is there a kind of order? Are all the doors along one row, windows on another?"

"Unfortunately, no. Vendor sites are first come, first served. Each vendor has a variety of items. Also, auction items are in the barn."

"I looked online at the offerings, too rich for my blood."

"I did not see anything I needed there, either. Before I forget, Management expects us for supper."

She bit her lip. "I know. I hope that is okay."

"Of course, but that means we have five hours. We need to be loaded and, on the road, no later than 3:30."

"Got it."

"If you need me, call, do not text, and I will find you."

"Ditto!"

He grinned.

She watched him stride away on his long legs before checking the new app.

Sure enough, she thought, she could track his movements and location.

Pulling her hair into a high ponytail, she re-adjusted her sunglasses, checked her list, and waded into the throngs of humanity.

∞∞∞

Two-and-a-half hours later, she was soaked with sweat, a bit sun scorched, despite a liberal application of sunscreen, and much lighter in the wallet, but she had purchased five old doors, each oversized with interesting details, half-worn finishes, or something else distinctive about it. She did not need that many doors, but she realized she could make a headboard out of one, a desk from another, or a bookcase out of a pair of them, which matched.

She had also come across an artist who took raw wood from old trees that had fallen or were otherwise rotted in the center. He cut two-to-three-inch-thick slabs and used resin to fill the void between the pieces of wood. They were absolutely stunning. She bought a huge slab, which was roughly four feet wide and twelve feet long. She hoped it would fit perfectly in the space next to the kitchen, just off the living area. While she did not anticipate having enough people over to warrant a table of that size, the space demanded it.

Plus, she thought, the resin had a subtle hint of cobalt in it, like a river channeling through the canyons made by the hollowed part of the tree. The cobalt would help tie the dining room to the kitchen.

As a bonus, the vendor agreed to attach the base she selected and deliver it to her by the end of the month, when he next traveled to San Antonio for a show. Thus, Zeke would not have to load and transport it.

She also found dozens of glass pieces she hoped her friend Andre could use to create light fixtures.

The one item she was completely unsure of was a massive armoire that had been part of a built-in wall unit. It was not exactly standing when she viewed it. She hoped Zeke or one of the other carpenters might be willing to help her install it, although she was not quite sure where it would go.

She could certainly use the armoire part in the bedroom, as there was no closet. Its original purpose was as an office. She really wanted to be able to use the piece downstairs because it was unique and incredibly beautiful. In addition to the armoire, it had shelves with a built-in secretary desk she could use for work.

The good news, she thought ruefully, is that she did not overspend her budget for the day.

The bad news, she had to laugh, she barely got half the items on her list and the armoire unit was not on the list.

However, she told herself, had she known such a thing existed, it would have definitely made the top of the list.

More good news, as she continued the internal dialogue, due to its size and the seller residing in San Antonio, he was willing to deliver for another $100. She hoped Zeke would be pleased it was one fewer thing to load and haul.

By the time she had finished debating herself, she had reached the food trucks. She stood in line for two water bottles and checked Zeke's location.

To save the remainder of her budget and curious as to what he was up to, she tracked him to a tent specializing in exotic wood veneers. She found him engrossed in conversation. Standing slightly behind him, she slipped her phone in her backpack, put her water bottle under one arm, while holding his bottle, and lightly grasped his left bicep with her free hand.

Without looking at her at all, he reached across his body with his right hand, removed her hand from his arm, and slipped her hand into his left hand with a reassuring squeeze.

She was startled by how smoothly and naturally he had repositioned her hand. She was also amazed at how nice it felt to have his hand swallow her own.

She stared dumbfounded at how slight and small, yet comfortable and protected, she felt just by the contact.

Within a few minutes, he wrapped up his conversation and turned to her.

Silently, she offered him the bottle in her left hand.

He took it with an appreciative smile and gently released her hand to open it.

After a deep drink he said: "Thanks, I needed that."

He watched her take a sip of her own before he asked: "How did you do?"

She beamed. "Great! You?"

"Fairly well."

"How much more do you have to do?"

"If this guy has what I need, I will be done."

"Excellent."

"Are you done or just getting started?"

Grinning, she admitted "I spent my money."

He mockingly groaned. "My back hurts already."

She playfully swatted his arm. "Actually, Mr. Buchanan, you should be pleased to know the two biggest things will be delivered."

He squinted his eyes. "Just how big, Ms. Lancaster?"

She pulled a face. "Twelve by twenty..."

"Feet?"

She nodded.

"What did you buy?"

Plucking her phone from her pack she opened the app and held it out to him. "It's two rows over and close to the front if you would like to see for yourself."

∞∞∞

Within ten minutes of concluding his business with the veneer guy, they were standing in front of the armoire unit flanked by shelves and desk.

Zeke's face was inscrutable, as his eyes traced the lines of the piece. He looked at it from different angles, front, sides, and back. He measured the height and depth. He walked around it twice before turning his attention to her.

"How much do you like it?"

Her heart filled with dread, as she anticipated he was going to suggest she abandon it.

He watched her bite her bottom lip as her gaze shifted from him to the armoire. Her chin was slightly tucked, as though she were expecting a reprimand.

She sighed and quietly revealed "I actually love it."

"Where would you put it?"

"While I need storage in the bedroom, I see it on the shared wall with the garage, on the right as you walk in from the back patio. I hope I am not wrong, but I thought that wall was thirty-feet long and something like sixteen-feet tall."

"Twenty-nine-feet long." He corrected.

He could see the disappointment creeping into her expression, as her deep brown eyes clouded over. "You think it is a bad idea."

It did not sound like a question, but she was no longer looking at him.

He turned to stand beside her, his focus on the armoire, too.

Evenly and quietly, he spoke "I think it is perfect, Bree."

He heard her sharp inhale and felt her slip her hand into his and give him a quick squeeze, as she whispered, "Thank you."

An hour later the trailer was loaded with most of their purchases. Zeke had everything tied down securely, and they were on the road back to Donovan's.

Zeke had teased her about the number of doors.

The glass for light fixtures were carefully wrapped and boxed. Zeke put them on the second seat of the cab to protect them. They were to be transferred to her SUV to be delivered to Andre.

He had purchased several large items, as well as two boxes of wood veneer.

While there was no rain in the forecast, he

methodically covered everything with a tarp and secured it.

Donovan and the twins were trimming the hedges when they returned.

Actually, Donovan was wielding the clippers and trying to instruct the boys on collecting the clippings. They were more interested in using the longer ones for play sword fights.

By way of greeting, Bree teased him "I see you have your minions helping you this afternoon."

Donovan deadpanned in return: "I don't care what Management says, military boarding school builds character."

"They are boys."

He rolled his eyes.

"Millie has the Hell Hound. She rescued him from..." He eyed the boys.

"Thank you."

He turned to Zeke. "You can clean up, if you like, then cocktails on the patio. I'm done with the manual labor thing for the day."

"Sounds great. I just need to move a few things into Bree's rig."

Once the glass was transferred. She watched him return to his truck and reach for his pack behind the truck seat. She was not surprised he was so well prepared.

She collected CoalBear from Millicent and returned to the cottage for a quick shower and change of clothes.

When she emerged half an hour later, she found Donovan nursing his signature Sazerac in a high ball, as he fired up the grill. He had changed into khaki shorts, an untucked tee shirt, and flip flops.

His companion held a beer bottle and was similarly dressed in a polo shirt tucked into khaki shorts, although he had leather deck shoes on his feet.

Bree had to blink twice before she registered that Zeke was clad in shorts and not jeans.

Zeke felt her presence before he turned to find her staring at him. Instead of her usual dark colors, mostly black, she had donned a simple sleeveless dress with a riot of colorful flowers on a dark blue background. The bodice was fitted through the waist, then flared to a full skirt with a hem mid-way between her calves and shapely ankles.

Her hair was once again down. She must have showered because there were a few damp strands around her face. She looked soft, feminine, and completely beguiling.

"I almost did not recognize you." She smiled breathlessly at Zeke.

Donovan pretended to ignore the exchange, but out of the corner of her eye, she knew he missed nothing.

"You are beautiful." Zeke quietly greeted her.

She was not sure, but she felt as though something had shifted between them.

"I am glad you think so." She touched his arm lightly when she walked past him on her way to help in the kitchen.

Donovan watched Zeke watch her walk away.

"You know," he advised, "she is special, right?"

Zeke faced the other man.

He detected no hint of malice or warning in Donovan's tone or words.

He agreed, "Yes, she is."

Chapter 9

Zeke found the meal delightful.

Evangeline was a lovely combination of beauty, wit, and grace. She was the perfect foil to balance Donovan's dark and dry humor.

The older child Millicent was her mother's mini clone, albeit quiet with the occasional "zing" of a comment to alert all, like her father, she missed nothing.

While boisterous, the boys were polite and respectful at the table.

Bree was exceedingly quiet throughout the meal, even though she was attentive and relaxed.

Donovan was a lively and entertaining host full of stories with a talent to regale.

The family, as a whole, operated as one. Once the meal was concluded, each of the children had a specific duty in clearing the table. Bree and Zeke were encouraged to inspect the dock while everyone else cleaned up.

Zeke expressed his appreciation for the fellowship and hospitality.

Donovan issued an open invitation for him to return.

When they were finally alone, Zeke offered Bree his hand and they walked toward the lake, as the sun began to set.

"You like it here?" He asked.

She faced him as they reached the edge of the dock. "I know I overthink things but are you inquiring whether I like this part of Austin, the lake, or staying here in the guest house?"

The way she looked up at him, standing so close, his brain was mush.

When he failed to respond, she continued, "If you are asking whether I like it here with you," she placed her hand on his chest and inched closer, lifting her lips toward his, "the answer is very much so."

While thoughts of kissing her had flooded his consciousness the prior few weeks, he had no specific intention of doing so. When his lips met hers, he knew this was the moment he had waited his entire life for.

For Bree, the initial contact was soft and light, then, in a breath, it was electric and consuming. She felt energized and light-headed. When her knees threatened to buckle, he pulled her to him and deepened their kiss.

The second wave of emotion brought with it a sense of urgency and need, making her bold and assertive in her response.

He raised his head slightly and searched her eyes with a smile on his face.

"Lady," he moaned breathlessly, "you are full of surprises."

She touched her fingertips to his mouth before running them through his hair and pulling his lips back to her.

Several more minutes elapsed, and he heard the dusk to dawn lights on the deck begin to buzz, as they slowly brightened.

"We are about to become a spectacle."

She was slow to open her eyes, but when she did, his heart sang at her bemused expression, her eyelids half-closed in a love-drugged fashion.

"You are beautiful." He kissed her again. "And sexy."

She lay her head on his chest, holding onto him tightly.

"Come on. Walk me to the truck. It is getting late."

Reluctantly, she allowed him to lead her back to the front, stopping briefly to release CoalBear from the guest house.

"I should walk you back and tuck you in."

"Why don't you?"

"I am afraid I may not leave."

She giggled.

He continued, "Then the Mafia Boss might have something to say to me in the morning. Plus, we have those young, impressionable minds to consider."

"He calls you Fly Boy."

"Of course, he does," he chuckled, "I guess it could be worse."

"Definitely, he called Clint twerp and, occasionally, twit."

"Ouch," he laughed. "I will take Fly Boy."

He kissed her long and hard, draining the breath from both of them.

Smoothing her hair and running his thumb along her bottom lip, he sighed. "Okay, I have to go."

She knew he had a two-and-a-half-hour drive ahead of him.

"I am sorry for keeping you."

"When will you return to the warehouse?

"Friday."

"Pack a bag. Bring the Hell Hound. Stay with me."

"I would like that."

"Good."

"Thank you for today."

"Thank you."

"Be safe."

"I will text you when I get in."

She kissed him again.

"Get your dog and go. I will wait until you are safely inside."

She hesitated.

He turned her around and swatted her backside to hasten her along.

He followed only far enough to have a clear view of her entering the guest house.

By the time he started the truck, his phone beeped.

She had texted: "Thank you for everything."

Chapter 10

Uncharacteristically, Bree slept in the next morning. Moreover, her sleep was not marred with disturbing dreams of an unknown woman crying for help or fear of a man with a form, but no face, threatening her. Instead, delicious images of Zeke touching her, holding her, and kissing her filled her head.

She was inclined to stay in bed and allow those nighttime images to cross over into her daydreams, but CoalBear had different notions. He had been patient long enough and desperately needed to go outside.

She knew she had a busy week ahead of her, especially, as she intended to take Friday off.

With an eye on her canine friend, she mentally considered her checklist. Tuesday and Thursday mornings, she had hearings. There was a staff meeting, and the following week, she had a brief due.

On the mundane side, she knew laundry and grocery shopping were overdue. She also had quite a few meals to cook, package, and freeze. Zeke had mentioned Jed's wife Darla was having a difficult pregnancy, and she thought a freezer full of prepared meals might be welcome.

When they retreated back to the guest house for a late breakfast, Bree checked her phone again, re-reading his text: "Home safe. Night-Night, Beautiful."

She grinned every time she read it.

∞∞∞

It was mid-morning when Zeke began unloading the trailer at the warehouse. Within minutes, he was soaked, less from exertion than the humidity, which saturated the air. Jed was supposed to have met him half an hour ago, but per his norm, he was running late.

Most of the items he could manage on his own, but an extra pair of hands would have been helpful.

Grabbing a water from his ever present and stocked cooler, he decided to create a punch list on what remained to be completed before Bree could move in.

In addition to the natural desire to see a project through to its end, he was motivated to have her closer to him, at least for a while.

There was no doubt he was interested in her; of that he was certain. What plagued him was how unsettled his future was at the moment.

Since he had separated from the military, he had been conflicted regarding his plans.

Actually, the plans were made a year ago, he had decided to retire from the Air Force, give himself six months to help Jed with his construction business, then take a position as a flight instructor with an elite group in Florida. He had shored up his network and contacts, made all the right inquiries, and set things in motion. He submitted his application, taken their tests, and made it to the final round of interviews, which he had already been assured were nothing more than a formality.

Texas was fine. He had spent a fair portion of his youth here. His parents had settled here for most of the year. They were both from Montana originally and preferred to spend their summers there.

Wiping his forehead, he did not blame them.

Jed, of course, was born here and had already set down roots. Zeke was proud of him and the life he had created for him and Darla.

Samuel, his middle brother, was also making noises about returning to Texas.

Zeke knew family was important, but he had not been convinced settling down in Texas was for him. Afterall, he had done that once. Although, that now seemed a lifetime ago.

Segregating his thoughts, as he drained the bottle and grabbed a pen and clipboard to begin his walk-through. He hoped Jed would show up by the time he was done.

Chapter 11

Nerves frayed; Bree checked her phone when she finally returned to her vehicle after an extraordinarily long day at the courthouse. Her 9:00 am hearing had been bumped to 10:30 am, rescheduled again for 1:00 pm. Then finally heard at 4:00 pm. As evidentiary hearings went, two hours was not bad for 165 different exhibits, but the corporate parties were extremely contentious. With the issues involving intellectual property, neither side wanted to share anything by way of discovery, she was completely done, tapped, and exhausted. She was ready for a day off and a long weekend.

Checking her text messages, Evangeline confirmed Millie had taken CoalBear out to play the moment she returned home from school.

Gratitude washed over her. She hated the thought of leaving her dog cooped up all day long, but with Millie around, she need not have worried.

She knew when she moved to the warehouse, she would have to secure arrangements for him on court days. She made a note to reach out to Dr. Kelty for a recommendation.

She continued to scroll through her missed messages when her phone rang. She answered immediately.

"Hello."

"What are you doing now?" Came the smooth and sexy voice.

She giggled.

"What are you doing?" she purred.

"Lady, I asked you first."

"Well, I am sitting in my ride in the parking garage at the

courthouse."

"I thought your hearing was this morning."

"We were bumped several times and finally put on a show at 4."

He whistled.

"Yeah. It was not fun, but it is done now."

"What would you like to do this weekend?"

She felt so comfortable with this man. He had called every evening since they last saw one another. There was no pretense and certainly no games with him. They did not have marathon conversations lasting hours on end, but they chatted and caught up. His time and effort letting her know of his interest and intent made her secure and comfortable.

Surprising herself, she allowed that security to embolden her. Dropping her tone to a husky whisper, she challenged: "Just how honest would you like me to be?"

She was rewarded with a hearty and deep throated laugh that made her giggle again.

"Okay, Miss Fancy Pants, I guess we shall see just how sassy you are in person when you arrive."

They chatted for a few more minutes, and he updated her on the renovations.

Chapter 12

His instructions were to pack light. She was able to get her stuff into her trusty backpack, but Coal-Bear required food and water bowls, bed, crate, harness, leash, toys, and treats. She had a Styrofoam cooler of frozen meals for Jed and his wife. She packed a second cooler with fresh roasted salsa, a package of her homemade marinara, berries, and heavy cream. With the berries, she decided to prepare a small round of pastry dough for a tart. Of course, she had to have tortilla chips for the salsa and pasta for the sauce.

It was a test, and she knew it. She had packed light, sort of.

She found herself giggling again, something she had been doing often in recent days, even though she had never once considered herself much of a giggler.

With all her preparations, she had not cooked any tacos or baked any treats, but she was determined not to show up empty handed. She made a stop in San Antonio for doughnuts and breakfast tacos.

When she pulled into the lot of the warehouse before 8:00, the place was abuzz with activity.

Zeke's dually was parked closest to the garage and indicated he had been the first to arrive.

Allowing the dog to roam free, she slipped her phone into her pack, swung it over one shoulder, balanced the two boxes of doughnuts in one hand, while she grabbed the bag containing the tacos, and closed the door with her foot.

With food in her hands, she was certain the dog would follow.

∞∞∞

Zeke had been tracking her on the app, just as he had done nightly. The last thing he did before closing his eyes was to check on her. He refrained from looking at it during the day, but he rested well knowing she was safe.

This morning, the second he woke, she came to mind, and he could not resist looking to see whether she was *en route* yet. Despite the early hour, he had been surprised she was already south of Austin and almost to New Braunfels.

The quickening of his heartbeat and extra spring to his step as he bounced out of bed only added to the anticipation of seeing her.

He had to admit, if only to himself, he enjoyed thinking about her and certainly enjoyed their daily conversations. She seemed genuinely surprised the first time he had called, but she quickly recovered, and they fell into an easy rapport. He could sense she was becoming more and more comfortable with him. She had even managed to surprise him with her flirtatious comment the evening before.

If he were correct and she actually became much more confident and bolder with him, he knew he would have his hands full because she already kept him on his toes.

He liked that about her. She was very much her own person, whether she fully realized it. She was somewhat shy with a propensity to remain quiet and aloof in crowds. He suspected she was actually quite comfortable in her own skin, and when pressed, perfectly capable of holding her own.

The weaving surprised him; however, her initial reticence to share surprised him even more. He wondered what other things interested her.

Fortunately, Jed spied her arrival and was happy to divest her of the sweets before she reached the patio door.

Taking the opportunity to speak to him privately, she asked him if he would help her with something in her truck.

They put the food down and he dutifully followed her back to her vehicle.

"Jed, how is your wife doing?"

"She is on bed rest. We have made 20 weeks and the baby is viable now. So, we just need for her to take it easy and see how far we can get."

"Would you be offended if I offered frozen meals I prepared for you guys?"

He was a bit dumbfounded and his knitted brows expressed it. "Offended by you bringing us pre-cooked meals? Are you serious?"

"Well, I know you guys can cook and neither of you know me very well, but I enjoy cooking, even though I do not have anyone to feed."

She opened the Styrofoam cooler and pulled out a package. "There are thirty or so vacuum sealed quart bags of food. There is gumbo, marinara, beef stew, etouffee, charro beans... Quite a variety."

"All that is for us?"

"If you would like it, Jed."

"Oh, yes, Ma'am. I just don't know how to thank you."

Bree smiled. She pulled a kraft paper envelope from the back seat. "Here is a list of what is in the cooler and how I serve it, just for ideas. You may have to make rice, pasta, or mash potatoes to go with some of it."

He opened the envelope and took a peek.

He shook his head. "You are the best, Bree. Thank you."

He hugged her tightly.

"Darla and I so appreciate this."

"Enjoy, Jed."

He carried the cooler over to his truck and slipped the envelope onto the truck seat.

"I will take this home and get it in the freezer in a bit. I will bring your cooler back."

"No need to worry about the cooler, that's why I used a Styrofoam one. Please keep it."

Making her way back in, she noted CoalBear scurried in just ahead of her. She guessed he was in search of Zeke, as Molly was nowhere to be found. A glance around the place brought her lips to form a perfect "O" as she realized how much had been accomplished.

A man who said his name was Juan appeared and raised a doughnut to her in appreciation. Others of the crew quickly helped themselves, as well. She returned their greetings with a smile and continued to assess all the changes.

The cabinets were installed in the utility room, and the tile was down in there. The room was almost complete. She knew the flooring in the rest of the place would have to be done before the other cabinets were set in place.

There were ceiling fans upstairs and down.

Her eyes drifted up the stairs and she found Zeke staring back at her, CoalBear in one hand.

He had been waiting for her, wanting to gauge her reaction at the work they had done. Her wide-eyed response was no disappointment. With a slight movement of his head, he bid her to join him.

She almost ran to the stairs and trotted up them.

Flushed and slightly breathless, when she finally faced him, she fought the urge to catapult herself into his arms.

He noted her dark eyes shone even brighter from three feet away.

He smiled broadly and lifted his hand toward the bedroom and bath.

She needed no further invitation.

He heard her squeal as he followed her. She immediately stepped into the free-standing tub and lowered herself into it.

"Oh, Zeke," she whispered, "this will be heaven." She leaned back and closed her eyes.

She looked tiny in the tub and he suspected once filled she would float around in it, but his second thought was there may be enough room for both of them.

"Shall we see if the taps work?" He teased.

She knew it was not yet hooked up but giggled anyway.

He realized how much he loved the sound. Her giggles reminded him of light little chimes singing in the breeze.

"Care to join me?"

He was pleased with her moxie and hoped this version of Bree were here to stay.

The look she gave him let him know he was in for a remarkably interesting weekend.

Instead of testing the faucet, he offered her his free hand. She took it and allowed him to pull her from the tub.

Still grasping his hand, she pulled closer to him and whispered, "I have missed you."

He exercised impulse control when she wet her lips and her eyes moved to his lips. His lower body tensed, and his breath caught in his chest.

"Careful, Lady," he cautioned, "there are eyes everywhere."

Her gaze returned to his and she raised her chin, along with an eyebrow. "Ashamed of me?"

"Never," he grinned, "but every one of these guys has a cell phone with a camera."

Her bravado eroded to sensibility. "Excellent point, Sir." She winked. "I concede."

He laughed that rich, deep throated laugh of his and pulled her in for a hug, kissing the top of her head.

"Are you pleased?"

She squeezed him tighter. "I am ecstatic with all the hard work. I cannot thank you enough."

She also felt as though she was taking advantage, especially when the massive built-ins she secured at the auction market came to mind.

"I understand," she told him, "the work with the built-ins is beyond the scope of our contract."

He grinned at her.

"No, I am serious. This is business."

He kept grinning.

She attempted to give him a stern look, but he reached out and pulled her to him, resting his hands just below her hips with his fingers splayed out on her lower back.

"Yes, Bree, the install of the built-ins is beyond the scope; however, that part is my housewarming gift to you, okay?"

She protested, hands flat against his chest, "You have done so much already."

"My brother's company and the crew, as well as all the sub-contractors are being and will be well and fairly compensated for all the work here. In fact, Jed was going to speak to you about having a photographer come in and take pictures for the company website, as well as ask you for a testimonial, when all this is done."

"Of course, I am happy to help," she paused, "but what about you?"

He moved one of his hands to gently rub her right upper arm. "That kind of runs parallel to one of the things I want to chat with you about this weekend."

"Sounds ominous."

"It need not be, I just want to be upfront with you about a thing or two."

He felt her body tense and stiffen.

She looked away momentarily before raising her chin and meeting his gaze again.

"Are you married?"

"No."

"Is there someone, somewhere waiting for you to come home?"

"No."

"Are you a fugitive from justice?"

"No."

She relaxed a bit, then almost smiled as she quipped. "Do you actually prefer men?"

Once again, she had caught him completely off guard and he threw his head back in roaring laughter.

"Hell no."

"Okay, we are good."

Tracing her lips with his thumb before tipping her face up to meet him, he kissed her, fully and deeply.

Once she completely melted into him, he murmured against her lips, "Yes, Ma'am, we are good."

∞∞∞

With her borrowed tape measure in hand, Bree referred to her phone for notes and photos about the built-ins. She had anxiety of where they were to go.

Zeke came up behind her and asked: "What are you doing?"

"Trying to decide if I made a mistake in purchasing those built-ins."

"You wanted to put them all along the shared wall with the garage, right?"

"That was my thought, yes. Where else would they go?"

"Well, it is in four or five pieces. There's the other side wall opposite where you had originally intended and behind the dining area."

"The east wall."

"There's also the wall outside the utility room. We could install just the armoire portion where you originally intended, along the shared wall with the garage, and you could use it as an entertainment center with storage. Combine the other pieces with the secretary desk over there." He pointed toward the utility room.

He had a good point. The area beyond the stairs on the way to the store front was a large space, which served as a passage area. Furniture would impede the flow, but there was a whole wall of nothing there now.

"What about the sides of the armoire? They are not all finished because they were attached to the other pieces."

"We will have to look more closely when they arrive. We may be able to stain what is there to match or use veneer, like what I picked up in Georgetown."

She considered the options.

He enjoyed watching the wheels turn in her head.

Her smile indicated she had reached a decision.

"I like your idea better, please."

"As you wish."

∞∞∞

She was sitting on a piece of plywood atop the island base after everyone else had left.

Zeke was doing a walk-through making notes on his clip board and locking everything up.

CoalBear was napping in his bed a few feet from her.

It had been a long and exciting day, but she was feeling the before dawn commute and most of the day spent on her feet. She did not know how Zeke managed to do it and surmised he must be in much better shape.

Unsure how much longer he would be, she decided to lie down for just a few minutes, until her second wind kicked in.

Half an hour later, Zeke found her curled up on the island, fast asleep.

He did not imagine the plywood was too comfortable, yet she looked so peaceful and angelic, he hated to disturb her.

The sun was low on the horizon, and he was anxious to get her home. He laid a gentle hand on her hip as he leaned over to kiss her forehead.

"Hey, sleepyhead, would you like to follow me home?"

She smiled as she unfurled into a stretch. "Best offer I have had all day."

∞∞∞

A quarter hour later, she was still yawning as she turned her blinker on and followed Zeke's white dually from the highway onto a narrow dirt road. He had indicated the short cut was actually the back way, which passed over his parents' land. She had been on this road before, but it was dark, and he had driven.

She had expected the scenery to be rural, but it was more wooded than she imagined. It was also bumpy, which explained the slow speed.

She checked the vehicle's navigation and was not surprised the path was not mapped. She doubted she would be able to retrace the route, and laughed, perhaps, that had been by design.

Another ten minutes found them driving beyond an electric gate. Two more minutes and the rutted road opened into a clearing with buildings along the tree line.

She realized when she was last here it had been dark when they arrived and also when they left the following morning. She remembered none of this.

Zeke rolled down his window and motioned for her to park next to him.

As she did, she could not look away from the structures.

The main one appeared to be comprised of two metal shipping containers. They were spaced at an angle to one another. The nearest ends were twelve or thirteen feet apart and joined by a structure featuring a covered porch with front door between the closest ends. There was a roof above them with clerestory windows on the front and along both sides, running the length of each container.

The light was low, but off to the left, she could make out a building, a barn or workshop, she was unsure.

Zeke had exited his vehicle and come around to her door to open it. Transfixed, she had not yet put the truck in park or killed the engine, which unlocked the door. When she finally did so, he opened the door with a smile, amused by her reaction.

"I missed all of this last week."

She collected the dog from the passenger seat and passed him to Zeke, who extended his free hand to assist her with stepping down.

"You realize," she advised, "this is a dream for introverts like me. I may never leave."

"That is why I told you to pack light."

He put the dog down as she reached for her pack.

"Well," she rolled her eyes, "I followed directions, but I cannot speak for my companion here."

"Oh," he began with mock surprise and opened the back of her truck, "the Hell Hound packed this cooler and bag full of food?"

"Note, Sir, the crate, bed, bowls, dog food, and treats..."

He unloaded everything.

"And," she continued, "if you say anything about the cooler, the Hell Hound and I will keep its contents to ourselves."

"Duly noted, counselor."

He deposited everything on the front porch and winked at her as he opened the door, gesturing for her to precede him. "Welcome."

She was delighted to see everything was just as it was the week before. The front door opened to a large expanse with wood floors forming a pie-shape the full length of the containers, one on either side of the large common area. The far wall was glass with a lovely view of a small open space before a thick tree line. The room contained a round dining table with four chairs closest to the entry and U-shaped leather sectional sofa. Everything was sleek and minimal, but comfortable and inviting.

She turned to find him holding the dog and watching her intently.

She reached for the dog and he promptly brought everything inside, depositing most of it on and around the table.

She knew the kitchen and utility were off to the right, while there were two bedrooms and a bath to the left.

Throughout he had used the same wood flooring with wide planks in a medium, almost greyed wood, similar to old barn wood. She reached down to run a hand over them.

"100% recycled vinyl planks."

"Really? I thought they were wood."

He used neutral tones throughout. While the bathroom and kitchen seemed a lighter shade, the bedrooms were slightly darker.

"This place is beautiful. I love the colors and finishes. You have maximized all available space without making it feel cluttered."

"I like it."

"You designed and built all of this."

It was more of a statement than a question, and he recognized it as such.

"It is a hobby of mine."

"Any chance you can make it a vocation? Are you on any social media platforms?"

He shook his head "no."

"I follow several tiny homes people on Instagram. This is every bit as good, if not better, than what they post."

"Are you into marketing now, too?"

"No, but I know good design when I see it."

"Are you hungry?"

She raised her eyebrows and grinned. "I can always eat."

"Good. I will let you get settled while I start a fire and clean up. Steaks okay?"

"Yes, please! What may I do to help?

"There are potatoes in the kitchen. Would you mind?"

"I am on it. I will walk him first, then get started."

Twenty minutes later, Zeke, freshly showered, found Bree busy in the kitchen. She had the steaks seasoned and on a plate. Potatoes had been through the microwave and were steaming in foil on the counter. She had cheese grated, green onions chopped, and freshly fried bacon cut up for toppings.

He noticed the oven was on and took a quick peek. Berries in some sort of pastry were bubbling away.

"Lord, woman, you do not waste any time."

"I like food," she grinned.

Wrapping his arms around her from behind, he pulled her hair aside and kissed her neck. "I like you."

"You smell good."

"You feel good."

"Do you have a mixer or a whisk, please?"

"Both. Electric?"

"Yes."

"Whipped cream?"

"How did you know?"

"Lucky guess. There are stainless bowls to left of the sink, bottom cabinet. Shall I place one in the freezer?"

"Please."

After he did so, he picked up the plate of steaks.

Before he asked, she said: "Medium rare, please."

"You got it."

Shortly, they were seated across from one another at the table.

Zeke had turned the sound system on, and Blues played softly in the background.

He had offered wine. She preferred water.

He selected a beer, which he poured into a glass, offering her the first sip, explaining a friend of his was into craft brewing. He called it a blond pilsner.

Unfamiliar with the beer, she was surprised the taste reminded her slightly of caramel.

The steak was tender and delicious, perfectly grilled.

Once they finished the meal and cleaned the table, Zeke distracted Bree from the dishes by inquiring about dessert.

"Oh, the tart!" she exclaimed.

"Don't talk about yourself that way," he teased.

She playfully swatted his back, as he rinsed their plates and added them to the dishwasher.

She had turned the oven off earlier and left the door cracked to keep it warm. She pulled it out and placed it on the counter before whipping the cream.

"Bowls or plates?" Zeke inquired.

While she had not thought being with Zeke at his place would be awkward, she was more than a little amazed at how natural and comfortable it was.

They enjoyed their dessert.

Zeke cleaned up their dishes while Bree showered. When she emerged fresh faced and sporting a tank with a sarong tied around her waist, he was relaxing on the sofa with a drink in his hand.

"Dinner was lovely, thank you."

His eyes traveled over her appreciatively, noting the bright smile, which reached all the way to her dark beautiful eyes, her toned arms, and her bare feet with dark pink tipped toes.

He raised his glass to her.

"Would you like a drink?"

"What are you having?"

"Bourbon and Coke."

She declined.

He placed his drink down and offered her his hand, "Come here, please."

She complied, moving to stand before him. He gestured for her to sit on his lap, but she only smiled.

Noting the impish grin across her face, he suspected she had something else in mind. Content to watch her, he simply waited.

Bending forward, she brought her face close to his, as she reached for his hands and rested them on her hips. Her lips lightly grazed one of his ear lobes, her breath soft and warm along his neck. Her scent was light and welcoming, as he inhaled.

She braced her hands on his shoulders as she tucked her

knees on either side of him deep into the cushions, straddling him with her bum resting between his knees, her face inches from his own.

"Better?" she inquired.

"Much," he approved, sliding his hands around her bottom and pulling her closer, curious as to her next move.

Without breaking their gaze, she shared "I like it here."

"I like you."

She rewarded him by cupping his face and began a slow, deep, exploratory kiss, successfully igniting every nerve ending from the top of his head to his toes and draining his breath from him.

Fighting the urge to deepen the kiss, he forced himself to relax his grip on her behind and begin to lightly caress her backside.

When their eyes met again, his lids were half-closed. Her lips were moist, swollen, and slightly parted. She dropped her hands from his face, content to bury her face between his neck and shoulder.

His breathing slowed. When his ability to think returned, he noted she had matched the rise and fall of her chest to his.

"You know I am really interested in you."

He felt her head nod.

When he did not continue, she sat up to face him with pursed lips and slightly furrowed brow.

"Well," she ventured, "you have my undivided attention, and you said you had something you wanted to chat with me about."

He squeezed her buttocks slightly.

She leaned forward with her hands on his shoulders, sinking deeper into his lap, and lightly kissed the edge of his mouth before moving to center and gently pulling on his bottom lip. His hands urged her closer into several minutes of deeper contact.

Regretfully, she pulled back from the distraction and pressed on.

"I think I have an idea of your agenda and would like to hear your concerns, please."

Her words were quietly spoken, but her tone was clear.

He studied her for several minutes before conceding.

"I really just wanted to be upfront with you about a couple of things."

"An attempt to manage my expectations?"

"Perhaps," he paused, "I know you have recently emerged from a divorce and long-term relationship."

She said nothing, tension descending into her body.

He suspected she was attempting to maintain a neutral expression and knew she had merely dropped a mask on her emotions.

She would have changed her position, as well, but his hands held her firmly in place.

She sighed.

"Let me spare you the trouble. I actually have no expectations. I learned how to protect myself from the bitterness and disappointment of shattered expectations a long time ago."

Her words were steady and even, though acerbic and biting.

"If you are interested, my relationship with Clint was over a while ago, I was just unwilling to admit defeat and failure."

Her focus was past him, on something beyond the walls behind him. Her eyes were dull, and he watched pain move across her face, as she contemplated her words.

"When I discovered the affair, the overriding emotion was not shock, surprise, or even anger. I was overwhelmed with this huge sense of relief. I knew people, like his mother, would blame me for his infidelity. For those people, I would never be good enough, so I tried not to let that get to me. I have no control over what people think, anyway. I know I did everything I could to be a good wife, and I worked hard to be what he needed me to be, but in the end, I was just not what he wanted."

She chewed on her bottom lip a moment before adding, "He was not what I wanted or needed, either."

Moved by her revelations, he had failed to notice the moment she had abandoned the mask. In doing so, she allowed him to witness her pain and vulnerability.

"We were not even good roommates. We were over a long time ago."

Her voice hardened slightly and took on an edge when she finally met his gaze again. "So, Mr. Buchanan, if you are concerned this is just a rebound infatuation on my part, you may be mistaken."

His expression surprised her. She had somehow assumed he would be uncomfortable with her admissions. Instead, she found concern and empathy in his dark blue eyes.

"Is it isolating to have no expectations of others?" He asked.

She had not anticipated that response.

"I think you discovered last week that I am an introvert." She smiled without mirth. "I am a socially high functioning introvert, but I basically live in an exceedingly small bubble. I have friends who I adore, but with whom I interact infrequently because I do not like to bother them. I know they have more important things in their lives than me. I am actually okay with that."

His brows furrowed and his lips formed a thin line. He shook his head slightly.

"However," sadness tinged her eyes, "I have an extremely rich internal life and have no problem entertaining myself."

"Why did you agree to come here?"

"As I asked you the other day, how honest do you want me to be?"

"Completely honest, please."

Her internal dialogue was triggered. One voice shouted it was unfair of him to ask her to share her innermost thoughts and feelings when he had yet to reveal any of his own. Her instincts told her to continue. As she most often did, she followed her gut.

"First off, you invited me."

His face had relaxed slightly, and his eyes softened, as he remembered how easily the request slipped from him and how quickly she had accepted.

"Secondly, I like you. I am attracted to you, and I want you."

If her veracity surprised him, he hid it well.

"The question remains," she pressed, "Why did you invite me?"

"I find you incredibly attractive, intelligent, and interesting. I wanted to give us a chance to get to know one another better."

Her face relayed her confusion. "I do not understand. What is the problem, then?"

It was his turn to sigh.

"My world is in a state of flux. A year ago, I decided when my 20 years were up, I would retire from the Air Force and do something new. I separated from the military three months ago. At that time, the plan was to take time off, spend six months or so helping my little brother continue to establish his business."

"Okay."

"As you know, I have done just that."

"And you have ninety days until you move onto the next thing and you do not want any strings or complications getting in the way."

Again, she made a more concerted effort to move away from him, but he held fast.

"Not exactly."

She set her jaw and the impatience and irritation which flickered across her face were unmistakable.

"For the past several months, I have been in contact with a flight school in Florida. This outfit is not the basic run-of-the-mill commercial flying school. They are a subsection of a security firm, which specializes in the wealthiest of the wealthy clients. They only hire elite military types, not just from the US, but most particularly from Israel, as well."

"Mossad?"

"Yes."

"I have the second round of interviews at the end of next month, provided I pass the extensive background checks."

She nodded and smiled. "Is this your dream job?"

"No," he admitted, "I had dreams a long time ago. They did not work out, and I kind of let them wither and die."

She was taken back by the bitterness lacing his words and considered them carefully before continuing their discussion.

"I appreciate your candor. I know how it easy it might be for someone else not to share, allow this to progress, then fade a couple of months down the road."

"I would not do that."

"I see that clearly." She kissed him softly. "This is what I know. I do not connect with many people, certainly not in a meaningful way. Not only do I work ridiculously hard not to expect anything from anyone, I actively choose to live in the present. Of course, I plan for the future and am conservative in my actions; however, I have learned that here and now are all we really have. Thus far, if my life is any testament, that can change in a heartbeat."

"What are you saying?"

"At this moment, I choose you and me, right here, right now. If you are interested, I would like to see how this unfolds and evolves, if at all. If you leave for Florida in three months, I have no desire to wonder 'what if.' Who knows, if you wanted me to, I might seriously consider following you."

The last of her words were spoken in hushed tones to the buttons on his shirt, as she absently fiddled with them.

For the first time in forever, Zeke felt a flicker of hope. In the extreme back of his mind and the bottom of his heart, he felt his old dreams were being dusted off, as the slightest bit of life was being breathed into them.

"You are amazing." He whispered.

She scoffed lightly. "Here I thought I sounded like a desperate old dog lady."

He chuckled and inched her forward, his hands still on her behind.

"Did you mean what you said?"

She narrowed her eyes: "Which part?"

"You want me?"

"I meant everything I said."

His eyes darkened and his voice became huskier. "What are we doing still sitting in here?"

Giggling, she kissed him; however, she sobered up just enough to address one more piece of business. "Just know, I am not on any kind of birth control..."

He groaned slightly, but she was unsure whether it was in response to her statement or her weight as he shifted them to the edge of the sofa before standing and carrying her off to his bedroom.

Chapter 13

By design, the bedroom was without windows, but with the door open, light from the common room and the window in the guest room poured down the hallway, invading the darkness.

With one eye cracked, he glanced over the body nestled into his side and checked the clock. It was a quarter of eight. Inhaling the essence of her, he smiled against her hair splayed across his pillow. Images from their night fresh on his mind and tempered with a gentle soreness in various parts of his body. Overall, he was content and wholly satiated.

She had surprised and delighted him with her sexual hunger and passion. While not aggressive, she was certainly not shy. In her eagerness to please herself, as well as him, she had exhibited an assertiveness, which easily matched his own; however, he grinned, many more nights like the last, and he may not survive.

More fully awake now, he realized what must have awakened him.

CoalBear had moved from the foot of the bed where he had been most of the night to his pillow where he sat watching him expectantly.

Loathe to wake her, he carefully lifted his arm from around her. He started to pull the covers up around her shoulders when marks across her skin caught his attention.

He refrained from tracing them lightly with his fingertips, but there were dozens of light lines, seemingly raised, across what he could see in the dim light of her upper back.

He frowned deeply, recognizing them as scars from whippings or beatings. He remembered she had said she was an orphan surrendered to foster care as a young child. He grimly hoped the marks were received before she entered foster care.

∞∞∞

Bree was floating in the arms of ecstasy. She felt decadent and free to indulge in the pleasures of the flesh. Her body felt fluid and warm, released from the pressures and stress of the daily grind. Images of Zeke were all around her. The feel of his hands on her body, as his mouth explored every inch of her. She felt a warmth emanating from the lower half of her and reached for him in the semi-darkness to persuade him, yet again, to sate her desires.

However, she could not find him.

Emerging from her dream, slightly heavy headed and groggy, she realized she was alone in his bed.

Lazily stretching, she rolled over to where he had been, his scent on the sheets, but they were cold with no hint of the heat he generated.

The clock on the bedside table read 9:15.

Rubbing her eyes, she could not remember when she had last slept so late.

Further thought revealed she could not remember a night so filled with passion and satisfaction.

She smiled when she realized just how sore she was. A giggle emerged when she wondered if she could walk straight. She decided a shower was definitely in order before she sought out her stallion of a lover.

∞∞∞

Bree was amazed to discover the glass wall opposite the front door in the common area was completely movable. The panels were seamless sliding doors, all on different tracts, which opened the room to the outside.

While it had been dark the night before, she had noticed patio furniture out there, she just had not known how to access it.

Zeke was sitting to one side, shirtless with jeans pulled up, but unbuttoned. CoalBear was at his feet, leash looped around the arm of his chair. A coffee mug sat on the table beside him.

She was smitten by how chiseled and handsome he was.

He must have sensed her presence because his head slowly turned. A sensual smile appeared as he caught sight of her.

Releasing the leash, he rose and stepped over to greet her.

"Good morning, Beautiful."

With mock skepticism, she teased him, "Oh, I bet you say that to all the ladies you invite to your slumber parties."

He knew she was joking, but his response was quiet and sincere. "Actually, Bree, you are the only lady to grace these particular walls."

Humbled, she closed the distance between them. "I appreciate your taking a chance on me."

When he moved to speak, she lightly placed a finger on his lips. "And," she purred, "Last night was amazing. Thank you."

Taking her hand, he pulled it down and kissed her, mumbling against her lips, "Last night was just the beginning."

All too soon, a day of laughing, lounging, and learning more about one another had passed. Saturday turned into Sunday, morning bled into afternoon, and Zeke was helping her load her SUV.

Holding her close, he asked "Is it too soon to ask you to come back next week?"

"I was hoping you would."

"Good," he grinned, "I will take you out to eat and enjoy some live music."

"I am perfectly happy to hang out here with you."

"Yes, but I want to show you off, so pack accordingly."

"Yes, Sir."

"Be careful."

"I will."

"I will call you later."

After another kiss goodbye, he got in his truck and guided her to the highway. With a smile and a wave, he watched her drive away.

Instead of returning home, he headed to town to get a jump on his tasks for the week.

Chapter 14

Zeke reviewed his punch list items and the schedule. The biggest job remaining were the floors. Several of the worn boards needed to be replaced before the floor guys could come in, sand, stain, and seal everything. Once that was done, they had to cover them with kraft paper to protect them while the light fixtures were installed, which reminded him, he needed to pin down Bree's friend...

As soon as the floors were finished, the remaining cabinets could be installed, as well as the appliances and plumbing fixtures.

The heating and cooling units were in, and everything on that end was up and running.

The propane tank had been delivered. Jed was supposed to bring a Bobcat by for him to dig a hole to bury it.

He made a note to check in with the plumber, electrician, and gas guy.

He needed to schedule delivery of the built-ins she bought, as well as the table.

Bree had already set up cable and internet.

He needed to clear it with her, but he found a little extra in the budget, mainly because she had provided most of the large light fixtures, to purchase and install a security system with cameras. He anticipated she would probably protest. Even though it was a small town, he did not like the idea of anyone knowing she was a young woman living alone, and he knew he could not be there all the time.

In fact, he had already decided the system and cameras were going in. She could decide whether to link the system with a monitoring service. At the very least, they could record and scan any activity on the cameras.

When he had mentioned this to Jed, his little brother gave him a knowing smile and parroted their father "Look after what you care about most."

His reflex had been to deny it, but he found he could not.

In the days which followed that conversation, he had given a great deal of thought to what was most important to him. His family, of course, was on that list, but other than Bree, there was not much else. He had friends, some close friends, in fact, but unless one of them expressed a need or desire for help, they were self-sufficient. Not that Bree was not, but she had become precious to him, and he was protective of her.

The job prospect in Florida loomed again. He received an email confirming he passed the background checks. Instead of excitement, he had begun to dread the interviews.

He had no problem flying to Florida and meeting with whomever, taking a tour of the facilities, and shaking hands. What he could not shake was the thought of leaving Bree behind.

Yes, he told himself, he knew she said she would consider following him there, but for what?

It could be the best job with excellent money, but everything and everyone she had known for the last decade was in Texas. She would have to take another bar exam, find another job, and make new friends.

He knew what the last was like. Unlike her, he was not an introvert, and it was still tough to connect with people and it took time to feel as though he belonged.

He did not feel he could ask her to leave what roots she had behind and start over somewhere new.

This, of course, left two options: go to Florida without her or remain in Texas.

Chapter 15

Bree had not signed into her work email since Thursday.

When she returned to the guest house, she texted Zeke to let him know she had arrived, then took care of laundry and other tasks, most of which involved daydreaming about one extremely kind and attractive man.

Unfortunately, she did not discover her email had blown up late Friday afternoon, until she returned to the office on Monday morning.

∞∞∞

Well after he had returned home on Monday, showered, had dinner, and sat down to relax, Zeke checked the tracking app to find Bree had at arrived at her office at seven that morning and, at 7:30 that evening, was still at the office. He shook his head, as there was no indication she had gone anywhere for lunch.

He called her.

"Hey," she answered.

"What are you doing?"

He heard her exhale. "One of the arbitrations we have been working on for the last four months blew up on Friday afternoon. I failed to check my email until this morning. So, I have been working to resolve some issues and get the parties back to the table. It is a mess."

"You okay?"

"I am fine, just frustrated."

"What can I do?"

"You are doing it. Thank you."

"Is it too soon to tell you I miss you?"

"No, Sir. I have missed you since I drove away."

"Go home. Get some rest."

"Yeah. Poor CoalBear. Thankfully, Millie rescued him when she got home from school."

"I actually wondered if the Hell Hound accompanied you to the office."

"I thought about it but decided not to push my luck with Donovan." She chuckled.

"Are you going to have a problem working remotely once you are down here?"

"I do not actually meet with clients in person that often. Most of what I have been doing can be done anywhere I have a decent internet connection and call coverage. I probably go to court four or five times a month, so once a week or so."

"That is still quite a commute."

"Well, we actually have cases in San Antonio, and I am transitioning to cover more of those."

"Perfect."

"Yeah. It was one of the selling points in convincing Donovan to agree."

"He was not going to stop you."

"No, but the issue for him was wider in scope. If he allowed me to essentially telework full time, he would have to allow others to do the same. His position is that I report directly to him, he wants to expand the San Antonio market, and my practice is largely appellate."

"Sounds good."

"Of course," she kind of chuckled, "He also announced it was me, he knew he could trust me to get things done, and no one else had better ask…"

"Mafia Boss."

"He is actually well loved."

"He plays to people's strengths, and I am guessing, he has a way of making each person feel special."

"Exactly. He cultivates loyalty."

"Should I be jealous?"

"Zeke."

"Yeah."

"You are my one and only."

"Go home. Take care of yourself."

"Yes, Sir."

Chapter 16

Bree's Monday continued for the rest of the week.

Her plans to be at the warehouse by noon on Friday were dashed completely. She and CoalBear did not make it to the highway where Zeke was waiting for them at the turnoff to the dirt road until well after nine.

When he opened her door to help her out of her SUV, she fell into his arms in exhaustion and relief.

He would have carried her inside, but for CoalBear begging for attention in the front seat.

He grabbed the dog and instructed her to go in. After he briefly walked the dog and unloaded her things, he found her stepping out of the shower.

He grabbed a second towel and blotted the droplets around her shoulders that she had missed. In the light of the bathroom, he could clearly see the scars on her back.

He also noticed how she tended to shift her back away from him. He was certain this had become an unconscious gesture over time.

"When was the last time you had anything to eat?"

She closed her eyes, shook her head, and admitted "I had a granola bar at my desk, but I am not sure if that was today or yesterday."

He grimaced and decided not to mention the dark circles under her eyes, although her sunken eyes gave him pause.

"I have salad, grilled chicken, and mac and cheese."

"Have I actually died and gone to heaven?"

He hugged her. "I picked it up on my way home."

"Thank you."

"Get dressed and join me in the kitchen."

∞∞∞

Zeke made plates for each of them and was setting them down on the table when she appeared.

"You have not eaten yet?"

"I wanted to dine with you."

As they sat down, she took a bite of pasta. "Oh, gosh, this is good."

They ate in silence, largely due to Bree's hunger. She finished everything.

"I may actually live." She announced, reclining back in her chair, and rubbing her stomach.

She watched him finish his meal, enjoying his presence.

"We have plans tomorrow night?"

"Dinner and music."

"I have been looking forward to it."

"Me, too."

"May I ask you a huge favor?"

"Sure."

"I have a flight out of San Antonio late morning Sunday."

He nodded.

"I will be in Baltimore through Tuesday, possibly Wednesday to present an arbitration agreement to the Labor Relations Board. If we do not obtain their blessing, this moves to litigation."

"You do not do a lot of labor law."

"No, I really do not. That is Ben's area, but he has been out. His wife is battling cancer, and she is not doing well."

"I am so sorry."

"I am familiar with the client, as I have assisted with negotiations in the past, and they specifically asked for me. With Ben out, I am it." She took a sip of her water. "In hindsight, Donovan was spot on to have Mitch work with me. I have completely relinquished that appeal to him to take this on."

"Do you need me to keep Coal?"

"Sort of. Doria works for the groomer in town. Dr. Kelty recommended her. I called and asked if she would consider boarding him for me. She agreed. The earliest she is available is after church on Sunday."

"And your flight is earlier..."

"Yeah."

"Sure. No problem."

"Thank you. She said she could meet you at the warehouse or the grooming shop, just let her know. I hope I am not making a mistake. I mean, I have only spoken to her on the phone."

"Juan is on our crew."

"Yes, I know him."

"Doria is his girlfriend."

"So, she is not likely to skip town and abscond with my dog?"

He chuckled. "I would say no."

"I did not tell you this, but when I first took him to the groomers in Austin, he must have thought I was abandoning him because they told me as soon as I left, he just laid down on his side."

She made a pitiful face. "The lady told me it was as though he had given up on life. It took two of them to bathe and clip him. One to hold him up, and the other to work on him."

"He totally has you wrapped."

She pouted.

"You know, a part of me can relate."

"Lady, you did not lie down and die."

"No, but I stopped talking for about a year."

Concern and confusion were written across his face.

She pushed her plate away from her and absently fiddled with the utensils. Her voice became low and hushed.

"When I was surrendered to foster care, I did not speak for a year, other than to say 'Bree' when anyone tried to call me by another name."

"Do you remember anything prior to that?"

"It is all a blank."

"Coal will be fine. If you would prefer, I will keep him with me."

She smiled her gratitude. "I so appreciate you, but you have enough on your plate without him under your feet."

Clearing the table, she put a hand on his shoulder to keep him seated. "How has your work been?"

He watched her deftly put away the food, rinse the dishes, load the dishwasher, and wipe the counter and table. The meal appeared to revive her.

"Your buddy Andre came by on Tuesday to deliver your custom light fixtures."

"Oh!" Her eyes grew wide and bright.

"He came back on Wednesday and installed them with the electrician.

Her surprise was genuine. "I did not expect him to deliver, much less return to install."

"Well, he is a fan of yours, and he said he wanted them done right."

"He is a good one."

"He said he owed his life to you."

"No," she shook her head. "He is exaggerating."

She had a distant look to her, as she recalled their history.

"He has had a rough life. He got into some trouble as a kid. I did some pro bono work in juvenile court a few years ago. We found him a mentor, someone who was able to help him see his potential. The rest he has done on his own."

"I like him."

"Did he leave you a bill?"

Zeke chuckled; he had known this was coming.

"Nope. He said it was on the house."

She shook her head.

"I have no intention of getting in the middle of this, but he did say he would like nice photos for his website when you were all moved in. He indicated the exposure would be good for him."

"Well, of course, that is the very least, but I will settle up with him after Baltimore."

"The floors are done, and the built-ins are installed."

"Squee!" she exclaimed, her face lively and bright. "Were they a huge pain and difficult?"

He laughed, delighted with her response. "No, they were fine. It just took time, tools, and a little know-how."

"You have a lot of know-how. Thank you." She leaned over and kissed him. "Where did you learn carpentry, anyway?"

"My dad did side jobs to make ends meet. Samuel and I went with him from before I can remember."

"You only have the two brothers?"

"Actually, no. We have a sister Rebecca."

Bree was flabbergasted. She had no idea there was a sister, too.

"Wait a minute. Why have I never heard about her?"

"I am the oldest. Samuel is two years younger than me. Rebecca is three years younger than Samuel, and Jed is six years younger than Rebecca."

"Did I hear an 'oops' before Jed's name?"

He grinned. "Yes, you did."

"You told Dr. Kelty Samuel was on mission in Africa."

"Yes, he should be back by the end of the year."

"Where is your sister?"

"My parents are originally from Montana. They were high school sweethearts who married when my father joined the Air Force. One of their duty stations was in San Antonio after I was born. They liked it here and returned once my dad was discharged. On one of their many trips back to visit family in Montana, Rebecca met and married a guy from there."

"She is in Montana, then."

"Correct."

Bree envied the relaxed and comfortable way Zeke spoke of his family. She sensed they were all close.

Perhaps, it was the exhaustion, but she was ill prepared for the sadness which overtook her and turned away when she felt the sting of tears in her eyes.

Zeke watched the flood of emotion descend, gained his feet, and wrapped his arms around her.

He was at a loss as she dissolved into quiet sobs.

"I am sorry," she murmured.

"You are okay, I have you."

Her tears where short-lived, and within minutes, she had them in check. He handed her a napkin to dry them, keeping his arms securely around her.

"What upset you?"

She shrugged.

"I am tired, I think. This whole concept of family and actually belonging to a unit of some kind is foreign to me. I have always wanted to be a part of something and to feel as though I belonged somewhere. You speak so fondly of your family, and I realized I really do not have anything to bring to the table."

He smoothed the hair from her face and lifted her chin to meet his gaze. "You are joking, right?"

"No. I am serious. You have done all the heavy lifting. You feed me; you are putting a roof over my head. You meet me at the highway to lead me back here because we both know I would never be able to find my way. Everything good in my life right now is directly attributable to you."

She could tell he was partly concerned and partly amused. "You did not strike me as the kind of woman to fish for compliments."

Her eyes were downcast. "I am not fishing. I just do not feel as though I am pulling my weight, and I do not want to be a drain on you."

"My day job at the moment is to complete the warehouse project. You happen to be the owner and beneficiary of those efforts. What I do with respect to that project is separate and apart from me and you."

"You say that, but the built-ins are beyond the scope..."

He cut her off, "of the contract, yes. We have discussed that, and I thought you understood it was my gift to you."

"Gosh," she warbled, "you sound like a lawyer."

"Logic and analysis, not even persuasion, are limited to the legal profession."

She exhaled heavily and rested her head on his chest.

"You are not a drain. I am sorry you have not benefited from the feeling of family. We are going to have to work on that."

Chapter 17

Bree woke with a start.

In the darkness, she held her breath and willed her racing heart to slow as she gained her bearings, allowing her senses to return.

She felt the weight of Zeke's arm across her, his hand cupping one of her breasts, his breath even on the pillow behind her neck, as they spooned.

Thoughts of his leisurely lovemaking brought a smile to her lips as warmth spread between her legs. She leaned her back into him, and he rolled onto his back, taking his hand with him. Raising her head, the clock read 2:40.

Fully awake, she decided to ease out of bed. Knowing she would not be able to sleep, she decided to dig into the pile of work she had shoved aside to deal with Ben's labor relations case.

Once her feet were on the floor, she searched for Coal, but he seemed content, curled next to one of Zeke's legs. She let him be.

Feeling her way out of the bedroom, she was glad she had left her bag in the guestroom, as she had taken to dressing in there, unwilling to disrupt the order of Zeke's bedroom with her things.

She donned a tee shirt and tied a sarong around her. Grabbing her laptop, pen, calendar, and notebook, she padded into the common room, moonlight streaming through all the windows, before electing to set up in the kitchen, where she was least likely to disturb him. Besides, she felt like a cup of hot black tea.

∞∞∞

From the depths of a sweet dream, he felt her tickling him with strands of her hair. He reached for her, as he struggled to open his eyes, but his hands could not find her among the sheets. He moved his hands to his face, and once again encountered the Hell Hound.

"Coal!" he laughed and wiped his mouth with the back of his hand as he sat up.

The clock read 6:17.

Bree was gone.

Her pillow was cold.

Pulling his briefs and jeans on, he stopped briefly in the bathroom before cracking the front door for Coal. He stood on the front porch as the little dog ran around sniffing and dutifully attending to business before trotting back to him. Zeke was grateful he preferred human company, particularly Bree's, to being outside.

The living room was vacant.

Entering the kitchen, he found her slouched in front of her computer, typing away.

"Good morning," he offered.

Her head popped around and she came over to greet him with a hug.

"Morning," she planted a kiss on his bare chest before moving her mouth over to one of his nipples and briefly rolling her tongue over and around it.

He groaned as desire surged through him. His hands cradled her head as she moved to inspect the other one. "You are going to be the death of me."

Purring, she asked, "Are you complaining?"

"No, Ma'am."

Moving her hands from his back, she gently pushed his jeans and briefs down as she kneeled before him, her eyes focused on his, a wicked grin on her face.

Words left him, his knees grew weak, and he could only watch as she slowly drew him into her mouth.

She heard him gasp as she rolled her tongue around him, exploring the folds of his tip while she continued to stare into his eyes. She noted his jaw was clenched.

There was a roaring sound in his ears, and he actually felt light-headed. His entire body was rigid and tense.

He wanted to reach out for her, but he kept his hands, white knuckled as they were, by his side.

Her hands were on his hips to give her leverage, as she kneeled before him. Slowly, excruciatingly slowly, she took him into her mouth, using her tongue to tease and excite him.

He struggled to keep from thrusting and tried to remain as motionless as possible.

She tested his control and changed her tempo and technique, edging him closer and closer to complete abandon.

Keeping her focus on him, she enjoyed watching him struggle. His breathing was in gasps and moans, teeth clenched.

When he reached out, he ran his fingers through her hair and relayed his urgency: "You are going to make me cum."

She hummed her satisfaction while continuing the attention in earnest and with renewed enthusiasm.

Moments later, he expelled a massive, agonizing groan and his entire body shuddered convulsively. Her mouth filled with warmth. She slowly and very gently eased off him and swallowed before wiping her mouth and rising.

His arms loosely wrapped around her as he hugged her, leaning heavily against her.

Stroking her hair, he whispered into her ear: "My God woman, you are amazing. Thank you."

Pleased he was satisfied, she hugged him back.

∞∞∞

It was mid-morning when they reached the warehouse. Zeke parked in the back. Once the patio door was unlocked, he stepped aside and allowed her entry.

He focused on her as she looked around, her eyes wide and full of excitement and wonder, as she noted the changes.

There was thick brown paper over the floors. She immediately knelt and pulled back the paper from one corner and allowed her hand to experience their silky smoothness. The coffee color stain was deep and rich, just as she had imagined. "These are amazing."

Looking up, she saw the armoire installed against the brick wall. She stood and ran her hands along the side of the armoire, her hands searching for the holes and gaps in the finish she knew had been there.

"It is so smooth."

He returned her smile.

"I cannot tell the difference in finish. You are a magician."

She opened the doors and gasped in delight. "You finished the inside, too?"

"It can be outfitted with shelves, unless you would prefer a television."

"I was thinking TV."

"There are hookups for cables, power, etc."

"You think of everything. I am so grateful."

She moved to the wall with the shelves and secretary. He followed and showed her a set of switches just inside the first unit. The first button turned on lights along the top shelves. The second lit the shelves on the middle tier. She had no idea what the third switch would do. She hesitated and cast him a glance.

He grinned. "Go ahead."

When she did, the kickplate along the bottom of the cabinets were illuminated.

"That's brilliant!"

"Inexpensive LED lights, nothing special."

"Extraordinarily special, Mr. Buchanan." She corrected.

She opened the front of the secretary and smiled. He had installed an ethernet cable and an electrical outlet for her laptop. He was thoughtful, her eyes glistened when she faced him and whispered, "Thank you."

He waved his hand toward the kitchen.

She looked past him and took two steps before she brought a hand to her mouth.

Andre had taken the glass she found and grouped three seeded glass bottles as pendant lights over the island, but he had somehow melted and stretched them into elegant, provocative shapes encasing long tubular bulbs. The choice of clear glass was perfect, as they would not compete with the bold blue of the range. The little seed bubbles caught the light, though, and made it dance in all directions.

Moving further to the left, she looked above where the dining table would stand. Above that space were two groups of fixtures suspended and linked by a six-foot-long piece of wood, which appeared to have been braided or made of intertwined branches.

In awe, she asked quietly, "What tree grows roots or branches intertwined?"

"I asked. Andre said that the wood was carved that way, although, in India, there were living bridges made of the roots of trees along riverbanks, which he was emulating."

Astonished, she nodded and affirmed: "I am okay with that."

On either side of the wood, five glass globes of different sizes and shapes hung. Like the island pendants, these had been heated and reformed in organic shapes; however, the bulbs in these were round and appeared to hover within their glass confines.

She had shared photos and the dimensions of the table with Andre, and she knew he had nailed it. They would work perfectly.

"Conversation pieces, no?"

"They are beautiful." Zeke agreed.

She studied him closely. She knew his words were sincere.

She walked over and hugged him.

"Upstairs?" he asked, prodding her along.

Pulling him by the hand, she climbed the stairs and stopped just inside the master bedroom, as something caught her eye over the tub.

She stood wide-eyed and open mouthed.

He explained. "Andre brought this with him on Wednesday. He said any woman worth her salt needed a chandelier over her soaking tub."

She brought both hands to her mouth. When she looked at him, her eyes and heart were full.

He flipped a switch, and the entire room was cast in multi-colored drops of light.

"It is magical," she whispered. Her voice full of awe.

The fixture was tiered. It was round in shape. The uppermost tier was the largest with each of the other two tiers smaller in circumference from the one above it. Clear icicle like pieces of glass hung from each tier with smaller multi-colored crystals and droplets of glass hung at varying heights all around each of the tiers. It was intricate and delicate, beautiful, and nothing short of spectacular. Alone, it defined the space.

"It appears I will have to find a professional photographer to do any of Andre's genius justice."

"Happy?"

Facing him, she appeared so small and vulnerable.

"Ecstatic, overwhelmed, and guilty."

His look quizzical. "Guilty?"

"I do not deserve any of this."

He frowned.

"No, truly." She searched for words. "I was handed the deed to this place. Yes, the house in Lakeway was worth more, but it had a mortgage. These renovations have been funded by the money and life insurance I received from the Lancasters. I have not worked for any of this. I have not earned this."

"You were with Clint for ten years. He received this in payment for legal fees. Those earnings were community property.

You said you gave up the house and everything in it, all of which were also community property."

"Are you sure you do not have a law degree, along with that engineering degree?"

"The inheritance from the Lancasters was separate property. They adopted you and were your parents. As parents, they wanted to provide for you. You are deserving. All this is yours."

She studied him for several minutes. When she spoke, her words were quiet and even. "Do you realize everywhere I look; I see you here. There is a part of you on every surface and in every square inch of this place. You have left your mark here and on me."

"Lady," he reached for her, "you have left a big mark on my heart."

∞∞∞

By noon, they had completed their inspection of the warehouse. The original plan had been to head to San Antonio to look at furniture, but Bree was tired. With an evening out ahead of them, she suggested they return to his home to relax.

After lunch, Bree took a much-needed nap.

When she stirred, she found Zeke in the guest room on his computer. As she approached, she saw he was using a 3-D design program to modify the interior of a container home, similar to his own.

"That looks interesting." She stopped next to his chair.

"Hello, sleepyhead," he reached out and rested a hand on her behind.

"What's this?"

"Just playing with a couple of ideas."

"Did you look at the sites I sent you on tiny homes and container homes?"

He nodded.

"I know it is a niche market, but good design speaks for itself...you are certainly qualified."

He squeezed one of her cheeks.

She dropped the subject, her eyes stopping on the calendar. "By the way, I have requested a couple days off beginning Thursday."

∞∞∞

Checking the time, Bree noted she had ten minutes, as Zeke said they should leave about six. As he had spent most of the afternoon working on his computer, she moved her stuff into the utility room to avoid disturbing him. She also realized the light at the kitchen table was perfect for makeup.

She knew dress was casual, but she wanted to look extra nice for him. She chose a black, sleeveless jersey dress, which skimmed her knees and accentuated her long limbs. Rather than heels, she selected strappy sandals.

While she preferred to pull her hair up and out of the way, she allowed it to hang loose. She knew her thick wavy mane was one of her best features; however, concerned with the heat, she kept a hair pin in her bag, just in case she needed to twist it into a bun.

Rather than just mascara and lip gloss, she made her whole face, as she anticipated meeting one or more of Zeke's friends. It was a small community, after all.

Gold hoop earrings and a dab of perfume behind one ear, her left wrist, and behind her knees, and she was ready.

Standing at the guest room door, she quietly cleared her throat.

When he turned around and stood up, she saw he had changed into a freshly pressed shirt and dark jeans with a nice pair of exotic skin cowboy boots, which made him even taller.

Her heart jumped at the sight of him. She was constantly amazed at how handsome he was.

He knew she was behind him before he heard her, as the soft

scent of her perfume gave her away; however, he was unprepared for the sight of her.

Gorgeous at any time of the day or night, even with sleep in her eyes and her hair untamed and unbrushed, but polished as she was now with extra care and effort just to be seen with him, blew him away.

Closing the distance between them, he stood before her and looked deeply into her eyes. "How did I get to be so lucky?"

"No, Handsome, I am the lucky one."

"Ready?"

"Always."

∞∞∞

Dinner at Maria's Cocina was a step up, establishment-wise, from Lupita's. Moreover, the food was excellent. One of the few restaurants in the immediate area, it was crowded. Their evening was punctuated by greetings and curious glances from all the people Zeke knew.

When she remarked on his popularity, he shrugged it off, insisting the attention had more to do with her presence.

As usual, conversation was easy, even when she pressed him on his past.

"How is it you are not married?"

His initial reaction was simply a raised eyebrow; however, she waited him out.

"Like you, I have been married before."

She tried to hide her surprise, and again, waited him out.

"Unlike your marriage, it did not last long."

"Would you mind sharing what happened?"

"There is not much to it, really."

He finished his beer and motioned to the waitress for another.

She waited.

"We dated my last two years of high school. She was a year

behind me. I joined the service. We dated another year, mostly long-distance. When she graduated, we got married, and I was deployed to Iraq for nine months."

"That is tough."

"Yeah. When I returned, she was six months pregnant with a friend of mine's child."

Her hand covered her mouth, and she gazed at him wide-eyed.

"I am so sorry," she whispered, "that must have been terrible."

"It was a rude awakening."

"I assume you divorced."

"Yep. They had a daughter, broke up, and she has been married a time or two since then."

"And you decided marriage was not for you."

"I let that dream go, yes."

"I regret that happened to you, although I appreciate your sharing."

He remained stone faced. "Allow me to also share, her daughter was the hostess who showed us to our table when we arrived."

He watched as her eyes moved to her upper left, searching her memory for an image. "Petite blonde, heavy makeup, low cut black blouse with tight black jeans, and heels."

"Very good."

"Does she resemble her mother?"

He nodded. "They are both bleach blonds."

She teased him, "Of course you prefer blonds, the only time I have ever been dumped, a blond has been involved."

He did not share her humor.

He reached for her hand and interlocked her fingers with his across the table. "Bree Lancaster, you are the woman of my dreams."

She brought his hand to her lips and kissed it.

∞∞∞

When they exited the young woman was nowhere to be seen.

After holding the door for her, he clasped her hand in his.

The drive to the Icehouse Tavern was brief.

It was packed, but they were able to find a spot to park. There was a breeze, and the walk pleasant, a full moon lighting their way.

The place was basically a bar with an outside stage. There was a porch at the back of the building. Wide stairs led to a grassy area with a stage twenty yards from the porch. The few tables present were occupied. It was obvious the place was set up, at least that evening, for a standing room only crowd.

She assumed he was leading her toward the bar, but their progress was halted every few feet as someone new greeted Zeke and chatted. He dutifully introduced her to everyone and provided her with a brief biographical report of how he knew each one. After the tenth introduction, she inquired if there were a quiz.

Once the opening band began to play, they were able to secure stools at the bar, as most of the crowd moved to the backyard.

"You okay?"

"Great!"

"Really?"

"I am with you. I am fine."

He leaned forward and kissed her.

She sat with her back to the bar, listening to the music and people watching. Zeke sat facing her with one arm on the counter, one leg behind her and the other brushed lightly against hers. His posture casual, but signaled she was definitely with him. She enjoyed being within the circle of his protection.

She relaxed and moved with the music.

As the headline group set up, more people moved outside. When they started to play, several of the remaining couples began to dance and the lights inside were lowered. She recognized the beginning of the next song. It was one she liked. She closed her eyes and swayed to it.

Zeke spoke in her ear. "Would you like to dance?"

The question startled her briefly because actually dancing was the last thing on her mind.

She turned to face him with a saucy smile "Where I come from, Mr. Buchanan, good Baptist girls do not dance."

The instant the words crossed her lips, he threw his head back and laughed heartily, tears in his eyes.

Still chuckling, he dropped his voice and inquired: "And, Ms. Lancaster, are you a good Baptist girl?"

She giggled in delight before admitting: "Now, not once in my life, have I ever claimed that."

"Will you dance with me?"

"Zeke, honestly, I do not know how to dance."

"Do you trust me?"

She nodded.

He stood and pulled her to her feet, wrapping one arm around her and taking her hand in his, holding her against his body.

"Lean into me and move with me." He whispered in her ear.

She complied, acutely aware of every inch where their bodies met.

"Relax," he said, "and breathe with me."

She closed her eyes and leaned into him, moving her legs with his.

The music faded, along with the people, and the world around them. All she knew was that she was in his arms.

"Bree."

She looked up quizzically.

He smiled. "The band is taking a break."

"Oh."

She looked around. The room was crowded again.

"Would you like a drink?"

"No, thank you."

"Shall we head home?"

She smiled and nodded. "If you like."

By the hand, he led her through the bodies and out the door. Someone called out to him. When he stopped to greet them, she slipped out of his grasp and trotted down the stairs and into the parking lot.

She looked back and he was engrossed in a conversation with two men. They must have been good friends because Zeke was animated and made no move to disengage.

She was grateful for the opportunity to watch him. He had an air of friendly confidence about him. He was neither arrogant, nor brash. His quiet demeanor appealed to her. Unlike Clint, Zeke was secure and did not require the constant approval of others.

She was so wrapped up in studying him, she failed to notice the approach of a man behind her, until she heard a snarl and felt someone yank her around by the arm.

"Whore!" he screamed at her.

She wrestled her arm from his grasp and backed up.

He moved to grab her arm again. This time she evaded him.

He was an older man, probably in his sixties with long, stringy, unkempt hair. His clothes were worn and dirty. He reeked of stale cigarettes and alcohol. He was at least six feet tall, thick, and stocky in a muscular way. His eyes were glazed and bloodshot.

He snarled at her and shook a finger in her face. "Whore," he repeated, "Your mother was a faithless slut."

She knew she should turn and run, but she was frozen and transfixed.

He lunged at her and the scream, which had risen within her, was stifled as he grabbed her by the throat, and the world went dark.

∞∞∞

Out of the corner of his eye, Zeke saw Bree standing in the parking lot waiting for him. He moved to disengage from the conversation when movement behind her drew his attention. He saw the man reach for her, and he was in motion, shouting her name.

He was a few steps away when she collapsed in front of him. His intent was to attack the man, who was already retreating, but he tended to Bree first. His friends were on his heels. One chased the man, the other kneeled with him next to Bree.

She was crumpled on the asphalt, unconscious. They gently rolled her over. Brian straightened her legs, pulled her skirt down and began brushing the dirt from her. Zeke checked her pulse and cradled her head, brushing her face from his lap.

Satisfied she was breathing, he stroked her cheek, and softly spoke her name.

She brought a hand to her face and came to with a quick intake of startled breath. Her eyes flew open in terror. She instantly flinched from them.

"Bree, you are okay. It is me."

Her breath came in short, shallow gasps. He was holding her wrist and felt her pulse pounding beneath his fingers.

"Bree, look at me."

He released her wrist and cupped her face, forcing her to look at him.

Her eyes were wild, and she did not appear to recognize him.

"Bree," he insisted, "It is me."

He continued to talk to her and slowly his words reached her. Recognition returned to her eyes.

Embarrassed, she brushed herself off and tried to stand. They helped her to her feet.

"I am sorry," she whispered, chin tucked to her chest and eyes downcast.

"Not your fault, Bree."

Brian followed them to his truck and helped secure her. "Is she okay?"

"She has had quite the scare."

"I hope she is all right."

"She will be fine. Thanks."

When he climbed into the truck, he looked over at her. Her eyes were closed. Her hands were tightly clenched in her lap. She was slowly rocking back and forth.

He reached over to place a hand on her lap, she jumped slightly.

He withdrew his hand and started the truck.

Chapter 18

Zeke had Coal at the groomers early. He checked her flight as the dog stepped over into his lap, front paws resting on his arm, his head straining to peek out the open window.

Zeke yawned and absently pet the dog, hardly noticing the softness of his fine, black fur.

Setting the phone aside, he rubbed his eyes before raking his fingers through his hair.

They had endured a restless night. Bree had not wanted to discuss the evening's events, other than stating the old guy had accosted and hurled slurs at her. She said she was frozen with fear and could not move or speak.

He thought he recognized the man as Henry Miller, known in the community as a farmer and alcoholic who lost his wife decades ago to drinking. Zeke and his father shared fence lines with the man.

He mulled whether he should confront him regarding the attack or simply have Bree file a report with the sheriff's office when she returned. His only hesitation about the latter was asking her to relive the event.

Her fear was evident and, he concluded, most likely related to childhood trauma. While threatening and unpleasant, with all the people around last night, she had not been in real danger. That; however, did not alleviate his guilt at having allowed her to wander that far from him at such a late hour. He knew the entire thing could have been avoided had he kept her close.

He also knew she was exhausted. She had pushed herself all week to stay on top of her regular caseload, as well as take on the labor dispute. She had stayed up half the night before.

He was surprised she had been able to sleep at all last night, but she curled around her dog and was able to finally drift off with his arms tightly around her.

He; however, had not been able to do the same. The image of Miller lunging for her was disturbing, but what haunted him more was how she retreated deep within herself. She reverted to an almost catatonic state and was nearly completely unresponsive. He recognized the rocking movements she displayed on the drive home as a soothing gesture, which she had continued once he had brought her in, and settled her on the sofa, but it was not until CoalBear was in her lap and began pushing her with his paws for attention, did she slowly re-emerge.

Refocusing on the dog in his lap, he scratched him behind the ears, surprised at how fond he had become of him. He had always liked dogs, but his impression of small dogs was that they were generally yappy and snappy. CoalBear was neither. He was completely chill and wholly devoted to Bree. Wherever she was, he could be found.

After she had left that morning, Coal had parked himself at the front door, staring at it, waiting for her to return.

Zeke sympathized. He knew exactly how he felt.

A few minutes later, Zeke recognized Juan's truck approaching. He and Doria pulled into the space next to him.

With Coal in his arms, he exited the vehicle and passed him through the window to Doria who cooed in delight at him. The dog was unsure, but Zeke was certain he would be fine.

Juan approached from the other side the vehicle and greet him: "Hey, Boss!"

They shook hands.

"Thanks for meeting me."

"Are you kidding?" He followed Zeke to the bed of the truck to receive the crate and box of stuff for the dog. "Doria has been on me about getting married and having kids, I am hoping she will decide she wants a dog, instead."

Zeke grinned. "There are worse things, my friend."

"Look at you, confirmed bachelor, fetching and carrying for

your girlfriend's dog."

Zeke's expression was wry, but nonetheless amused.

"I guess we are two of a kind."

Juan laughed, "What's that French word?"

"Touché."

"That's it! In Spanish we say *'Tienes razon.'*"

Once all the paraphernalia was transferred, Zeke walked back to Doria and reached in to pet the dog again. "We keep him on a leash."

"Yes, I know he was a stray. I will love him like my own. Tell Bree not to worry."

"Thank you."

Once he waived them off, he drove to the warehouse. With clipboard and punch list in hand, he walked around the space. Instead of detailing the items remaining, he thought about what Bree had said the day before, except wherever he looked, he saw pieces of her. Everything was imprinted with her smile and energy.

His interviews were inching closer, even though Florida seemed a world away.

Chapter 19

Sunday bled into Monday. By Tuesday morning, Zeke was exhausted. He had not been able to rest well. He texted Doria and asked if he could collect Coal at the end of the day, explaining Bree might like to see him when she arrived. Doria understood. Arrangements were made.

His days were long, but full and busy. The cabinet guys were delayed until Thursday, which pushed back deliveries until the following week, but the project was headed toward completion. The punch list had shrunk considerably. He had even had time to install the security system.

He dragged out an old laptop and replaced the hard drive with a new Tera byte one. He set the cameras to motion activate, rather than have them run continuously. The images would be stored on the laptop. Depending on activity, even though recordings would eventually save over older ones, he anticipated months would pass before anything was copied over.

Bree checked in via text in the mornings, and he called her in the evenings. He knew she was preoccupied with work, but despite her chipper disposition, he felt it may have been a little forced.

He was only faintly surprised when his phone alerted to a text about eight Tuesday evening, as he and Coal were relaxing on the couch.

"Donovan here. Call me."

He answered on the first ring. "Thanks."

"Of course."

"What's going on?"

"Context, Donovan."

"Our girl is not sleeping. Three of the last four nights she has accessed VPN to my servers between one and three in the morning. She is on for hours at a time."

"In addition to covering for Ben, she is trying to stay on top of her own files."

"I am aware of her workload. Good try, but I have a sixth sense when it comes to her. Let us just say I detect a disturbance in the force."

Zeke knew Donovan was not a threat to Bree. He hesitated only briefly before sharing Saturday night's events.

"So, Friday night to Saturday morning was an anomaly and the last two nights she may be having nightmares."

"What do you know about the nightmares?"

Donovan took a turn at pausing briefly but appeared to come to the same conclusion as Zeke. "She has described them as dark, hearing a woman calling for her urgently and begging for her to run for help. There is a man whose face she just cannot make out, who terrifies her."

"The dream never varies?"

"Not from what little she has shared."

Donovan interrogated him about the incident and pressed him to describe in detail her response following it.

Like Zeke, he considered the benefit of pressing charges versus speaking to Miller in person.

While the word catatonic had come to Zeke, he did not speak of it.

Donovan, his fingers typing away as they spoke searched her behavior and said: "Hmmm... catatonic... unresponsive, agitated, repetitive movement... related to catatonic schizophrenia. That does not sound good."

"You are off base. Try PTSD."

There was more typing.

"Extreme physical reactions to reminders of trauma, nightmares, detached from others, difficulty remembering important aspects of a tragic event... Yeah. I agree."

"She shuts down when something triggers a feeling or

memory. Miller scared her and she completely froze. There was no flight or fight. When he lunged and grabbed her throat, it was too much, she fainted."

"Jesus. She has been through enough already."

Zeke decided against mentioning the scars on her back.

"Will she be safe in the warehouse, if this guy decides to come at her again?"

Zeke had been grinding on that possibility. He described the cameras with alarm system he had installed.

"Good thinking. I do not have anything like that, but I will dig into Miller to see if I can find leverage."

"Let me know what you discover."

"Of course. Keep me posted on our girl."

Once they rang off, Zeke stared at his phone. Had he not already met Donovan, he might be concerned about the relationship between him and Bree, but he could detect no sexual chemistry or connection. The affection and friendship were certainly present.

He acknowledged he could be jealous. His reaction to his wife's betrayal proved he was quite capable of jealously and rage; however, her relationship with Donovan did not trigger that response from him. At most, he envied the length of their relationship. He wished she had been in his life for as many years.

Activating the tracking app, he could see she was at her hotel. He cleared his throat and called her. She answered immediately.

"Hi, Handsome. I was just thinking about you."

"Good because I think about you all the time."

She sounded tired, but upbeat. She inquired as to his day before sharing her flight would be mid-afternoon the following day.

He omitted mention of Donovan, instead letting her know he had retrieved Coal early. She squealed in genuine delight, which immediately raised his spirits.

Not long after they said goodbye, he and CoalBear settled

into bed. The dog curled into his side with his hand on him, gently petting him. Zeke could not deny how soothing he found the dog. For the first time in days, he drifted to a peaceful slumber.

Chapter 20

When there were few workers at the warehouse, Zeke allowed the dog free roam; although, he stayed near him.

With a flurry of activity, he moved the crate to the top of the stairs and out of the way to the far left, but where the dog had a full view of the activities. Despite his confinement, CoalBear was fine. Zeke took him out often, and even shared his lunch with him. He was content with surveying the area between naps.

By late afternoon, Zeke was engrossed with the HVAC subcontractor. One of the zones was not registering properly. They were checking each intake to ensure proper airflow.

An excited yip from the Hell Hound alerted him to her arrival.

He watched her quickly scan the lower level before looking up and meeting his eyes. The smile which spread across her face warmed him from the inside out. He moved to release the dog and trotted downstairs to greet her.

She threw herself into his open arms, hugging him tightly. CoalBear jumping at her legs. She reluctantly pulled away to scoop up the dog, but she leaned heavily into him, content just to feel him.

Standing behind her to allow her to survey the continued improvement, he had an arm wrapped around her upper chest and the other on her hip as he bent his head to hers, whispering in her ear the details of all the progress.

The crew had grown accustomed to their relationship and largely ignored them to attend to their own tasks. Juan, though, took a quick photo to send to Doria.

Once he caught her up on the status, he turned her around and studied her. Despite the makeup, she had dark circles under her eyes. He was not certain whether she was dehydrated or had lost weight, but her cheeks were hollow.

"Not sleeping?"

She started to deny it but shrugged instead.

"Have you been eating?"

"I have not been hungry."

He tickled her rib. "You have not had me around to help you work up an appetite. I get it."

"Ha!" She laughed and hugged him. "I have missed you so much."

"I tell you what," withdrawing from her arms, he took her hand and led her to the kitchen, where his clip board lay on the counter. He flipped it to the back and extracted a piece of paper. He passed it to her.

He had drawn a map from the highway directly to his place with distances noted in tenths of a mile with handwritten notes in his very precise, all caps print denoting an engineer. She loved his handwriting.

"I can follow this!"

He beamed. "Good. When I met Doria yesterday, in addition to the Hell Hound, she gave me a dish of homemade enchiladas. I saved them to enjoy with you tonight."

"OH!"

"Go ahead, head over, unpack, and relax. I will be home as soon as I can."

She liked the word 'home.'

She nodded.

He loaded the dog crate and bed, as well as his bowls, noting silently he would need a second set of bowls to leave at his place.

He also brought out a Styrofoam cooler and put it in the back of her SUV.

"What's that?" she inquired.

"Jed asked me to return this to you."

She gave him a blank look, unsure what to say.

He opened the cooler and handed her the envelope that was inside.

Her name was across the front.

"Open it."

It was a note from Darla expressing how much they were enjoying the meals and thanking her.

She handed the note to Zeke.

He scanned it and gave it back to her.

"I appreciate what you did for them."

She shrugged. "It was the least I could do."

"She would very much like to meet you."

"How do you feel about that?"

"I would love for you to meet my whole family." He grinned at her, "You would be doing me a huge favor by meeting her, too."

Noting Bree's confusion, he explained, "She interrogates me about you every time I see or speak with her. I am sure she does the same to Jed."

She nodded.

"I will have time in the next couple days to fill the cooler up again and, perhaps, we can deliver it?"

"I would like that, and I am sure she would, too."

Once she was loaded up, he helped her into her SUV and gave her a long kiss. He reached into his pocket and handed her a key. "This is for you. Come and go as you please."

She turned it in her hand, dazed, but happy. "I was going to ask if you would mind if I washed a load of clothes."

He kissed her again. "What is mine, is yours. Please make yourself at home."

"Thank you."

"Of course." He smiled. "And just so you know. On Wednesdays, house rules are no clothes."

Giggling, she asked, "I am scared to ask what the house rules are for Thursday."

"I will let you know when I think of something."

∞∞∞

Opening the door, the aroma of cooking greeted him warmly and humbled him. It reminded him of returning home from school and his mom having snacks ready for him and his siblings, as well as any friends who had accompanied them.

His parents were always warm and affectionate with one another, as well as with him and his siblings. After he joined the service, he had wanted that for himself.

He had given up that dream almost twenty years ago, but now, with Bree, it was calling to be dusted off and reinvented.

He found her in the kitchen with her back to the door. She looked adorable with her hair hanging down her back, outfitted in one of his tank undershirts and another one of her brightly colored sarongs tied around her waist. CoalBear was curled in the corner, just a yard from her bare feet.

"Ummmm," he said, "What smells so good?"

Beaming, she turned to him, wiping her hands on a towel. "Welcome home, Handsome," she purred.

She was without a bra. He tweaked a nipple as she approached. "We need to discuss your flagrant violation of the dress code."

"So says the man fully dressed."

He kissed her deeply, his hands roaming her body freely.

"Nice," he whispered, "I approve the lack of underwear."

Nibbling his bottom lip, she reveled in his attention.

Perhaps, he was nostalgic for the happy home his parents had lovingly provided, but he was overcome with a sense of contentment. He realized everything he had ever wanted was standing before him in the form of Bree.

Cupping her face gently, he concentrated his gaze into her eyes. His voice was low and serious. "Bree, I need you to do something for me."

Concerned with his tone and demeanor, her brow furrowed,

she did not hesitate. "Of course, Zeke, anything."

"I need you to help me take better care of you."

She lowered her head to his chest and sighed. "I know. I am sorry."

∞∞∞

After a relaxed meal and once the kitchen was clean, they settled into the sofa. She was officially on vacation until Monday. For the first time since they had met, her phone was not in her hand or within arm's reach. She looked relaxed, her feet propped on the ottoman, stretched out next to him. The internet radio was set to her favorite Amos Lee station. He held her hand, a whiskey and Coke in the other.

"I have been thinking about Florida."

She sat up and folded a leg under her, as she turned to face him, one arm over the back of the sofa cushion.

"When do you go for your interviews?"

"They are scheduled to begin two weeks from Monday; however, I have decided to call and cancel."

Her eyes narrowed, she pressed him. "Why?"

"I do not think Florida is where I want to be." He was surprised by her reaction.

"What has changed between when the interviews were scheduled and now?"

"You and I happened."

She closed her eyes and took a breath.

"Zeke," she said quietly, "I am thrilled with you and me, but I do not want to be responsible for holding you back from your dreams and aspirations."

"You are not holding me back from anything."

"Really? Then why are you considering cancelling the interviews. Do you not think you should go, gather as much information as you can? Are not the best decisions made with the most information available?"

"Are we actually arguing about this?"

She blinked twice, considered his question, and dropped her head with a smile.

"See what happens when I have time on my hands?"

He opened his arms and invited her into them. She was only too happy to comply.

"You are right." He conceded quietly. "I will go to Florida, see exactly what it is all about, get a feel for things, and we will discuss it when I return."

∞∞∞

Bree followed Zeke to the warehouse early the next morning. As she parked, Brett was walking Molly on a leash and waved at them.

She waved back with a warm smile and promptly slipped the harness and leash on CoalBear; however, he was relentless when she put him down, trying to get to Molly.

Molly led Brett over to them. After half a minute of trying to untangle the leashes, they acquiesced and released them to play.

Brett was again outfitted in scrubs and looked as though he had been up all night; however, he was pleasant. "How are the renovations coming?"

"We are closing in, everything looks great."

"That is wonderful. I am looking forward to having neighbors."

Looking over at the short row of bungalows, she asked: "Are any of those occupied?"

"A couple of them, but like normal people, I think they work during the day."

"You are still on graveyard?"

"Yeah."

"Forgive me for asking, but what brings you to this part of the world? You do not sound as though you are from here."

"I was an Air Force brat. My dad was stationed in San Antonio when I was a kid. My parents liked it here and when he retired, they moved back."

"Do they live here?"

"They live in Bandera. They are getting older, and I am an only child. I wanted to be closer to them."

"Surely you could have found something a bit less remote, but still close."

He smiled. "Well, I have always wanted to be one of those country doctors..."

They continued to watch the dogs play chase.

"In fact," he continued, "Seeing what you have done with this building, I have been daydreaming of turning one of these other ones into a clinic."

Her face brightened immediately.

"I believe I know of someone who could do that for you."

"I bet you do." He chuckled. Her response leaving him in no doubt of her affinity for Zeke.

"I have no idea who owns any of these other buildings, but if neither of the Buchanan brothers do, a quick search of the courthouse records would tell us."

"Are you a real estate agent?"

"I am actually an attorney."

He was surprised. "Oh. Are you opening a law office in the front of the building?"

"No, I have no desire to hang out my own shingle."

"Do you think your boyfriend would mind if I picked his brain?"

"Not at all, I will keep an eye on the dogs."

"Thanks."

Brett jogged over to the warehouse while Bree whistled for the dogs who dutifully ran over to her. To reward them, she pulled treats from the truck.

She knew CoalBear had missed his training class that week, so she had him practice his "Sit." She was delighted to find Molly knew the maneuver, as well. She rewarded them each in kind, impressed either was able to perform with the distraction of the other, but she guessed the dried liver was incentive enough.

Ten minutes later Brett returned with a slip of paper in his hand.

Holding it up, he smiled brightly: "Bingo!"

"Three buildings, two different owners. I have names and numbers to call. Zeke even said he or his brother could make themselves available to do a walk through with me to advise, which may be in the best condition for my needs."

Bree was elated. "That would be amazing!"

She loved the idea of a neighbor, as well as the small step in returning more life to the main street of this small town.

"Listen," she began, "I usually bring breakfast on Friday mornings, if you are interested, stop by tomorrow."

"Ah, food and the chance to let these two lovebirds burn off some energy, that's a date!"

"Good!"

Reattaching the leash to his dog, he waved. "See you tomorrow."

She gathered CoalBear in her arms and headed for the warehouse.

Zeke was watching as she came in.

She noted he had a weird look on his face.

"What is wrong?"

He shook his head.

She followed his gaze out the window and could see Brett and Molly enter their bungalow.

She put the dog down and stepped over to wrap an arm around Zeke's waist. "Is there a problem?"

"He seems like a nice guy."

"Yes, he does."

He looked down at her, and she slowly realized he may be jealous.

She hugged him tighter. "But he does not make my heart skip a beat when I look at him, as it does when I look at you."

He sighed and finally smiled.

"He is not a cardiologist, is he?"

"I do not think so, why?"

"It sounds like you may have tachycardia, and I have no desire to have him examine you."

She laughed. "You have nothing to fear. My heart beats for you."

∞∞∞

The arrival and installation of the appliances took most of the morning. Under Zeke's direction, everything went smoothly.

Jed was actually the owner of the company, but even he looked to Zeke for instruction. Bree could not help but compare him to the other men. Physically, he was among the tallest, but with his broad shoulders and quiet air of confidence, he was obviously the leader. She appreciated he did not bark orders at the men. Instead, he carefully laid out the overall plan and individually ensured each person knew his role.

When they broke for lunch, Bree sought out Zeke and presented him with a pair of sandwiches and chips on a paper plate she had made that morning with a thermos of iced tea.

Her reward was a big smile and a quick kiss.

As he ate, he shared the plans for the afternoon.

Because he was on site and in command of the schedule, she had provided the contact information for him to schedule the deliveries.

"Your table should arrive this afternoon."

She had planned to go to the market and spend the afternoon cooking, but she scratched that entirely, excitement rising within her.

She smiled at him broadly.

He studied her openly, enjoying how she nurtured and cared for him. He especially enjoyed how neither of them felt the need to fill every lapse in conversation. He was a lucky man.

He drained the thermos. “By the way, you make the best iced tea.”

∞∞∞

The table arrived. She felt bad for the men because it was so large and heavy. It took four of them to carry it in.

To protect it, the top had been covered in thick, brown paper.

She had not said much about the design of the top and knew Zeke had no idea what she had chosen, except for the size. She held her breath as the delivery man carefully removed the paper and wiped it down.

She thought it was spectacular, although she was aware it may not suit everyone’s taste.

Zeke walked around it, taking it all in. He ran a practiced hand over it and even bent down to study the details.

He paused at the other end of the table, farthest away from her, where he could look past her into the kitchen.

“Amazing,” he finally said. “There is just a hint of that cobalt in the blue running between the two wood pieces.”

“Do you like it?”

“The craftmanship is superb. The size is perfect for this space. I cannot imagine another table here. Well done, Bree.”

She beamed with pride.

“In fact,” he walked back toward her. “I think you have missed your calling. You should have been an interior decorator.”

She blushed and teased him. “So, you think I am a crap lawyer?”

He laughed and pulled her into his arms. “No, Ma’am. I am just saying you have options.”

∞∞∞

With the floors done, cabinets and appliances in place, Zeke had advised the plumbing fixtures needed to be installed, the propane tank had to be buried and filled, then the tankless water heater she wanted had to be installed. Things were actually moving ahead of schedule, in no small part to Zeke's efforts and dedication.

It was three in the afternoon.

Bree decided she still had plenty of time to the go the market and have a nice meal prepared for him when he got home.

Checking her list, she searched him out and found him in the store front.

She had not been in that part of the building since that first day.

He was alone, just standing off to one side, looking around.

"Hey."

He turned and offered her a hand.

She walked over and he wrapped his arms around her.

"What are you doing?"

"Enjoying the feel of you in my arms."

"Ha!" she laughed, "I mean, what are you doing in here."

"Just thinking."

"What about?"

"It might be nice to see a little more life in this town."

"Brett's clinic?"

"Yeah."

"I am about to pick up groceries. Do you have anything you would like to eat the next few days?"

He looked down at her. "What are my options?"

"Braised short rib stew, chicken and sausage gumbo, etouffee, baked ziti with homemade marinara..." She shrugged. "I do not know. I was hoping you would give me some ideas."

"I assumed with that big range you chose that you liked to

cook."

"I love to cook."

"So, you enjoy cooking, weaving, and making love?"

"No."

"No?"

"You have it all wrong. I enjoy making love to you. Cooking and weaving are a toss-up by comparison."

∞∞∞

Bree left CoalBear with Zeke for the afternoon. It was far too warm for her to leave him in the truck while she shopped. She could have carried him around in her tote, but he was worn out from his playdate with Molly. She thought he was content to snooze in his crate and had even entered it on his own. To ensure he did not go in search of her later, she secured the door and made sure Zeke knew where he was.

She had driven past the market several times, but this was the first time she had entered.

She had not been sure what to expect, but she was pleasantly surprised. They stocked beautiful fresh produce. The proprietor was busy unpacking tomatoes when she arrived. He made a point of introducing himself to her as Mr. Honsinger. He revealed he bought from local farmers as much as he could, making every effort to source Texas vendors to ensure the freshest products for his customers. He explained this was why he tended to offer a number of items only seasonally.

When she inquired as to beef short ribs, he relayed his butcher was employed part-time and mostly worked evenings; however, if she would call at least a day ahead, he could ensure they would cut whatever piece of meat she wanted. She placed an order for the short ribs, as well as for pork baby back ribs. He assured her they would both be ready for her the following day.

With seafood, he regretfully explained there was not enough of a demand for fresh, unfrozen, but he did stock frozen. He also recommended a fish monger in San Antonio who had had deliveries from the coast several times a week.

She found Mr. Honsinger quite kind and knowledgeable.

As to the dry goods, instead of a dozen different brands of flour, there were only two, but she assumed this ensured a higher turnover on what he stocked, which meant they were fresher as well.

Overall, she was pleased and knew this grocer would be able to meet 90% of her needs. The specialty items she preferred with balsamic vinegar and anchovy paste, she could pick up in Austin or order online.

Pushing her cart out of the store, she knew she was going to enjoy living in this town.

Once she had loaded her vehicle, she returned the cart to the store and retraced her steps back to her truck when she suddenly felt a chill and the hair on her arms and at the back of her neck stood straight. Her steps slowed and she looked around.

To her right and fifteen feet away, she saw him.

It was the man from the tavern, his hair and clothes still dirty and disheveled.

A shiver ran through her, but this time she did not freeze or stop. She was within feet of her truck, and she knew the door was unlocked.

She reached for the handle, opened it, jumped in, and locked the door.

She started the engine and pulled through the empty parking space in front her, refusing to look back.

It was not until she was safely at Zeke's, groceries unloaded, and door locked did she feel safe enough to draw a full breath.

∞∞∞

Zeke arrived home with the dog a few hours later.

He had difficulty getting in, as the deadbolt had been engaged from the inside.

He knocked and Bree dutifully appeared a moment later, mortified and apologetic.

She was dressed in one of his tank undershirts and a sarong with bare feet. He was delighted to discover she had opted completely out of underwear once again.

Her hair was pulled up in a high ponytail, revealing a slender neck he felt compelled to explore with his lips.

It was obviously an erogenous zone for her, as she completely melted in his arms with a soft moan.

Pleased with her response, he made a mental note to discover more of those.

Allowing her to return to the kitchen, he made his way to clean up before supper.

When he returned, he found her busy stirring not one, but three large pots on the stove. He peeked in the oven, and she had a Dutch oven cooking away in there, as well.

"Whoa, that is a lot of food."

She turned and smiled, wiping her hands on a towel.

"I have been busy."

He rubbed his stomach. "Is any of this for us?"

"You may have whatever you like." She motioned toward the oven, "I did not find a slow cooker, so I have a pot roast with potatoes, onions, and carrots in there."

Pointing to a soup pot on the stove, "This is marinara. I have pasta, as well as a couple of flattened, seasoned, and pan-fried chicken breasts for chicken parmesan, if you like."

"Yum!"

"I prepared a salad that is in the fridge."

"Excellent."

She opened another pot on the stove. "This is etouffee base. I have shrimp in the freezer that goes with it."

He pointed to the largest pot. "This?"

She opened it. "Here are two chickens I cut up with celery, onions, bell pepper, and garlic for broth and gumbo tomorrow."

"Impressive."

"Do you happen to have a vacuum sealer?"

He shook his head.

"No problem, I picked up quart size freezer bags I can package meals in for your brother and sister-in-law," she smiled, "as well as for your freezer."

"Do you cook like this all the time?"

"Yes and no." She waffled. "It depends. Sometimes I am hungry for something and I make a batch of it. I eat what I can, then tuck away the rest for another day. Other times, when I know there may be a need, Ben and his wife as she fights cancer, Jed and Darla as she is on bed rest, or when a friend has a baby, or whatever, I like to send food to help out and let them know I care."

"You are amazing."

She dropped her gaze and shook her head.

"I am not a hands-on kind of nurturing person. I kind of like to keep people at arm's length, even those I genuinely care about, but at the same time, I feel compelled to help if I can. This is kind of my mission, feed people. Donovan loves to cook, too. He and I have a saying 'Food is love.' It is one of the ways I express affection."

He reached out and wrapped her in his arms, kissing her forehead, grateful to have her in his life.

"I am okay with all the ways in which you express affection."

She hugged him tighter.

They enjoyed the salad and chicken parmesan.

After the meal, he helped her clean up and package all the meals, filling his freezer to the brim.

She had inquired if the freezer she had just purchased for the utility room were up and running.

He advised while the refrigerator in the kitchen was not, as the plumber needed to attach a water line, the freezer was actually plugged in and operating.

They decided the first half of the meals for Jed and his wife would be transferred to that freezer in the morning, and she would have room for the other meals she was planning on

Friday.

Once everything was settled in the kitchen, Bree showered and joined Zeke on the sofa. He was lounging with one leg on the floor and the other bent with a foot on the ottoman, drink in hand. He raised the other arm to allow her lie down with her head in his lap. He brought his arm down around her, his hand on her stomach.

Interested in how she was settling into the town, he asked how she had found the market.

He immediately felt her body tense as a slight tremor ran through her. Looking down, he saw goosebumps form on her arm.

"Bree, what happened?"

She sat up, and he straightened.

He set his drink down and turned his body toward her, raising her chin so her eyes met his.

He leaned down and rested his forehead on hers.

"Talk to me."

She shrugged, pulling back, she crossed her arms in front of her.

"The market was great. I met Mr. Honsinger. He is having the butcher cut meat for me tonight, and I can pick it up in the morning for more dishes..."

"Great. What happened?"

"After I loaded everything into my truck, I returned the cart to the store..."

"And..."

"When I came back out, he was standing in the parking lot."

"He, who?" He asked, but he already knew.

When she did not reply, he filled in the blank. "The guy from the tavern?"

She nodded; her gaze fixed on her lap.

"What did he do, Bree?"

She absently shook her head.

"Nothing. He just looked at me. I ran to my truck, got in, and drove straight here."

"Locking all the doors behind you?"

He now understood the deadbolt.

He pulled her to him and held her tightly.

"You are fine. Everything is all right."

He did not have the heart to tell her Miller was a neighbor and lived less than a mile away.

Chapter 21

Bree was up early and had breakfast tacos well underway by the time Zeke joined her in the kitchen and the sun rose.

CoalBear's arrival actually signaled he was up, and she had a cup of coffee and a plate ready for him.

He took both and placed them on the table before pulling her close.

"Good Morning, Beautiful."

She beamed under his attention.

"What time did you get up?"

"I woke up about 4:15 and checked my email. Donovan must have had George code an alarm to his phone, he called me before 5."

Zeke raised an eyebrow.

"Yeah. He chastised me for being on the server on a day off..."

"Good man."

She smiled.

"It seems Mitch has been talking to him about my files."

"Oh?"

She expelled a heavy breath.

"He had George give him access, which is not a problem, because we had done that originally, when I first started putting them together."

He was relieved George had not betrayed her.

"What did he say about your work?"

"Your breakfast is getting cold. Eat while I share."

They sat at the table, and she waited until he had taken a bite.

"Donovan took the 'Bree' file, which is at the top of the folder tree and is basically an outline for what I have organized and put together. He printed it out and when he lunched with the dean at the local law school, shared it with him."

"Why would he do that?"

"He thinks it would be a feather in my cap and his if I guest lectured at the law school about appeals. According to Donovan, I have a primer on appellate work."

Zeke smiled, despite the forlorn expression on her face. "It would be prestigious for the firm to have the leading expert on appeals on staff."

"He thinks I need to publish it, as well."

"That is impressive, Bree."

"I am not that interested in sharing, though."

"What about teaching?"

"An introvert with social anxiety, teaching is not panic attack inducing at all..." Her reply laced with sarcasm.

"It is not that different from litigating cases or arguing in hearings, is it?"

"Actually, it is. When I appear at the bar, I am representing a client. It is so much easier to fight for someone else."

He nodded. He understood that.

"Well, you can publish without teaching, and you do not have to publish at all; however, it has to be nice knowing how much faith Donovan has in you."

"You have such a nice way of putting things. Thank you."

"Of course, I have a great deal of faith in you, as well."

She looked at him and hoped everything in her heart shone through her eyes because she did not trust herself to speak.

He reached for her hand and squeezed it, acknowledging her message had been received.

She stood and placed a gentle hand on his shoulder as she reached down to kiss his temple.

"Do not be surprised," she quietly cautioned, "if Brett shows up for tacos this morning."

∞∞∞

As he followed her to town in his own vehicle, the radio played a song by the Turnpike Troubadours that brought a wry smile to his face as he listened to the lyrics "...The whole damn town's in love with you..." He knew it was only a matter of time before the whole town was in love with his Bree.

∞∞∞

Half an hour later, the Golden Retriever Molly appeared at the back door of the warehouse, her master not far behind.

Zeke was unimpressed with the fact Brett had showered and wore jeans with a button-down shirt, instead of scrubs or that he carried a bouquet of flowers in his hand.

Bree was gracious, of course, and delighted with his gallantry.

She invited him in and fussed over him for a few minutes, ensuring he was fed and made to feel at home.

He knew she was not interested in Brett.

He knew she was sincere and completely loyal. He had seen how devoted to Donovan she was.

He had also seen flashes of a temper, particularly at the waitress the day they discovered CoalBear, but she truly operated without malice or ill-will toward anyone.

He knew he had no issues with Brett, either. His issues were his own insecurities.

He knew he was a lucky man.

He decided he should act like it.

"Good morning, Brett, glad you could join us." He extended a hand in greeting, one arm around Bree.

"Thank you again for that information yesterday, I contacted both owners. If you have a few minutes next week, I was hoping we could do a walk through?"

Zeke nodded. "Absolutely. I am here most all day every day during the week."

"Fantastic. I have some days off early in the week. I will confirm later today and let you know."

Bree fussed over the bouquet, grateful Brett had had the foresight to bring it in a vase, as she had none on site. She displayed it prominently on the island.

She knew Zeke was anxious to get to work, so she called the dogs to her and took them outside.

Brett followed shortly.

She thanked him again for the housewarming gift.

They chatted for several long minutes, as the dogs played.

Someone drove by on the road between the warehouse and bungalow, they honked briefly and waved. Bree smiled and waved back with no idea who it was.

Brett was equally perplexed.

Once the dogs began to wind down, he took it as signal it was time for him to leave.

Bree told him she hoped they would see them again soon.

His response brought a smile to her face, "We are neighbors, of course we will be seeing more of one another."

Collecting CoalBear, she carried him toward the warehouse, looking around the expanse of the yard. Reflecting on her conversation with Mr. Honsinger, she wondered how hard it would be to create a container garden, as well as plant a few more trees. She had heard people had problems in town with deer eating their landscaping, but she had not seen any. She decided fencing the yard would not be a bad idea, at all, especially with CoalBear.

Looking at the buildings adjacent to her, she wondered whether she would enjoy having more traffic and people around her home, then decided it would not matter, a fence would give her privacy and once she was inside, the whole world was kept away. She smiled at her good fortune.

∞∞∞

Bree kept Coal with her in the utility room most of the morning.

Zeke had brought the cooler in. She was able to unload its contents directly into the upright freezer.

She was deliriously happy to have it.

She and Clint had had an overflow refrigerator/freezer in the garage, but it was older with a small freezer on top. She never quite had enough space to store the packaged meals she made.

She had splurged on this one. It was huge with double doors and had so much room. She looked forward to filling it soon.

Once she secured the cooler back in her truck, she returned to the utility room, made notes, and mentally organized the space and the cabinets. But for the hookups for the washer and dryer and the plumbing fixtures, the room was actually complete.

She ran her hand over the counter, pleased with the quartz. She hoped the salesman was correct and the acid dyes she used on her cotton and wool threads for weaving would not stain them.

Absently, she wondered if she could actually begin loading this room or at least using it on the weekends to dye warps while she waited to move in properly...

Her head spun with all the possibilities.

Zeke looked up when she and the dog emerged from the utility room.

His heart swelled at the radiant smile she sent his way. He could see she was becoming more comfortable and confident in the space every day.

When she had stated she strove to live in the moment, the concept had not resonated with him. Although, the more he considered it, the more he came to realize he did not know how to do that. He discovered he operated from mission to mission, project to project, almost wishing his life away. There was no real thought of making the most of what he found before him at any given time.

Watching Bree, he recognized she had opened his eyes in so many ways.

At that instant, she was conversing with Juan. He strained to catch the conversation. While he could not hear every word, he had the impression she was asking about Doria and sharing how much they had enjoyed the enchiladas the other night. The way she gave him her full attention resonated with Juan who grinned broadly at her. It was obvious she had made a connection.

Sincerity.

In a word, that was Bree. She was completely sincere in everything she did.

∞∞∞

In an effort to stay out of the way, Bree moved over to the pantry area and was delighted to find someone had already installed the shelves and baskets.

She was basking in the space when Zeke appeared at the open threshold where a door should go.

"Hey, you." He smiled.

"When did all this happen?" Her palms were up and gestured to the shelves around her.

"Sometime early this week."

"You have been busy."

"I have been motivated."

"Ready to have your bachelor pad back?"

He pursed his lips and advanced on her. "I think you know better than that."

With wide eyes and huge grin, she mocked him. "What other reason could it possibly be?"

He pulled her to him and kissed her deeply, oblivious to the activity all over the warehouse.

She gave herself to him completely, allowing him to set the heat and tempo, ready to meet him heartbeat for heartbeat.

Groaning with frustration, he lifted his head to gaze down at her half-closed eyes. "You will be the death of me, Lady."

Licking her lips, she coyly responded: "Was it something I said?"

He chuckled and eased his grip on her. "What did I do to deserve you?"

On the tip of her tongue were those three words she longed to express to him, but she feared putting a label on their relationship, especially as they really had not known one another for all that long, despite the time they had spent together.

She swallowed the words and again hoped her feelings shined through her eyes as she gazed at him.

Their moment was interrupted as Jed arrived, calling Zeke's name.

As he started to turn, she told him: "I am going to go to the market to collect my meat and head home to start cooking, unless you need me here."

He wanted to tell her to be careful, but he did not want to spook her, and he doubted Miller would be hanging out at the market waiting for her to return.

In fact, he was more concerned with Miller making his way here to the warehouse or his home. Afterall, it was a small town. He was well known, and just about everyone who cared was probably aware they were an item. She would not be hard to track.

He made a mental note to reach out to Donovan. He was leaning toward a personal confrontation with the man and wanted to chat with him before he did anything unwise.

"I need you wherever I am, Bree."

She raised her palm to his cheek and gently touched her thumb to his mouth.

"I left your lunch and thermos on the counter in the utility room. I hope to have braised beef short ribs with carrots over mashed potatoes for you when you get home."

He kissed her again and watched her collect the dog, as she left.

He smiled as he remembered her words "Food is love."

Chapter 22

As promised, Mr. Honsinger had her cuts of meat prepared for her.

When she exited the store with her dog in the tote under her arm, she was relieved to find no one in the parking lot; however, she did not dally and hopped in her vehicle without delay.

She was becoming more confident in negotiating the route home, grateful for Zeke's detailed map. She knew it would be a while before she was able to do it at night.

Setting up her laptop on the kitchen table, she streamed music to entertain her, as she prepped several meals.

∞∞∞

Reaching for the knob, Zeke's heart skipped a beat when he realized it turned freely and had not been locked.

Moving directly into the kitchen, he expelled the breath he had been holding the instant he saw her. She had her back to him and was washing a cutting board at the sink, her hair pulled high on her head, exposing her slender neck in a cropped tee and ever-present sarong tied around her waist. With her gold hoop earrings, she looked bohemian and sultry.

Not wanting to startle her, he cleared his throat quietly.

Her head popped around and a bright smile covered her face.

"Welcome home, Mr. Buchanan."

She dried her hands and sashayed over to greet him, wrapping her arms around his neck, and pulling him in for a kiss.

He groaned in pleasure, his nerve endings rapid firing.

A timer "dinged," and Bree pulled away slightly, murmuring, "My bread is ready."

He immediately recalled a euphemism from his military days "making bread," and smiled as she cut the oven and pulled out two loaves. They smelled like heaven.

In fact, he mused, everything before him was heaven, the woman in his kitchen, the dog at his feet, the aroma of home cooking, and the love in his heart. He wanted time to halt and allow him to enjoy what he had right this second much longer.

Once she had the bread on racks to cool, she checked a pot on the stove, gave it a quick stir, and shared over her shoulder: "You have about fifteen, maybe twenty minutes, before supper is ready."

When he did not move, she stopped and looked his way.

His lips were slightly upturned at the sides, and he appeared to have a deep, brooding look about him.

Approaching him, she placed a hand on his chest, concern across her brow. "Are you okay?"

Covering her hand with his own, he opened his heart to her. "I have never been better, thank you."

Her smile hesitant, she was unconvinced, allowing her eyes to probe his more deeply.

"Zeke?"

He wrapped her in his arms and kissed the top of her head briefly before disengaging and retreating to clean up.

Bemused, she set the table and continued cooking.

When he returned, he had showered and donned a tee shirt and loose pair of grey athletic shorts. His bare feet silent on the floors.

She glanced at him when he retrieved a beer from the fridge and held it up in askance.

She shook her head with an appreciative smile.

"Do you mind eating in the kitchen, I need to keep an eye on the gumbo?"

"Not at all."

He took a seat, and she filled their plates, serving him his before collecting her own.

"This looks amazing, Bree. Thank you."

Beaming, she asserted: "I hope you like it."

As they ate, they discussed plans to drop by Jed and Darla's for a quick visit and to deliver the frozen meals. Despite working all day, Zeke was happy to assist with the packaging and freezing of food. He even insisted on righting the kitchen and sending her off to clean up.

∞∞∞

He was waiting with a towel as she emerged from the shower.

Her eyes widened slightly when she realized he intended to dry her off.

Wrapping it around her, he used the ends to blot the rivulets cascading down her body.

"Thank you," she softly murmured as she pulled the towel from his hands and side-stepped away.

He knew she was modest, perhaps shy about her body because she was diligent about cutting the lights down low, if not off before they made love. During the night, after he was asleep, she usually got up to don panties and a camisole before returning to bed. He realized he had not yet seen her fully nude in daylight.

Even now, she kept one towel tightly wrapped around her while using a second to finish drying off before wrapping her hair in it.

She shot him a smile before collecting the fresh undergarments from the counter.

She approached him, laid one hand on his upper arm, and pulled up onto her toes, offering her lips.

"You are beautiful, you know that, right?" He assured her.

She lowered her head and rested her forehead on his chest.

But for the turban, he would have kissed the top of her head.

Instead, he wrapped her in his arms tightly.

"I want nothing more in this world than for you and me to work out."

She nodded.

"For that to happen, you must trust me."

The weight of her heavy sigh tore at his heart.

Her hands rose to his chest, and she gently pushed off him. She dropped the towel and allowed it to pool at her feet before she slowly turned around. Her head bent, she stared at the floor.

Running his index finger from one shoulder to the other, he traced the lines of long healed scars, which crisscrossed her entire back. They were heavier and more pronounced at her buttocks and upper thighs, but the lines extended almost to her calves.

Nearly smooth to the touch, he marveled at how extensive they were. He had noticed faint lines along her upper back before. Thinking back, he did a mental inventory of her outfits and realized she wore jeans, black leggings, and occasionally sweatpants. With her suits, she wore hose. Any casual dresses or skirts, including a vast array of sarongs, all had hems that reached between her calves and ankles.

"Who did this to you?"

She shrugged.

He turned her around and cupped her face gently between his hands. "You are the woman I love. Everything, good or bad, you have experienced and endured, makes you the person you are today, right this second. I am so sorry you have been hurt and abused. I would not have thought it possible, but I love you even more right now because you have survived this."

She shook her head, as the tears rolled down her cheeks.

"Yes, Bree, despite this, you give of yourself and do for others without thought or obligation. You have a freezer full of cooked meals for God knows who. But when you hear the call of someone in need, you step up and provide. I do not know another human being like you."

"You do not understand, Zeke."

"Baby, what do I not understand?"

He felt her shiver and held her close to warm her.

He could barely hear her mumbled words, as her face was pressed tightly against his chest.

"Hold on," he smiled, pulled the towel off her head, dropped it to the floor, and led her to the bedroom. He grabbed one of his tee shirts and pulled it over her head. As she poked her arms through the over-sized sleeves, he handed her a sarong.

When she was covered, he led her to the sofa.

Once she was settled back in his arms, he repeated "Tell me what I do not understand."

She fidgeted with the hem of a sleeve.

"There's nothing special about me. If there were, I would know."

From her tousled wet hair, cheeks bright both from the shower and tears, she looked much like a child in his shirt. He found her irresistibly charming, cute, and sexy, all at the same time.

"Of course, you are special."

At his teasing tone, she almost giggled and mock punched him. "Not short-bus special," she retorted.

"Oh!" He laughed.

He continued to study her.

"Did you mean what you said?" She asked quietly.

"Look at me, please."

Once her gaze locked with his he slowly and deliberately shared "Bree Lancaster, I love you."

Her eyes filled with more tears, she kissed him and said: "Thank you. I have been in love with you since the first time you smiled at me."

"Thank you for trusting me."

"No one knows."

He narrowed his eyes. "No one knows what? About the scars?"

She nodded.

"How long were you with Clint?"

"Ten years."

"Did he never see you naked?"

"If he noticed them, he never said anything. He certainly never asked about them."

Confused and deeply disturbed, he once again wondered what kind of man Clint was, but he decided not to voice his concerns.

"Donovan?"

"No reason for him to have any idea."

"Do you suppose these have anything to do with the nightmares?"

"I don't know. In them, there is someone else screaming and asking me to run for help, but I am not being attacked or beaten."

"These were before the Lancasters?"

"Oh, definitely. They were nothing, but good to me. Their idea of punishment," she interrupted herself with a chuckle, "was basically to discuss any transgression to death with me. It was awful, everything had a life lesson in it. When I was 9 or 10, I remember asking why they could not just ground me or force me to stand in a corner, instead."

"Ha! I bet that went over well."

"Oh, geez. I received an incredibly detailed lecture on how unevolved the parents of my contemporaries were and if they only understood the benefits of rationality and positive reinforcement on the psyche of young minds."

"That is horrible, you poor thing." He laughed. "But that certainly explains a lot."

"You are terrible."

"I just declared my undying love for you, and you call me terrible."

"I do not recall any undying declarations, Mr. Buchanan."

"I love you with all my heart now and forever more."

"I love you."

Chapter 23

Like Jed, Darla was born and reared in the county. Her parents had a farm with cows and alpaca, as well as chickens, pigs, and a few goats. As Zeke explained, her parents gifted them ten acres when they became engaged on which they built a home.

As it was on the other side of town from Zeke's place, it was convenient for them to drop by the warehouse to empty the other freezer.

Bree was exceptionally quiet, and Zeke assumed she was anxious.

Reaching for her hand, he gave it a squeeze and asked, "Nervous?"

Holding it between both of hers, she kissed the back of his hand. "A little."

"Everyone loves you, Bree."

"I am glad you think so."

"Darla is the female version of Jedidiah. They are two peas in a pod."

She repeated Jedidiah in her head and whispered in surprise "Ezekiel?"

His grin affirmed she had hit the mark.

Revelation dawned on her, and she connected the dots: "Ezekiel, Samuel, Rebecca, and Jedidiah."

Her brows knitted thickly, she gazed upon him anew. "What does your father do?"

"He is retired now, but he was a Baptist preacher."

"What did he do in the military?"

"Chaplain."

"Oh, gosh," she giggled, "You are the son of a preacher man."

He broadened his grin.

"And as we both know; you are not a good Baptist girl."

Their laughter completely released all of the anxiety and tension she had hoarded.

Zeke was absolutely correct in his assessment. Darla was a doll. If possible, she had less of a filter than Jed, but she spoke without a hint of malice.

While on continued bed rest, Darla was parked in a recliner in the living room, something she was not pleased about, but she was resolute in her effort to care and protect their baby.

Bree joined her in the living room, while the brothers put away the food and served refreshments. The cookies she had baked, along with the extra loaf of bread, were a hit and much appreciated.

Fifteen minutes into their visit, Bree's apprehension about being forced into idle chit-chat, which she loathed, completely faded. Darla was so starved for interaction; she dominated the conversation.

Bree was amused with her gregariousness, but she was also a wealth of information. She discussed how happy the family, as a whole, was Zeke had finally found his someone special. They had had a family meeting via Skype about everyone getting together, just as soon as she had this baby and Samuel was back from Africa. Rebecca and her husband were looking forward to coming down, and she was unsure where everyone would stay with the baby coming and all, but she was sure Zeke would join Bree at the warehouse and Samuel could stay at Zeke's place while Rebecca and Declan could stay with the Buchanans... She even added she so hoped Bree and Zeke would have children soon so their sweet baby would have cousins to grow up with... She had everything planned and everyone sorted.

Bree was overwhelmed and exhausted by the time Jed offered to give her a tour of the property before they left.

Zeke helped her disengage from the socially starved Darla by promising to bring her by again very soon.

When she finally stepped outside, Bree closed her eyes and took a deep, cleansing breath. When she opened her eyes, Zeke was smiling sympathetically at her. He offered his hand. She took it, and they allowed Jed to walk them around.

In addition to the lovely ranch-style home they built in the middle of their land, there was a small barn housing a tractor and a chicken coop. Other than a handful of Rhode Island Reds for eggs, the only other animal was a miniature donkey name Sally.

Bree wanted to go over and pet her long, wild mane, but Zeke held her back and shook his head 'no' in warning.

According to Jed, Darla rescued it from the slaughterhouse at a livestock auction when she was ten. "Cute, maybe," he had asserted, "but meaner than a hornet and better than any watchdog Rottweiler."

Bree had laughed, but secretly sighed in relief they had elected to leave CoalBear home for this visit.

Jed described their plans and aspirations for the place. Their neighbors to the west were an older couple whose children had moved to the city and had no plans to return, at least not permanently. He was hoping he could buy their land, a whole 250 acres, on which to rear their children.

He revealed once the baby was born healthy and Darla was back on her feet, he would have more time to till a piece of ground to create a garden for them next year.

She had no doubt how devoted he was to his wife or how concerned he was with her welfare and that of their child. She was humbled by his depth of affection for them.

As they prepared to depart, Jed came over to her and gave her a big hug. "Bree," he began quietly, "you are one of the best things to happen to this family."

Startled, her brow furrowed.

He continued, "Not only have you helped take care of me and my wife, you have breathed much needed life into that big, surly brother of mine."

Tears sprang to her eyes, and he hugged her again.

"This family already loves you," he whispered in her ear. "Don't you forget that."

Several feet away and just out of earshot, Zeke watched her wipe a tear.

Jed walked her over to the truck, opened the door, and helped her in.

Zeke assumed the driver's seat and found she had slid over to sit next to him. He started the engine and squeezed her thigh before resting his hand in her lap for the drive home.

∞∞∞

By Sunday morning, Zeke began to miss her already, even though she had not yet left for Austin. In the few days since she returned from Baltimore, they had fallen into an easy, comfortable routine. She fit perfectly into his home, his family, and his life, especially his heart.

CoalBear had even become his morning and evening shadow.

Instead of alerting Bree when he wanted to go out, he came over to Zeke, rested his front paws on his leg, and gave him a look, which was an intense stare, until Zeke made eye contact with him. Then the dog would plant all four feet on the floor and make his way to the front door, looking back every few feet to ensure Zeke was watching. Dutifully, Zeke followed, and they made their way around a perimeter marked by the dog. When they returned, he led his human minder to the counter where the dog treats were kept, sat, and waited. Zeke was uncertain which of them was better trained.

While Bree collected her things and prepared to load her truck, Zeke went over the schedule and checked the remaining items on his punch list. Looking at the calendar on his desk, he counted the days from their meeting at Lupita's to sign the contract and through the upcoming Friday. It was exactly five weeks.

Smiling, he stood and moved to carry her things outside.

Once everything was tucked away and secure, CoalBear safely on his bed in the front seat, he circled her with his arms.

"You look happy to see me go." She teased.

"Not at all," he assured her, "I have something to tell you."

Eyeing him suspiciously, she waited.

"I expect to have your occupancy license by Friday."

Her eyes grew wide and she held her breath, unsure she heard him correctly.

"That is well ahead of schedule."

"Yes, Ma'am."

She squealed and jumped to hug him more tightly.

"Oh, gosh," she exclaimed, "I have so much to do. I need to schedule the movers and pack up the guest house... Donovan is going to kill me, but I want to take a couple weeks off to get completely settled."

Her mind raced as she mentally went through her calendar, before she hit an item, which gave her pause. "Two weeks from tomorrow you fly to Florida, right?"

He clenched his teeth absently, and she saw the muscle above his jaw twitch again, as he did when he was upset about something.

"Let us get you settled first." He suggested.

Not wanting to upset him further, she kissed his chest. "I am so grateful for you. Thank you for making this happen, Zeke."

He cupped her face and kissed her tenderly.

Chapter 24

Bree was at the office bright and early Monday morning, CoalBear carefully secured in her tote. She stopped by with cookies and a smile for George before knocking on the side of Donovan's open door.

"Good Morning, Sweetheart," he stood to greet her. "Close the door."

As soon as she sat down, Coal's head popped out of the top of the bag.

In mock sternness, he ground out "Hello to you, Hell Hound."

She placed the tote on the carpet and allowed him to step out. He immediately ran over to Donovan who picked him up and placed him on his lap, smiling and scratching behind his ears. For all his gruff, she knew he adored the dog.

"Millicent seems to have found a young female at the Havanese rescue group. They are sending people over to perform a home inspection before we are allowed to adopt. Management insists we keep the driveway gate closed to show them we have a fenced yard to contain it."

She smiled at him, knowing how soft-hearted he really was.

Redirecting his attention, he put the dog down and faced Bree across the desk. "What brings you in?"

"I know I have been out quite a bit lately."

He shrugged, "You have over a month of accrued vacation. Your files are current, and Mitch is off and running with your research files. I have no complaints."

"Donovan," she hesitated, suddenly overwhelmed with emotion, tears springing to her eyes.

Not unaccustomed to weepy females in his office, he opened

a drawer and produced a box of tissues, which he unceremoniously placed in front of her. His face inscrutable.

She took two and dabbed her eyes. Coal was ready to jump in her lap. She reached over and picked him up.

"I just needed for you to know I how much you and the family mean to me."

"Sweetheart…"

She held up her hand.

"Seriously, Donovan. You have been my lifeline all these many years. You have believed in me, encouraged me, and been there for me every step of the way. I know I do not always listen to you."

"Yeah, I have kids, I am accustomed to being ignored."

She chuckled.

"I am at a crossroads."

"Fly boy?"

She nodded.

"You are not thinking of dumping him, are you? I am not sure I can come up with a more suitable contender on such short notice."

As always, his humor kept her grounded.

"In a nutshell, he has a job interview two weeks from today in Florida with an outfit specializing in security and transportation for the ultra-wealthy. Apparently, they only hire former elite military, like from Mossad."

He gave a low whistle. "I wonder if they need a crack legal team in Texas?"

She knew he was only half-joking with that remark.

"Is Zeke thinking about piloting for them?"

"Flight instructor."

"Not a bad gig, although I am not sure the commute for court is practical, but I assume that is the rub."

She nodded. "If he asks me, I will go."

His expression grave, he nodded. "You have my blessing. I will help you in any way I can."

She lowered her head, tears falling freely. Hugging the dog

to her, she wiped them from her face.

Reaching into the same drawer, he produced a bottle of water, opened it, and placed it before her.

She took a sip and regained most of her composure.

"However, if he chooses to stay or go without me, I will come back to work settled, focused, and ready to do whatever you need of me."

He leaned forward in his chair, searching her face.

"You have a guest lecture gig at the law school in town for the fall, if you would like."

"Thank you."

"At the very least, I would like to see you publish what you have whether you stay or go to Florida. It will make you one of the most sought-after appellate attorneys in forty-nine of the fifty states. I am not sure what they do over in Louisiana."

"I would not even know how to begin."

"That is what I am here for, darlin'. Say the word, I have a publisher lined up to work with you, care of the dean over at the law school."

"Word."

He nodded. "Done."

"Take three weeks, beginning right now."

She could only smile in return.

"Will you be at the guest house this evening when I get home?"

She nodded.

"I will help you load that loom in the back of your rig. Do you need help with anything else?"

She shook her head and mouthed: "Thank you."

"Do we need to break his legs or sabotage his background check to keep him grounded? I have people."

She grinned. "I think he has already passed the background."

He snapped his fingers. "Two days late and a dollar short."

They exchanged a long, meaningful glance.

"Okay," he broke the moment, "hide that dog, straighten

your face, and get out of here. I have work to do."

∞∞∞

Bree spent the remainder of the day cleaning the guest house from top to bottom. Her hosts kept the kitchen fully equipped, so there was nothing for her to box up, but her clothes and toiletries. The loom folded slightly, allowing it to pass through a door without having to take it apart, unlike the bigger ones she had in storage.

She folded the seats down in her SUV and cleared the back for the loom.

Surveying the small cottage, she decided to wait until morning to empty the fridge and wipe it down. She would also wait to wash the bed linens and remake the bed before she left in the morning.

Checking her watch, she had a couple of hours before Donovan returned home to help her load the loom.

She decided she really needed to make her final furniture selections if she wanted to have something to sit and sleep on in a week.

She placed her order moments before Donovan appeared at the sliding door.

At less than 150 pounds, the small loom was no problem for them to load. They had to lay it on its back, but that was how she had driven it from California when she bought it.

She thanked him for everything, assured him she would leave the guest house in pristine shape, and see him soon.

He cautioned her about taking wooden nickels and returned to the main house.

She loaded everything, except what she and Coal needed for the night.

Once she had a shower and a bite to eat, her phone rang.

"Hello," she smiled.

Zeke's deep, smooth voice greeted her. "Good evening, Beautiful."

She inquired as to his day. He assured her things were on track for a Friday move-in.

"Do you like surprises?"

He responded, his voice guarded, as a number of things came immediately to mind. "It depends, what do you have in mind?"

"Donovan told me not to come back to work for the next three weeks."

"Ha!" he laughed, much relieved. "Outstanding! When will you be here?"

"In the morning. Is that a problem?"

"Not one bit, I have missed you."

"You are not tired of me, yet?"

"No, ma'am, not even a little."

"What would you like to eat this week?"

"Bree, I love that you cook and have enjoyed everything that you have made, but you do not have to cook every day, at least not for me. I can cook, and I know how to make a sandwich."

"Well," she teased, "how would you have me fill my time?"

"Ummm," he grinned, "I can think of several interesting things..."

"I am a little slow, you may have to provide diagrams."

He chuckled. "That sounds like evidence to me."

Giggling, she assured him, "Think hard on that Mr. Buchanan and remember it may be difficult to perform effectively on an empty stomach."

He laughed heartily. "You win, Ms. Lancaster. I thought I would grill jalapeno burgers for us this week. How are your onion rings?"

Delighted, she admitted, "I have no idea. I guess we will find out."

She had been apprehensive earlier in the day whether he would be ready for her to return so soon. As it was, she was unsure how much she would actually be seeing him once she was moved into the warehouse and he was at his place. It was not something she was prepared to discuss, as she feared pressuring him, especially with Florida looming.

Promising to see him soon, she bid him a good night and hung up.

Chapter 25

Tracking her, Zeke realized she would not arrive until mid-morning, which put her half an hour or so out.

He ran down his list.

The plumbing fixtures were all installed and operational.

Jed was on the Bobcat and digging the hole for the propane tank. It would be buried shortly. The gas technician was to return after lunch to attach the lines. The gas company would send a truck to fill it in the morning.

The only appliance not online was the refrigerator. One of the water lines must have been pierced when they nailed down the flooring before staining and refinishing.

He loathed the thought of pulling up any of the finished floor. Instead, he had his guys prepared to remove planks in the store front, hoping there was enough crawlspace under the two buildings to find and replace the damaged water line.

One of the tile guys was working on the kitchen backsplash that instant. There were actually two sets of tile guys. One group did vertical surfaces only, and the other strictly worked horizontal surfaces. It was frustrating, as he had had to schedule them both and have them work around one another; however, the bathrooms and utility room were complete. Both groups were to return on Wednesday to seal the grout. Bree would have to wait 72 hours for it to cure, until she showered, but he did not anticipate that would be a problem.

He was excited about her moving in soon, but he was torn. He enjoyed having her to himself at his place. He wondered how it was going to work, each of them with their own place.

Then, he shook his head, he really did not care where he slept, as long as she was beside him.

"Boss," Juan called him.

Turning toward the voice. "Yeah."

"There's actually a floor panel in here."

Following him into the store front, Juan knelt in the northeast corner along the shared wall with the warehouse. He outlined a rectangle in the dusty wood. Zeke pulled out a hammer and they tried to pry it open to no avail.

He called to Jose and asked him to bring a broom, a bucket of water, and a rag.

Within minutes, Jose returned.

Zeke swept the caked dust away, as Juan dipped the rag in water and began wiping down the planks.

He identified several screws.

Zeke nodded.

One of the other men produced a drill, and Juan began removing the screws.

Bree carried Coal to the back door and put him down, as she entered. There was a flurry of activity, but no sign of Zeke.

Following the dog, she entered the store front and found him with a few of the other men, working on the floor.

She moved closer to see what they were doing, as the men pulled up a floor panel to reveal a dark crawl space or cellar.

She inched forward to peer down when the dank, musty odor hit her, and she was instantly seized with a paralyzing and deep-seated hysteria.

Out of the corner of his eye, Juan saw her drop. His head snapped around as her body hit the floor and curled into a ball. "Boss!" he shouted and moved toward her.

Zeke turned; his eyes focused on the woman on the floor. In an instant, was kneeling beside her. Her eyes and hands were tightly clenched. Her arms were cold to the touch and covered with goose pimples, despite the late spring heat. Her breath was shallow and labored. She seemed to rock back and forth slightly.

Glancing over to the hole in the floor, he noticed a thick, musty smell. "Close that thing up, now!" He ordered. Pulling her to his chest, he scooped her up, and strode onto the patio with her.

Sitting down on one of the chairs with her in his lap, he whispered quietly, "You are okay. I am here. I have you. You are okay," as he rocked her gently in the sunlight and fresh air.

Tremors ripped through her body, as her breath came in short, shallow, forced bursts. He finally made out what she was saying, "No, no, no" with each rapid exhale.

Instinctively, he knew something about that hole, either the smell or the darkness, triggered a distant memory or trauma.

As they rocked slowly, a favorite hymn came to mind, and he began with quietly humming it in her ear, but by the second rendition, he was softly singing it to her.

Slowly, inch by inch, he felt the tension begin to leave her body. While her breath was far from normal, she was quiet and stopped the repetition of "no."

Eventually, her body sagged against him and her head came to rest at the crux of his shoulder and jaw.

As her breath steadied, he fell silent.

When she finally spoke, her voice was faint and breathless. "I am so sorry."

He shushed her and comforted her with "You are fine."

Then the tears began to fall. For several minutes soft sobs shook her and quaked his soul with her hurt and despair.

He felt entirely helpless, but kept holding her firmly and rocking her gently, letting her know she was not alone in this emotional tempest.

He realized they had company, as a pair of paws insistently pushed against his shin. Releasing her with one of his arms, he picked up her dog and placed him on top of her arms, which had been folded across her stomach. She lifted one to hold her beloved CoalBear.

Several more minutes passed before she finally took a deep breath and shifted slightly in his lap.

"Thank you," she whispered against his neck.

He smiled and kissed the top of her head. "Anytime."

He felt the tension completely leave her body. She was spent, and he was content just to hold her in his arms.

"Where did you go, Bree?"

He felt her shrug before she answered. "I am not sure," she paused, "that smell, just..." she shuddered, and it rippled through them.

Her muscles tightened again.

"You are okay. I will not let anything happen to you."

She sighed and straightened, her eyes seeking his. He found her face tight. Her eyes, red and swollen entertained a haunted expression that deepened his own frown.

She looked away.

He released his hand from the back of her knees, allowing her legs to dangle from his lap. He kept one hand behind her back and brought his free one to rest on her lap, next to Coal-Bear.

He remained silent, anticipating she may need to share.

Studying her profile, he watched her chew on her bottom lip before taking a deep breath.

"There's something there, a memory or an image. I can almost see it. It's like if I peer just a little harder into the darkness, my eyes will acclimatize, and it will reveal itself."

"Have you spoken to anyone about PTSD?"

She faced him again, sensing the subject was deeply personal to him. She knew he had been in the military for the prior twenty years, but she just realized he probably had quite a bit of combat experience with Iraq and Afghanistan.

"From what I understand, PTSD relates to flashbacks, nightmares, and racing thoughts about a terrifying incidence or event."

He nodded.

"I have no memory of a specific event."

Very gently, he asserted: "You bear the physical scars of abuse."

She knew he was correct.

"It is not a stretch to assume your five-year-old self buried the memories of a specific event or, heaven forbid, a series of traumatic events."

"With Dr. Lancaster, we did cognitive behavioral therapy, art therapy, and even hypnosis...to no avail."

He rubbed her back. "You know what?" He smiled.

"Your legs are asleep, and you are dying for me to get off your lap."

His smile turned into a broad grin, grateful for her humor.

"No, ma'am. I like you just where you are." He pulled her closer to him.

"What I was going to say is that there is nothing wrong with you. Whatever it is that you have had to endure as a child, you have overcome. You are kind, considerate, big-hearted, and a wonderful human being to be around."

Her heart swelled with his words, but she was cautious.

"How are you?" she probed.

He was unsure how to respond.

Right that second, he was content because he was with her. He knew his brother and the crew were probably watching and insanely curious about them, but he did not care.

He also knew he had an interview in Florida with the promise of a new life and another adventure before him, but the thought of being anywhere without her filled him with dread.

He searched for the words to adequately convey all the things he felt.

When he finally answered her, he did so with absolute sincerity. "As long as you are okay. I am okay."

Crushing the small dog between them, she wrapped her arms around his neck and kissed him.

∞∞∞

Once she was mostly recovered, he encouraged her to go home and relax. He told her he would unload her clothes when he got there, so they would be able to move the loom in the next day.

He wanted her away from the warehouse when they opened that panel again.

She complied with his request.

She did not argue, when he insisted on picking up a pizza on his way home, either.

When she and CoalBear arrived at Zeke's place, she brought in the boxes with her clothes and neatly stacked them in the guest room. She undressed in the utility room and walked naked to the bathroom and took a shower. Once she dried off, she gathered the dog, closed the door, and crawled into Zeke's bed.

∞∞∞

After she left, Juan opened the panel again and as the smallest man on the crew, he was elected to search out the problem line.

Fortunately, there was no barrier between the buildings and enough space for him to maneuver. He located the line and within an hour had it replaced.

Zeke did not wait for the plumber, he hooked up the refrigerator himself while Juan sealed the panel once more.

∞∞∞

Leaving Jed to lock up, he called in a pizza and picked it up before driving home.

He again found the front door unlocked. It further tested his already frazzled nerves. He made a mental note to speak with her about it when she was feeling better.

He checked the kitchen first with no sign of her.

Glancing into the utility room, he noticed her clothes in a basket on the floor in front of the washer.

The guest room was filled with boxes.

The door to his bedroom was closed.

Easing it open, CoalBear lifted his head.

Zeke left the door cracked to allow in a thin stream of light. He reached over and gently pat the dog, willing him to remain still.

Bree was on her side, curled into a ball. Coal lay behind her knees in the crook between her thighs and calves.

Her arms were folded to her chest, covers wrapped tightly around her.

He kneeled beside the bed and smoothed the hair from her face and gently kissed her forehead.

She smiled and opened her eyes.

"Hey, Beautiful," he whispered.

She reached out and placed her palm on the side of his face, her thumb caressing the edge of his mouth.

He kissed her.

"You okay?"

She nodded and sat up, the sheets falling down around her, exposing her.

One hand moved to cup her breast, his thumb and forefinger gently rolling her nipple between them.

"You should greet me like this every time I come home."

She pulled the covers to the side and swung her feet to the floor.

He stood to give her room to stand, his hands settling on her bare bottom, as he pulled her to him.

She ran her hands over his back, tugging his shirt tail free of his jeans.

She moved her hands to his waist and undid his belt buckle before unbuttoning his jeans and pulling down the zipper. Without breaking their gaze, she unbuttoned his shirt and pulled it off his shoulders, holding it as he pulled first one arm, then the other free of it. Allowing it fall to the floor, she pulled his undershirt up and over his head, as well. Turning him around, she pulled his jeans and brief down before she pushed him to sit on the bed. She turned her back to him, straddling one leg, bent over, and reached for his boot, tugging it off. She did the same with the other. Facing him again, she reached down and tugged his jeans and underwear off, until he was as naked as she was.

Pulling her to him, he buried his face between her breasts and feasted upon them, as his hands roamed her body. He eventually leaned back onto the bed with her on top of him.

He pivoted gently and rolled her onto her back, moving to kiss her deeply.

She did not resist and ran her fingers through his hair, squirming to get closer to him.

Moving from her lips, he concentrated on the sensitive area at the base of her neck, just above her shoulder blade, one hand stroking the inside of her thigh. She moaned.

Revisiting her breasts, he kneaded them with his hands, as he rolled his tongue around one nipple and gently suckled before showering attention on the other.

Her urgency intense, she struggled to pull his lips back to her mouth, but he resisted, content to explore her navel, before raining small kisses along her inner thighs.

Placing his palm on her mound, he encouraged her to part her thighs by gently running his thumb between her nether lips. She squirmed and writhed.

Using both thumbs, he parted her lips slightly and tasted her with his tongue.

He heard her breath catch in her throat. His head rose slightly to look at her face. Her body was tense with hands clenched in the sheets. Her eyes closed, and her teeth gritted.

He smiled and applied himself to gratifying her, gently teasing the small nub of her pleasure center until she began panting, then increased the pressure, changing his technique, as he gauged her response.

His hands continued to roam her body, caressing her breasts, but as he deepened the pressure and she began to squirm in earnest, he slipped his hands under her bottom to steady her as the tremors and shocks rippled through her and she cried out in release, her hands trying to simultaneously push him away and hold him in place.

Persuaded she could take no more stimulation for the moment, he moved beside her and cradled her to him, as the aftershocks slowed and faded.

As her breathing normalized, she mumbled into his chest, "God, Zeke, I thought I was going to die." She kissed him. "Thank you."

He smiled into her hair.

Recovering, she moved a hand to his erection to return the favor; however, he halted her advance by placing a hand over hers.

When she looked at him, he said: "Ride me, please."

Without hesitation, she raised to her knees and straddled him. She leaned back with her hands on her own calves and rubbed her swollen lips against him as the tension built immediately within her.

He enjoyed watching her, her head thrown back, long hair hanging down, and her breasts bouncing. Her face was contorted in ecstasy. His hands fondled her breasts, as she continued to rub against him; however, when she began grinding against him in earnest, he lowered his hands to her hips and steadied her for a brief moment to allow him entry when she cried out again "Oh, God, Zeke," she panted, an instant before a new set of quakes shook her.

He held her tightly as she crumpled on his chest, tiny aftershocks rippled through her.

Still erect, he allowed her to catch her breath before gently moving his hips against her.

She lifted her head with a mischievous grin and kissed him deeply, her tongue inviting his to dance.

She moved her hips against his, slowly, almost gingerly.

"Are you okay?" he whispered.

"So sensitive," she responded.

"Roll over."

She did and remained on her hands and knees, head resting on the mattress, as he gently entered her from behind.

"Ahhhh," she moaned.

"Better?"

She rocked against him in answer and his brain turned to mush with all the nerve endings flooding his senses.

He clenched his teeth, trying not to thrust too hard or too fast, as he wanted it to last, but Bree, high on endorphins, coaxed him to abandon. He released a loud grunting, groaning growl before convulsing and shuddering uncontrollably before falling onto the mattress beside her, spent.

Several minutes later, once he caught his breath and found his voice, he uttered: "Lord, help me, woman, you will be the death of me."

She giggled and squirmed her behind against him.

Much later, they emerged for a meal of cold pizza and colder beers.

Chapter 26

For once, Bree did not stir at all the entire night.

Zeke woke first and collected Coal as he eased from the bed. It was not quite five, so he was in no rush.

He stepped onto the porch to allow the dog a brief run before padding barefooted into the kitchen to start a pot of coffee.

He filled Coal's bowl with a partial scoop of kibble, rinsed the other, and filled it with fresh water.

By the time he poured the first cup, Bree had joined him in the kitchen.

Neither of them had a stitch of clothing on.

Turning to her he greeted her with an appreciative smile.

She grinned back and automatically moved into his arms.

He kissed her neck, his hands lightly caressing her back, leaving a trail of heat wherever he touched.

His voice low and resonated over her skin, "We are not going to get anything done today, if this keeps up."

"Well, it is no clothes Wednesday..."

By the time he had showered and left, Bree was still naked and in bed, dreamily spent and satisfied.

∞∞∞

Shortly after he opened up the warehouse, Brett appeared sans Molly. He was dressed in jeans and a button-down shirt with sneakers. He carried a couple boxes of doughnuts.

Setting them down on the island, he offered Zeke a hand. "Good morning, Sir."

"Morning, Brett."

"I appreciate your doing these walk-throughs with me."

Zeke nodded. "Do you have an idea of your needs before the agent arrives?"

"Reception area, two waiting rooms – sick and healthy, perhaps a smaller room for newborns and their mothers to wait safely, a restroom, at least four exam rooms, a private office for me, one for billing, and a file room. If there is an upstairs for a loft apartment for me, even better."

He knew Bree's building was the largest of the four, two others on her side of the street and one facing them. Each of them had a second floor, as it was common in the era in which they were built to have the proprietors live above their shops, rather than build a second structure somewhere else to house them.

"What about room for growth?"

"I believe the agent mentioned the two on this side of the street are connected."

Zeke had not been in any of them, he nodded.

Checking his watch, they had a few more minutes before their appointment, but not wanting to waste time, he suggested: "Let's walk around the two on this side while we have a few minutes."

Brett nodded.

Zeke grabbed his clipboard, outfitted with a new pad, and a pen. His measuring tape was attached to his hip.

He called to Juan as they made their way to the store front: "Juan, I will be next door or across the street, if you need me."

"Yes, Boss," was the reply.

An hour later, Bree arrived and backed her truck all the way up to the patio door.

She allowed the dog to run around for a few minutes, as she unloaded his crate and bowls in the pantry, certain it was the safest place for someone not to trip over them.

Calling him to her, she lured him into the crate with a treat and closed the door.

Zeke was nowhere to be found, so she asked Juan if he would help her unload the loom.

He and Jose brought it in, and she directed them to place it along the east wall, closest to the windows, to the far left of the kitchen, as she stood facing it.

She thanked them and brought in a weaving bench, and a basket of weaving-related items before she moved her truck to her regular spot along the garage.

Releasing Coal, she pulled his bed from the crate and brought it over to the loom before placing it on the floor. Coal-Bear carried his treat with him, and as soon as she deposited the bed onto the floor, he climbed on it, content to chew on the bully stick for a while.

She squared up the loom to the walls and opened her up, adjusting the tension on the warp carefully. When everything was in place. She moved the bench, grabbed a handful of bobbins, her shuttle, and sat down, ready to weave.

Brett and Zeke were deep in discussion as they walked back into the warehouse.

They had completed a thorough tour of all three buildings, and it was obvious to both of them, the one across the street was the least suitable for what Brett had in mind. It was in the worst condition, it was the smallest, and the configuration of load-bearing walls was unworkable as a medical clinic.

In contrast, the buildings adjacent to the warehouse were in significantly better condition structurally with a larger lot for parking, both in front and along the east side, which preserved outside space for private, personal use directly behind the building.

Moreover, the owner of the adjacent buildings was motivated to sell, the larger lot and both buildings being offered for less than the decrepit one across the street.

While Brett was not ready to make an offer, as he needed

to know from Zeke what it would cost to convert it, he was excited.

Zeke washed his hands at the sink, allowing Brett to follow suit, before indulging in the doughnuts, as they continued to chat.

The rhythmic thud and clank of the loom caught Zeke's attention first.

Following the sounds, the sight of Bree lost in her task warmed him. She appeared relaxed, calm, and completely engrossed.

He missed the last sentence or two from Brett.

When he failed to respond, Brett turned and followed the direction of his gaze.

"Is that a loom?"

"Yes. She's weaving."

"I have never seen anyone create cloth before."

His curiosity led him over to inspect it more closely. Zeke followed.

When he crossed her line of vision, Bree looked up and greeted him.

"That's amazing, Bree," he bent beside her and ran a finger over the woven fabric. "Who taught you how to do this?"

"I read several books."

"Autodidactic, huh?"

She smiled modestly.

"How long have you been weaving?"

"Six or seven years now."

"How did you get started?"

"My former mother-in-law collects Lalique glass. It is expensive. My ex liked to go to estate sales in search of it for her. I went along one afternoon and encountered a loom for sale."

"This one?"

She grinned. "Uh, no. One similar to this, but much larger. This one has a 24" weaving width," she moved her hands two feet apart, "the one I bought has a 56" weaving width." She stretched her arms out wide.

"Whoa."

"Yeah. I call him The Beast. He weighs over 450 pounds." She glanced at Zeke. "He will be delivered tomorrow afternoon."

Zeke rolled his eyes.

"So," Brett continued, "You have two looms."

Again, she looked at Zeke, a silent apology in her eyes. "Not exactly."

Zeke chimed in, "Just how many looms do you have?"

"I have a third one like this one, but it has a 32" weaving width. I have a table loom, which is much smaller than this one, as well as two rigid heddle looms, which are basically lap looms."

Brett counted on his fingers, as he kept track. "That is six, right?"

She bit her bottom lip. "Well, a friend of mine discovered a barn loom, coincidentally in a barn that was to be torn down. He borrowed a trailer and picked it up for me a couple of years ago."

Brett looked at her quizzically. "What exactly is a barn loom?"

Again, she looked at Zeke before answering. "It is called a barn loom because of its size. It was far too big to fit in a home."

Brett looked at Zeke, too, and laughed. There was an unspoken 'Better you, than me' aspect to the exchange.

Bree continued, "The thing about the barn loom, though, it came to me in pieces, I never saw it put together, and I have no idea whether I will be able to resurrect it or even if I have all the pieces."

Zeke inquired, "Will it be delivered tomorrow, too?"

"Everything I own, which really is not much, aside from the looms, will be delivered tomorrow. I tried to put them off until Friday, but the movers have a job to pick up a load in San Antonio tomorrow afternoon that is going to Denver, and I reluctantly agreed without speaking to you first. I am sorry."

"How much stuff, Bree?"

"Basically, my spring and summer clothes are at your house.

I have two pods coming. One-and-a-half of them contain weaving related items. The remaining half of a pod has boxes with kitchen stuff, my winter clothes, shoes, and personal items/ books. I have not a stick of furniture, I left all that with Clint and the Lakeway house."

He nodded, "We will make it work."

Brett looked at her, "What are you going to do about furniture?"

Grinning, she cast another glance at Zeke. "What I have purchased should be delivered on Friday."

Brett was enjoying the conversation at Zeke's expense. "Do tell, does any of it have to be put together?"

She giggled. "Other than a Murphy bed, no."

∞∞∞

Long after Brett left and Zeke returned to his dwindling punch list, Bree continued weaving until she had exhausted the warp.

Returning to her basket, she unwrapped a pair of scissors and carefully cut the finished fabric from the loom.

Coming down the stairs, Zeke saw what she was doing and came over to check on her.

"You finished it?"

"Yes!"

"What do you do now, pull it off?"

"Yes, would you mind doing me a favor?"

"Not at all."

She pulled her phone out of her pocket and set it to video.

"Would you mind standing over here," she directed him to the right side of the loom. "Pull up on this lever with your right hand, it releases the ratchet on the cloth beam, which allows me to unroll it."

He did as she instructed.

"Now, hold my phone in your left hand. I like to video it

coming off the loom."

She pulled the end of the cloth between the front beam and beater with one hand.

"Okay," she steadied his left hand where she wanted him to film and hit the record button and unfurled the cloth.

It took a whole minute to pull all the fabric off.

She nodded to him, and he released the lever to press the stop button before handing the phone back to her.

"Thank you!"

"What do you do with the video?"

She pulled a face, as though reluctant to share a secret.

"I have a website about the weaving and maintain a presence on social media."

He raised an eyebrow, uncertain quite what to think.

"What is your website called?"

She licked her lips before chewing on her bottom lip.

"Breezy Handwovens."

"Is that your social media handle, too?"

She nodded.

"Show me."

She pulled up Instagram and handed her phone to him.

He spent several minutes scrolling through the photos. "You have almost two thousand posts."

"Really?" she replied, "I did not realize I had that many."

He noted most all of them were weaving related, but Coal-Bear had made a couple of appearances.

Inspecting a Coal post, he noted the hashtag #coalbearchronicles.

"He has his own Instagram page?"

She laughed.

"No, silly, that would be weird. I just gave him a hashtag."

He continued to scroll the photos, reading one here and there.

"You dye your own thread?"

"Yes."

He tapped her bio, which sent him to her website.

He scanned a few of the posts.

"You write about weaving."

"I share what I enjoy, Zeke, please do not make fun of me."

He put the phone down and studied her. All levity had abated from her expression.

He reached out and placed a gentle hand on her arm, rubbing her forearm with his thumb.

"I am not teasing you. I am surprised, that is all. My little introvert is all over social media. You have over six thousand followers, I am more than impressed."

He handed her phone back to her.

"However, are there any other websites and Instagram profiles I may like to know about?"

She smiled. "No, Sir. I am all about the weaving and that is about it."

He hugged her to him, kissing her on the forehead.

"Hungry?"

"What time is it?"

"1:30."

"I packed sandwiches and chips before I left this morning. I think I left the cooler in my truck. Let me get them."

"Awesome. I will meet you on the patio."

Someone, one of the crew she presumed, had brought a small table with a few chairs, and left them on the patio.

Zeke was wiping off the table when she returned with the small cooler.

She pulled out his thermos of iced tea, a bottle of water for her, a couple of sandwiches, and two small bags of chips.

"What do you think if I fence in back here?"

"From the property line or just around the patio?"

"I was actually thinking to the property line."

"CoalBear?"

"And privacy?"

"Six- or eight-foot privacy fence?"

She nodded.

"That would be really nice, but a lot of fence. Expensive."

"I was also thinking of a container garden using troughs or raised beds."

"Juan's dad has a landscaping business. I am sure he could set you up. He and his brothers also do odd jobs, I feel like they would do a good job on a fence, as well."

"It's mid-March now. I saw plants appearing outside the feed store the other day."

"Check the almanac for zone 8b." He took another bite of his sandwich. "What are you thinking, tomatoes?"

"Basically, a salsa and marinara garden with tomatoes, habaneros, tomatillos, cilantro, jalapenos, basil…"

He smiled at her. She was planting all kinds of roots.

Bree considered her options as they continued to eat in comfortable silence.

Zeke opened his thermos and took a long drink.

"You really do make the best tea, Bree. Thank you."

"How did it go with Brett this morning?"

His eyes brightened and he smiled with excitement. "These two next to you are perfect for what he has in mind. According to the agent, they were last renovated in the 70's, which may sound like a long time ago, but your buildings were vacated sometime in the 40s. There was a lot less damage and decay inside."

She smiled at his enthusiasm.

"I am going to work up an estimate and get back to him sometime next week if I can. Between this project and that one, we could establish Jed's company in a big way."

"No disrespect to your brother, at all, but can he manage a project like that without you?"

He knew she was right. Teaching Jed how to remain focused and efficiently run a project was exactly why he had taken six months off between separating from the military and finding a job.

"He has been distracted with Darla's health and the baby."

She nodded knowingly and decided not to pursue it.

Jose stepped out and asked if Zeke could look at something.

He jumped up, but not before thanking her for lunch and giving her a wink.

Bree cleaned up and retuned the cooler to her vehicle before seeking Juan out.

∞∞∞

By mid-afternoon, Bree had wiped down her loom and removed all thrums, readying it for a fresh warp, just as soon as the rest of her weaving equipment arrived. She carefully folded the handwoven fabric she had removed earlier and tucked it into one of the cabinets in the utility room.

She thought about sweeping the floors, but she knew with the foot traffic and continuing work, it would be wasted effort.

She walked through each of the rooms, upstairs and down, imagining how she would decorate each one.

Zeke found her standing in the bedroom staring at the empty space.

"Everything okay?"

She held out her hand to him, and he stepped over and intertwined his fingers with hers before raising them to his lips and kissing her hand.

"How are we going to do this?"

"Arrange this room?"

She shook her head.

"You and me?"

She nodded.

"I do not care where I sleep, as long as I am next to you."

She leaned into him. He rested his free hand on her hip.

"Do you mind if I leave Coal with you? I would like to go to the market on my way home."

"Not at all."

"I will put him in his crate. It is in the pantry."

"Good idea. I will not forget him"

"Thank you."

He kissed the top of her head and released her.
"See you later."

Chapter 27

Zeke and Bree hit the ground running on Thursday.

The movers were expected before eight, and Zeke had the final inspection for occupancy later in the day. He was concerned the inspector would think she had already moved in, which tended to create issues, but fortunately none of the furniture was due to arrive until Friday.

Both of the pods with Bree's items fit on the back of a single semi. The truck had a small crane-type winch, which off loaded each pod for loading and unloading.

The driver was able to back straight up to the back door, which made unloading a straight shot into the warehouse. Bree had done a great job of labeling each box and once they identified where they should go, the movers took care of everything.

The looms required more care.

Zeke had them place the pieces of the barn loom in the store front for the time being.

Bree supervised the handling of her precious looms.

In less than an hour, everything was completely offloaded, and the movers were gone.

Bree produced a small red toolbox from her SUV and set about putting her looms together.

The middle sized one was intact, but for one of the two back beams she described as a sectional. Instead of smooth and round like the top one, the sectional had four flat sides attached to it with metal pins sticking out along the edges of the flat sides, one inch apart.

He had noticed the small loom Meg had two beams on the back of her as well, a smooth round beam on top and the boxy sectional beam on the bottom. It appeared each of the three floor looms was constructed the same way.

The largest loom, the one she referred to as The Beast was a monster. She had mentioned it weighed over 450 pounds, and he did not doubt it.

She had taken most of it apart to move, and it was in several pieces. He had offered to help, but she declined, explaining she would only need help with attaching the sectional beam, but it would be the last thing, so he left her and her toolbox alone with the dog at her heels. She was happy and very much in her element. It warmed his heart.

For the third time in recent days, he checked the taps on each faucet and shower for hot and cold running water. He made sure the toilets flushed and the drains drained. He checked the burners on the range and ran the air conditioner. All the ceiling fans were operating. The vent and exhaust fans worked. He had his permits in order. He had certificates from the gas technician and the electrician. Everything was lined out. He had dotted each "i" and crossed each "t." Yet, he was nervous as a cat at a dog fight.

Jed's presence and incessant chatter did not help.

He pulled his little brother aside and handed him copies of his notes from the walk-through with Brett. He tried to impress upon him what an important project this could be for him and his company, before suggesting he go somewhere quiet, like home, and begin putting together an estimate.

Jed did not like the paper side of the business. He much preferred to work with his hands. Neither did he have the patience to develop schedules. He also did not have the stomach to stay on top of subcontractors to keep them on the timeline.

Zeke had bristled a bit when Bree had asked if he could manage a big job like a medical clinic, but he knew she had a valid point.

He had had a heart-to-heart talk with Samuel a few weeks ago about his concerns with Jed and the business. Samuel had expressed an interest working with Jed, just as Zeke had, but he was committed through the end of the year, and it was only March.

Without him, Zeke was unsure he could continue to remain afloat by then, and it tore him up.

Fortunately, Jed was excited about the prospect of the clinic and agreed to take a stab at the estimate. He took Zeke's copies and headed home to work on them.

Zeke was relieved. He hated to admit it, but he was afraid Jed's gift to gab would throw a wrench in getting the all clear on occupancy.

∞∞∞

Lost in her own world of weaving-related things, Bree was completely oblivious to Zeke's nerves, the inspection, the window washers, or anything but CoalBear and her looms.

She wiped down every piece of The Beast's wood with a feed and wax, dusted each metal part, and carefully put him together. When it came to the sectional beam, she knew it was too large for her to install alone.

Looking around, she saw Zeke was giving someone a tour, she assumed it was the inspector.

Rather than pull Jose or Juan away from their projects, she decided she would wait until someone had a moment, and moved onto the middle loom, the one she had named Lil Miss.

Once she, too was rubbed down with feed and wax, as well as dusted. She did the same to Meg.

Zeke remained occupied, so she delved into the boxes labeled studio until she found one containing the pieces for her warping mill and put that together. There were only five pieces, so it did not take much time.

In another box, she found the pieces to her warping square. It involved a bit more work, but soon she had that together, too

Most of the other boxes contained her thread stash she used to dress her looms.

With the built-in secretary along the utility room wall, she no longer needed a day job workspace, but the area she had originally dedicated as an office behind the kitchen would be perfect to house her weaving stash and equipment, especially since she had decided to place the looms between that space and the east wall of the building.

Surveying the looms, all clean and neatly lined up in the natural light coming from the windows, she was thrilled. It was the perfect space.

As she was taking it all in, Zeke and the gentleman approached.

Zeke introduced the man as the building inspector. She extended her hand and thanked him for coming. He told her everything was in order and they could collect the occupancy license later in the day.

She was so excited, she almost hugged him, but she refrained and thanked him again.

Casting a quick glance at Zeke, she could tell he was awash in relief and pride.

Zeke walked him out and promptly returned. He completely surprised her by reaching down, picking her up, and spinning her around a time or two.

She giggled uncontrollably at his antics.

He put her down and kissed her.

Holding onto him, she squeezed a little tighter. "I am so grateful for you."

"Just doing my job, ma'am."

Pulling back slightly to look up at him, "Perhaps," she raised an eyebrow, "it is a good thing you may be looking into a different line of work."

Puzzled, he narrowed his eyes.

"I do not think I could sit at home wondering how well you would take care of the next lady owner."

"Jealous, are we?"

She sobered for a moment; the joke was actually on her as she thought about it. She tucked her chin slightly and placed a hand on his chest. "Yes, actually."

He studied her carefully. "Well, the next job may be for Brett, and I can promise you, he gets no special treatment or attention."

She nodded with a small smile.

"Can I help you with this beam now?"

"Please."

They moved back over to The Beast.

"All I really need for you to do is hold it for me. I cannot pick it up and attach these nuts at the same time."

He did as she instructed and held it in place while she secured. It took all of two minutes.

"That's it?"

"Yes, Sir."

He looked around and noted the other two pieces of equipment.

"What are those?"

"One is a warping mill, and the other is a warping square. They are used to prepare the warp, which are the vertical threads on the loom."

He nodded, it made a little sense to him, but he had no idea how they were used to do anything.

"What do you need me to do?"

"What do you mean?"

"I mean once we pick up the certificate of occupancy, Buchanan Construction will have fulfilled the contract with you, eight days early."

She grinned. "Two things, Mr. Buchanan. First, you are the most amazing man I have ever met. Thank you. Two, if you will give me the bill on the last change order, I will settle up with you."

Zeke nodded, "However, on a personal level, we still have a lot to do to get you settled here. I believe you mentioned something about a Murphy bed. I assume you also need shelves. What did you decide about storage in the bedroom?"

"Slow down, please. Take a deep breath. Live in the moment.

You have done an extraordinary job getting this place ready. Enjoy this."

He breathed deeply as he gazed into her beautiful brown eyes. He rested his hands on her hips and enjoyed the feel of her beneath his fingers. He inhaled the scent of her and felt the desire rising within him at her nearness. He slowly counted his blessings, most of which directly involved the woman standing in front of him.

"I love you, Bree."

"I love you."

Chapter 28

Friday morning, Zeke and Bree rose with a purpose. She had deliveries from several different places arriving, beginning at eight.

The first truck was timely and carried several area rugs, the largest of which went directly into the space designated as the living room. The second largest rugs were placed in each of the bedrooms upstairs. The last three were to go under the looms.

The delivery guy had no problem helping Zeke place them under the smaller looms, but he balked when it came to moving The Beast, until Bree produced two pairs of furniture slider coasters and placed them under the corners of the loom, which allowed them to move the loom with ease. Zeke smoothed things over with the man with a generous tip, as well.

Zeke praised her for her taste in rugs and ensuring they were delivered first.

She christened her newly acquired vacuum cleaner on the rugs while they waited for additional deliveries.

The Murphy bed arrived next. Fortunately, two men were involved with that, and they were able to get everything upstairs without assistance from Zeke.

The third truck held most of the furniture.

A simple bed frame went into the master, Bree still had no idea how she wanted to handle the absence of a closet. A desk and a bookcase went into the spare room.

An L-shaped leather sofa, two club chairs, and an ottoman were moved into the living room. End tables, lamps, and a coffee table were still to be discovered.

Three bar stools found a home at the island and twelve dining chairs surrounded the table.

The final delivery contained mattresses for both bedrooms.

By two in the afternoon, they were exhausted.

Bree collected two bottles of water from the refrigerator and joined Zeke on the sofa.

He looked around and nodded. "You have quite the impressive home, Ms. Lancaster."

She took a sip and graced him with a smile.

He noticed she had been unusually quiet and subdued all day.

"You know, sometimes, it really does help to talk to someone about what's bugging you."

She found him gentle and kind. Unlike his brother, he was quiet and comfortable in his own skin. She noted he was content to observe and learn with no desire to prove anything to anyone. He provided a steady and calming influence on her. Whenever he was near, she experienced a sense of comfort and wellness. Had anyone else nudged her to share, even Donovan, she would have changed the subject or avoided it a dozen different ways, but she felt compelled to open up, if only a little.

"Today is something of a milestone for me, in addition to the gloriousness of this place."

She stood and fidgeted with straightening things and wiped an already spotless counter before glancing at him again. His clear blue eyes darkened and became more intense as he studied her. She felt drawn to them and him. Reticent to break the gaze, she continued "I was surrendered to foster care on this date 28 years ago."

His brow furrowed more deeply. He made no move to speak.

"According to the paperwork, the man who brought me in was a neighbor. He said my father had died and my mother had abandoned me on his doorstep early that morning and left."

"I am sorry, Bree."

She shrugged, looking away. CoalBear was at her feet. She bent to collect him and cradle him in her arms, grateful for his warmth and affection.

"The man did not know my name, much less my birthdate. They thought I was about five years old and listed that date as my date of birth, minus five years."

"At five, you probably knew your name and birthday." He offered quietly.

"One would think, no?" She gave an empty, mirthless chuckle.

"Well," she continued, "I think I may have already mentioned I was actually non-verbal the first year or so after my surrender. In fact, I actually have no memory of anything prior to foster care."

His eyes never left her face. They had spoken briefly of this before, but not in as much detail. "Wow," he breathed softly, "that is rough."

Again, she shrugged.

"You know the Lancasters adopted me and left me an inheritance."

He nodded.

"Dr. Lancaster died when I was in law school."

Her face scrunched in pain, and she began rocking slightly, as she pulled the dog close to her cheek, her eyes threatening to overflow.

"He had a heart attack the week before finals. His wife did not want to upset me or interfere with my exams. They were very practical people. She had a stroke and passed a few days after he did. I was unaware until the funeral home contacted me."

He moved to gently wrap his arms around her, careful not to crush the dog, and rocked with her for several moments.

Bree felt stupid for becoming emotional, but she was compelled to continue. "I never had the chance to say goodbye to either of them or thank them for all they did for me. Looking around this place, I am so grateful to them. I hope they knew I really did love them."

Chapter 29

The following day, Bree had a long list and shopping date in San Antonio with her friend Priscilla. Their mission was to acquire bedroom and bath linens, cleaning supplies, as well as stock her pantry and fridge. With a full day ahead of her, she left before eight, promising to let Zeke know when she was on her way back, to allow him to help her unload.

Zeke had plans to design a clinic and create an estimate for Brett.

They agreed CoalBear was to supervise and remain with Zeke.

By half-past three, Bree texted Zeke she was on her way. He tracked her location, printed his progress, and headed to the warehouse.

When he arrived, Brett was playing fetch with Molly on the grounds behind the buildings adjacent to the warehouse. Zeke released the Hell Hound, grabbed the roll of plans he had been working on, and strolled over.

They chatted for several minutes while the dogs romped. Zeke explained Bree was headed in with supplies. Brett took Molly home and promised to return to help.

Whistling for the little dog, Zeke opened up the warehouse, dropping the plans on the dining table.

Brett returned as two vehicles backed into the patio area.

Bree was dressed in a tee shirt, jeans, and sneakers.

Her friend Priscilla wore a red dress with large print flowers over it and sandals. It was fitted through the waist, accentuating her ample cleavage and hour-glass figure. Like Bree, she had dark hair, which hung past her shoulders, but it was a beautiful riot of curls. Her olive complexion was smooth and supple. When she turned her full dark red lips smiled at him, her liquid brown eyes shined. She was stunning and vivacious.

Bree stopped, staring at both men as they gaped open-mouthed at her friend. She was accustomed with the manner in which her friend was able to completely stop traffic.

Priscilla was oblivious, intent as she was on filling her arms with bags of sheets and towels to carry in.

"Hang on, Pris," Bree whispered, patting her arm to release the goods. "I would like to introduce you to a couple of gentle-men."

Following Bree's instruction, she turned around.

Motioning for Zeke, "Zeke, this is my dear friend Priscilla."

He stepped forward and extended a hand, "Nice to meet you, Priscilla, Zeke."

Gesturing to the other man, "This is our friend and neigh-bor, Brett Parker."

In his haste to make the introduction, Brett stumbled over the loose gravel and broken concrete on the patio, but managed a relatively dignified, "It is a pleasure, Priscilla," as he took her hand gently.

Brett recovered and immediately asked, "May I help you with those, please?"

The ladies exchanged glances.

Bree laughed, "Why don't we allow these guys to unload, and I will show you around?"

The ladies scurried off, leaving the men looking at one an-other.

"Wow," Brett breathed the moment they were out of ear-shot.

While Zeke found her extremely attractive, as well, his eyes followed Bree exclusively.

He turned back toward Brett, "Snap out of it, man, you look like a deer in the headlights."

By the time the ladies finished their tour, the men had brought everything inside.

The women moved like a well-oiled machine.

At Bree's request, Zeke presented a knife to Priscilla to remove all the tags from the linens and immediately retired to the utility room to begin washing them for use.

Bree loaded the refrigerator with the cold items and immediately began filling the pantry. She had picked up a frozen lasagna for supper, which she left on the counter to thaw a bit, as well.

Once she was done, she joined Priscilla in the utility room and together they opened, sorted, and put away all the cleaning supplies, including the big box store paper goods.

The guys had unrolled the plans and had their heads together going over them, when the girls returned for a quick break, as they waited on the washer and dryer.

Bree collected water bottles from the fridge and passed them around before assuming a club chair.

The moment Pris sat down, CoalBear appeared, ready to join her.

She squealed at the sight of him and invited him up. He charmed her immediately and settled down beside her on the sofa.

It was nearing six.

Bree stood, turned the oven on, pulled a bag of salad she had just purchased from the refrigerator, and opened the dish washer. It was full, as she had unpacked her dishes directly into it the day before and ran it before they returned to Zeke's for the night.

Priscilla washed her hands and began helping her unload, asking briefly where she wanted a few things.

The moment they had returned, Brett's ability to concentrate on the plans faded, and he watched Priscilla's every movement.

Zeke understood, Bree had the same effect on him. He rolled the plans and sat back in his chair, content to observe.

Bree stepped back into the utility room. She found the utensil tray and crock she had just purchased and handed them to

Pris before emptying the dryer into a basket and reloading it and the washer.

Priscilla had the utensils squared away by the time Bree set the basket on the island.

They each reached in and began folding towels and stacking them.

Bree handed a small stack to Pris for the bath under the stairs and carried the larger one to the upstairs bath.

Zeke noted they hardly spoke, each anticipating what the other wanted or needed. He was amazed.

Brett leaned over to Zeke and whispered, "What do you know about Priscilla?"

Pursing his lips in thought, Zeke called up what scant information he had, "She lives and works in San Antonio. I think she is a bank manager. She is divorced with two young boys. Beyond that, you know what I know."

Priscilla returned to the utility room with Zeke's knife and a handful of bamboo place mats. She carefully removed the tags and closed the knife. Carrying them all over to the table, she smiled and handed the knife back to Zeke. "Thank you."

He nodded and smiled. "Anytime."

She set out the mats and returned to the kitchen before coming back with plates and silverware, as well as a roll of paper towels under her arm.

Setting the table nicely. She tore a towel, folded it twice, and added it to the left of each plate.

Bree had opened a box of inexpensive wine glasses and was washing them in the sink.

Pris opened a drawer and pulled out a tea towel. She dried each one, after Bree rinsed them.

Curious, Zeke stood and stepped into the kitchen, opening the same drawer Pris had just closed. He picked up a towel and inspected it carefully, noting on the underside, along one hem there was a tag: "Breezy Handwovens – Made in Texas." He smiled, folded it neatly, and returned it.

He waited for Bree to glance his way before stating, "Impressive," and giving her a wink.

She beamed but said nothing.

The dryer dinged again.

As Bree was putting away the glassware sans what she set at the table, Pris moved to the utility room, removed the items from the dryer, and put the last load in the dryer.

Bree noted Pris had sheets in her hands. She looked around but did not see the pillows she had purchased. Remembering she had them in the front seat, she returned to her vehicle for them, as Pris headed toward the stairs.

Brett saw his chance and quickly made his way toward her. "Hang on, one end is about to drag. I would hate for you to trip."

She stopped and he divested her of the light load.

"Let me help you," he insisted.

She smiled and he followed her upstairs.

Bree returned with the pillows in time to see them enter the bedroom.

She looked at Zeke with a bemused expression.

He shrugged.

She carried the pillows over to him, removed them from their plastic covers, and asked him to cut the tags for her.

He complied without complaint.

"Is Pris available?" He inquired when he was done.

A saucy expression on her face, she teased "Depends on who wants to know, Mr. Buchanan."

He leaned in for a kiss, then explained, "What kind of a wingman would I be, if I did not do a little recon?"

"Brett," she giggled, "Bless him."

"Indeed."

"To my knowledge she is not dating anyone. She has been burned more than once. She has become exceptionally picky, and I do not blame her."

"I like her, you two are very much in sync."

"I adore Priscilla. She is sweet, whip smart, and practical. She has a huge heart. She is also the best mother and completely devoted to her boys. She attends every baseball, basketball, football, and soccer game and practice, as she can. Despite her issues with her ex-husband, she strives to work with him for the benefit of those kids. I am constantly amazed by her."

"And here she is helping you today."

"Exactly," Bree agreed, "the boys are with their dad this weekend and she did not have to work half a day at the bank. Instead of relaxing for much needed 'me' time, she insisted on helping me. Gosh, Zeke, left to my own, it would have taken me two days to do what we did today." She hugged him.

"I hope we see more of her."

Pris and Brett were descending the stairs when a timer beeped.

Priscilla returned to the kitchen and began assembling the salad, while Bree removed the lasagna from the oven.

Zeke found a bottle of red wine Bree had just stored in the pantry. He presented it to Bree who nodded.

He had not noticed into which drawer Pris had loaded the utensils, but he made a logical guess and found a corkscrew on the first try. It was a small victory, but he took it as he worked on living in the moment.

As the ladies dressed the plates, he washed up.

Brett quickly followed suit.

With everyone seated at the table, Bree raised her glass. Her eyes full, she smiled and looked at each of her companions "To life, love, health, and happiness."

There was a round of cheers, then she turned quietly to Zeke. "I was never brought up in a church and have no formal knowledge of any kind of religion, but it seems appropriate if someone would bless our first meal in this new home."

He reached for her hand on his left and Brett's on his right.

Brett took his hand and offered his other to Priscilla, who smiled gently and took it. Her other hand linked with Bree's.

Once the circle was complete, everyone lowered their heads and closed their eyes.

His voice low, but rich and smooth, Zeke began, "Dear Heavenly Father, thank you for the fellowship with which you have graced us and the blessings you have bestowed upon us. We appreciate your light and guidance as we walk through this life to spread your word. We humbly ask you bless this home, the people within it, and the food we are about to partake. In your name we pray, Amen."

∞∞∞

With no commitments, Bree and Zeke spent a lazy Sunday lounging. Bree caught up on laundry and cleaned at a leisurely pace while Zeke retreated to his workshop with Coal.

By late afternoon, Zeke's place shined. To his credit, she noted he kept everything neat and tidy, which made her efforts mostly redundant, but she wanted to lighten his load, he had done so much for her.

Borrowing a ruler and note pad from his desk, she sat at the dining table and began sketching out a floor plan for the bedroom. She could have used the notebook she kept in her pack, but she liked the grid design on the pads he used.

The office they had converted to a bedroom was actually a large waiting or meeting room off which a restroom with three stalls had been originally planned.

Fortunately, the bathroom was large enough to accommodate two sinks, a single water closet, roomy standing shower, and free-standing tub. To store linens and supplies, she hoped to find something of an antique piece on legs with glass doors. In her mind, it would be metal with chipped paint and a lovely patina from age. It should be three- to -four feet wide and could stand anywhere from four- to six-feet tall. She knew the odds of finding a vintage piece were slim, but she could dream.

As to the master bedroom, it was partially open on two sides to the landing at the top of the stairs. The ceiling on the mezzanine level was lower that it was downstairs, probably eight- or nine-feet.

The doors she purchased at the auction flea market were oversized in height and width. She had not measured them specifically, but she wondered if they could be hung, one on each of the partial walls like barn doors and slide together to form a right angle to give that bedroom privacy.

With respect to storage, she was almost resigned to ordering a streamlined wall of units to install opposite the bed from a boxed furniture store. She recalled Brett's chiding of Zeke about putting furniture together. She had a feeling if she invited Pris over, Brett would be only too happy to help with that task.

She had not had an opportunity to speak with her friend about her doctor neighbor, but she recognized the quiet reserve Priscilla had adopted toward him. She suspected there was some attraction, but she was very wary of men these days. Bree hoped Brett would exercise patience and understanding if he were genuinely interested in getting to know her.

Moving on to the pantry, Bree thought another one of the doors would be perfect to hang barn door-style there, too.

Swinging over to the space behind the pantry, she knew she needed more storage; however, she also needed a post for her overlock and sewing machines to land. She thought how convenient it would be if she did not have to pull them down from the top of a closet each time she needed to use them or box them up and hide them away when she was done.

She decided a built-in desk along two walls would accommodate her equipment with storage underneath one of them. Above the desks, she would need hanging shelves. She left one wall open where she could place the warping square. The mill was redundant equipment, as the square did everything the mill did and more, but she was emotionally attached to it. She was not prepared to sell it. As it was easy to break down and put back together, she knew she could store it in the utility room.

Smiling to herself, she realized the utility room with its abundance of space and cabinets may be her favorite room, at least for storage purposes. Any overflow weaving stash or equipment could easily find a space to hide in there.

Satisfied with her plan of attack, she tore the sheets off the pad and returned the items she borrowed to the desk.

∞∞∞

Monday found Bree up and moving just after five. She wanted to stop by the warehouse to take precise measurements before heading back to San Antonio.

She decided she could purchase the bedroom storage units and all the weaving storage at the same Scandinavian chain well known for their boxed furniture. She decided against a built-in desk for that space because her online search revealed the same store carried pre-made desks with additional under-counter storage units, which would suffice. They also had hanging shelves, which matched.

While she would still need assistance from Zeke, she thought it might be easier and faster than asking him to construct something from scratch.

With Zeke in mind, she also decided to load what she could in the back of her SUV. Whatever did not fit, if anything, she would either return for or have them deliver/ship.

She knew, if she asked, he would be happy to drive over with a trailer to pick everything up, but he was preoccupied with designing and creating an estimate for Brett's clinic. Before she left, he indicated that was his priority for the day.

Coal was content to hang with him, even though she was willing to tote him around with her.

∞∞∞

Zeke was at the warehouse when she arrived and backed her truck to the patio door.

She had only been able to load the items she needed for her weaving storage; the wardrobes were too long to fit inside her SUV. She paid extra to have those items delivered the next day.

Zeke had picked up dinner from Lupita's on his way over.

Once they unloaded the boxes, they cleaned up and had a bite to eat, catching up with the other's day over the meal.

CoalBear sat on the top cushion of the sofa and stared longingly in the direction of Brett and Molly's house.

Zeke was closing in on an estimate and had a good working plan for the clinic. There were a number of specialty medical-related items; the names and prices of which were beyond him, but he had contacted a supplier who sent him a list of commonly used items for a general medical practice. He excluded those items from his estimate.

He had texted Brett, who was off that evening and agreed to come by and visit with him about it.

When he arrived without Molly, Coal was heartbroken and completely ignored him.

Bree left them to their discussion and began putting together the desk units, anxious to have her things around her and on display once more.

The men talked for over an hour, and by the time Brett left, she had the two desks assembled, as well as one of the three under counter units.

Zeke offered to help with the other two, but she knew she had those, what she needed him to do was install the shelves.

Nodding, he retrieved his tools from his truck and had them up by the time she was done.

Bree would have liked to unpack and load all of her supplies, but Zeke insisted it was after nine and time to go home.

Reluctantly, she agreed.

Chapter 30

Mid-week found Bree back at the warehouse, happily ensconced in organizing her dozens and dozens of cones of thread. By noon, she had everything in place.

Zeke arrived to find her basking in the joy of her accomplishment.

It was not lost on him her priority had been weaving related and not getting any of her other things moved in and sorted.

When he trotted upstairs, he noticed the wardrobe boxes had been delivered. He knew what his plans were for the afternoon and smiled.

However, by two, he heard voices and stepped over to the landing to look down to find Donovan standing just inside the door.

He came down and joined them.

Donovan made eye contact and extended a hand, "Forgive the unannounced intrusion Zeke, I had a meeting in San Antonio this morning and could not resist driving over to check out your handywork."

"You are always welcome, Donovan. Good to see you."

Slowly looking around, Donovan assessed every detail. After several long moments, his eyes came to rest on Bree. "I am impressed, young lady. This is a far cry from the time warp in Lakeway."

She laughed, "So, true!"

"It suits you, Sweetheart. I see that rich and sparkling personality you work so hard to hide in every detail. Those light fixtures are amazing, but I think this table may be my single favorite thing."

He moved to inspect it closer.

"Iced Tea?" she offered.

Both men nodded.

His eyes fixed on the table as he bent down and ran a hand over it, Donovan spoke quietly, "I walked the perimeter before I knocked, nice job on the cameras."

Bree returned, "Here you go," and handed each man a glass. "Donovan, have you had lunch?"

"Indeed." He nodded, "I see you have your torture racks lined up and waiting for their next victims." He motioned toward the looms.

Zeke raised an eyebrow, and Donovan explained. "Have you not heard the noise they make when she gets going. The only thing missing are the screams of agony."

He chuckled. Now that Donovan had mentioned it, the looms, at least the smallest one, was noisy, but in a rhythmic way. He found it soothing.

Staring at her, Donovan asked: "What is different is about you?"

Perplexed she turned wide eyes toward him.

Brows knit, he assessed her from head to toe.

"Your legs."

"I have always had legs, Donovan," she corrected.

He continued to study her in earnest.

"You are wearing shorts." He surmised. "Why have I never seen you in shorts?"

Zeke's chest tightened. He was unaware he held his breath, until she turned around in front of Donovan and said: "I have scars all over the backs of my legs."

To his credit, Donovan was Donovan. He lifted the back of her top and asked: "Here, too?"

She assisted by pulling her shirt up to her bra in the back. "Yeah."

He released a slow, low whistle. "You must have been one feisty kid... You think this kind of corporeal punishment would work with my hellions?"

Dropping her shirt, she faced him with a smile. "Probably not."

"Good," he agreed, "I am not sure Management has the stomach for it."

Pride and relief surged through Zeke.

Aware of his scrutiny, Bree beamed her own pride back at him.

Crisis averted, Zeke asked if he wanted a tour.

Donovan said "Absolutely."

Bree led the way, heading to the store front.

After surveying the space, he asked: "Are you interested in opening a satellite office or hanging a shingle of your own?"

She shook her head but offered no other response.

He kneeled before the pile of old lumber which comprised her barn loom. He picked up one long piece and inspected the craftsmanship of the join. "Is this the one George found and brought to you?"

"Yes."

"What are your plans?"

"I have no idea. One of these days, I will have to research barn looms and try to assemble it. To be honest, I am more than a little intimidated. I had hoped I could find a museum and a curator with knowledge, but the closest one is in Maine."

"I understand lobster rolls are divine."

"I may have to do that."

Zeke enjoyed the shorthand in which they communicated, he envied it, actually.

After the tour, Donovan took a casual seat at the bar. "I have a question."

Bree filled his glass and waited.

"Interns."

She knew Donovan knew she was at a crossroads. She also knew Donovan hated having balls in the air. He liked all his ducks in a row and was somewhat OCD about it. She suspected this was one way for him to gauge Zeke's plans, which, in turn, would reveal her plans.

Instantly feisty with daggers in her eyes, her back straight, and her hands on her hips, she fired off emphatically, "Please do not assign any more interns to me."

Donovan persisted; his tone amused. "Each department gets at least two, you know the drill."

"Fine," Bree conceded, "but let me interview and select my own."

"I have a short list for you to choose from. I will give you picks of the litter."

"Sounds great, unless they are all like that Mayorga drip you chained me with last summer."

"Hey. Now wait a minute," Donovan interjected, "his father's company is one of our largest clients."

"He was still a total drip."

"I think he was sweet on you."

She groaned. "Did I share exactly what happened with him?"

"I meant to ask. He was the only one to quit half-way through the summer."

"Well, as you know, I had three interns," she relayed for Zeke's benefit, "I gave each a specific point of appeal to research and draft memos. I was hoping to mine them to use in the brief I was drafting at that time."

"Okay."

"Corrections and redirection are common; however, the third or fourth draft is usually fairly decent."

"Good."

"Not for your Mayorga, though. Edits basically meant re-writing every single sentence." Her voice uncharacteristically rose, "Is subject-verb agreement too much to ask?"

"He could not have been that slow, he was in law school."

"A big thanks to his family's endowment, no doubt." She rolled her eyes dramatically. "Seriously, Donovan, grammar is one thing, but he had zero ability to grasp how to analyze anything. He was completely incapable of recognizing a legal argument, much less formulating one. After the tenth revision, he had the gall to suggest I was picking on him because I was attracted to him."

"Now, Bree," he laughed, "we do not need any sexual harassment claims..."

"Have no fear, I looked him dead in the eye and said, 'You know I am lesbian, right?'"

Hearty laughter erupted from both men.

When her boss finally caught a breath, he shared, "Perhaps, I need to rethink how we assign interns..." He continued to chuckle, "I will have to get back to you on that."

Checking his watch, he made a motion to leave. Looking directly at Zeke, "Would you mind helping me? I have a house-warming gift in the back of my ride for this lady."

They returned with several large, flat, table-sized boxes, a big bag with "Lump Charcoal" written on it, as well as one exceptionally large and heavy box, which required a dolly Zeke had in the garage and both of them to move.

When she looked askance, Donovan explained: "These Komado style ceramic grills are all the rage."

She protested: "I do not know how to grill."

"Perfect! You can learn. Besides, how do you plan to snag a husband, if you do not know how to cook?"

"You know quite well I know how to cook."

"Yes, Sweetheart, and grilling is cooking. Until you learn to grill, you really do not know how to cook."

"You are terrible!"

"Just thank me, I have to get back to Austin."

"Thank you!"

Once he left, Bree turned her full attention to the man before her. His features relaxed and amused, she was amazed at how attracted to him she was.

"Lesbian, huh?" he smiled.

"His statement caught me off-guard, I panicked. It was the best I could do under duress."

"Ah, so I am not your beard?"

She wanted to tell him he was her reason for living, but as she stepped over to him, the words were lost the instant their lips met.

Chapter 31

Once the wardrobes were assembled and Zeke bolted them to the wall, it was time for her move her clothes and the remainder of her personal items into her new home.

She did that on Thursday.

As with most things these days, she was torn. She loved being at Zeke's and enjoyed the time they spent together, but she was also excited about having her things, specifically her looms, around her. She felt as though she were behind in her weaving goals for the year, as she usually made items as gifts for her friends. She also wanted to weave a baby wrap, blankie, and a few other things for Jed and Darla's child.

She had a few more days off, she mused.

With Zeke in Florida, she truly did not want to think about Florida, she hoped to dye new warps and dress each of her looms.

Once the last of her things were loaded, she and CoalBear walked through the house. She had washed the sheets on his bed soon after she rose and remade the bed. She checked the bathroom. She had debated whether to leave any of her toiletries but realized she had not acquired a second set and would need them in the new place. She removed the lint from the dryer and emptied the trash cans. She wiped the counters in the kitchen once more.

The dog's items were in a box by the door. She picked it up and opened the door. Coal scurried past her and waited by the truck. She closed the door and locked it with the key he had given her. Looking down at it, she knew she would be back. She loaded the box and the dog before looking back on the house.

When she reached the warehouse, Zeke had assembled the table Donovan had gifted her with the grill. The spot he had chosen to the right of the patio door, in the corner made by the junction of the warehouse and garage was perfect. There was a slight overhang where the roof of each structure met.

She knew the ceramic grill was far too heavy for one person and offered to help him put it in place, but he assured her he would get Brett or Jed to help him later.

He noted her quiet, melancholy expression. "Are you okay?"

She forcefully brightened and offered him a smile, but it stopped far short of her gorgeous eyes.

He knew what was bothering her, it was eating at him, as well.

However, strong, stoic Bree had made no mention of it all.

He desperately wanted to cancel his flight to Florida. He knew he did not want to take the job, no matter how much money they offered him, but he also knew she did not want to be the reason he did not explore the option. Not wanting to allow that wedge, no matter how seemingly small, between them, he would follow through with the interviews, report back, and allow them to jointly reach the conclusion he had already made. He was staying in Texas.

He and Samuel had engaged in several more email conversations and another phone call. His brother had a serious girlfriend and was ready to move home and establish roots. He wanted to invest in the construction business and take a guiding hand in running it with Jedidiah.

Knowing Samuel was returning permanently, Zeke was thrilled, and the clinic build for Brett excited him. He did not think there was enough room in Buchanan Construction for all three brothers, but Bree had planted a seed with the container home design side of things. He had explored her website and her Instagram more closely. He tracked a few of the small home profiles she followed, and he knew his ideas and designs were every bit as good as the ones posted.

Looking at the garage, it was certainly large enough to

house two units at a time.

Ratcheting down his enthusiasm, he reminded himself to live in the moment and not get too far ahead of himself. At the moment, the most important person on earth to him was a bit down, and he needed to assure her how precious she was to him.

Chapter 32

With their limbs tangled and wrapped around one another, Bree gently woke to the soft light of dawn coming through the windows. Without the benefit of a bedside table or clock, she had no idea what time it was, but she was sure she had slept much later than she normally did.

Zeke was snoozing peacefully next to her. CoalBear had not budged from his spot between their feet.

She breathed deeply, content with the first night in her new place behind her.

There was no discussion of who was sleeping where, Zeke had merely adopted to sleeping wherever she was, and she was grateful.

Shifting slightly, she moved where she could observe his face clearly.

She found he appeared almost boyish, despite the stubble, when he slept. The lines on his face relaxed and disappeared. She tenderly ran her finger along his jawline. As she reached his lips, he kissed her finger and opened his eyes.

"I love you, Ezekiel Buchanan."

He smiled and kissed her.

Chapter 33

Fridays were about food at the warehouse.

As afternoon rolled about, Jed and Brett sat across the island from Bree, as she continued to prep the meal.

She had candied pecans in a bowl on the counter. Brett was enjoying his iced tea, while Jed nursed a beer. Zeke was working on the Murphy bed upstairs. He had already had Jed help him position the grill.

Charro beans with ham hocks, tomatillos, tomatoes, chorizo, onions, and jalapenos had been simmering in a large pot on the cooktop most of the day, filling the building with a delightful aroma and the promise of a full belly. A large loaf of artisan bread was rising on the counter close to the beans.

Bree had roasted the vegetables for a fresh salsa and run them through a food processor. The men watched as she filled a quart jar, as well as serving bowl, before carefully packaging and vacuum sealing the remainder for the freezer.

Bree found Jed to usually be the most outspoken of her visitors. He had little impulse control and generally shared whatever thoughts came to mind. His wife Darla was doing better, and they were inching closer to their due date. Understandably, Jed stayed close, but he needed to get away here and there.

She offered tortilla chips and fresh salsa to the men.

Jed took one bite and exclaimed: "Wow, Bree, you must really enjoy cooking, you do it all the time."

She smiled. "I actually like to eat."

"Not from what I have seen." Zeke's smoothly deep voice came from the stairs, as he closed the distance.

Her impulse was to argue with him, but she stood silent,

drinking in the sight of him. His wavy hair was tousled from where she imagined he raked his fingers through it, as she had observed on more than one occasion, while grinding on how to address an issue. The tendrils around his face, moist with sweat from exertion. His mouth was relaxed with lips slightly parted. Reflexively, she ran the tip of her tongue over her own.

She must have stared at him a bit too long because as she moved her gaze to his eyes, she found she had his undivided attention.

His eyes were wonderous. When they were outside, they were the palest blue, much like the sky over a bright beach. Now, they were the deepest of blue, an abyss in which she was most willing to drown.

Fighting her way back to the present, the best she could offer was a slightly breathless "No?"

"No," he smiled. "What you enjoy is feeding people."

Brett joined in, "I agree, and you do it exceedingly well."

Not to be left out, Jed added, "If my wife cooked like you, I would never leave her."

His statement shocked her, but knowing him, she half-teased: "Are you actually considering leaving your pregnant wife?"

Jed looked momentarily confused, then explained himself. "Oh, heavens, no," he almost stuttered. "I was just thinking if you cooked for your husband like this, why on earth would he ever leave you."

Zeke rewarded him with a quick hand to the back of his head.

Jed apologized, "No offense, Bree."

She looked down and sighed, as she considered his words. Emotionally, she had not completely processed the reasons behind the divorce, although intellectually, she had a fairly good idea.

She was almost surprised at how comfortable she felt with these men. She thought she should feel awkward about discussing any part of her personal life, but she did not.

She picked up a knife and an avocado and began preparing guacamole, as she spoke.

"I think most of you are aware I am an orphan and came out of foster care."

Without looking up, she saw the brothers nodding. Zeke pulled out a stool and joined the others at the island.

She glanced at Brett. He was in the dark, and she directed her next comments to him. "According to my records, when I was five my mother abandoned me on the doorstep of a neighbor. He surrendered me to foster care. He was unable to provide a name, birthdate, or the names of either of my parents, other than he thought my father was deceased or unknown."

Brett's face was grave, his brows knitted, as he inquired: "At five, you could have provided some of that information."

She agreed. "One would expect; however, I was largely non-verbal at that time."

"Wow." Jed whispered.

Out of the side of her eye, she caught the twitch of Zeke's jaw muscle as he clenched his teeth.

"I was fortunate, though. The clinical psychiatrist assigned to my case took an interest in me. He and his social worker wife offered to foster me. They eventually adopted me."

Brett inserted: "You said largely non-verbal, implying you were not completely non-verbal."

"Correct. The first year following my surrender the only time I became agitated or spoke at all was when people tried to address me by a name, I did not consider my own. Apparently, I would have a fit and say 'Bree.'"

She stopped what she was doing, washed, and dried her hands, then stepped over to a stack of boxes in the back corner. As always, Zeke appeared to assist and once they shuffled a couple around, he produced a knife to cut one open, she reached in, and retrieved a leather-bound journal. Returning to the island, she placed it in front of Brett.

"These are Dr. Lancaster's notes beginning at the time we met."

"May I?" Brett asked.

"Of course." She shrugged. "I have tried reading them a time or two, but the memories are not pleasant. Plus..."

After a significant pause to allow her to continue, but when she could not, Zeke suggested "Plus, reading them made you wonder whether they adopted you for you or for a case study?"

Watching the pain settle in her face and the tears collect in her eyes as she turned away from them, Zeke kicked himself for his words.

"Yes," she agreed softly, "that is it exactly. Thank you."

She reached for her glass and took two full sips of water.

Clearing her throat, she added "The Lancasters were extremely good to me. They gave me their name, a home. They provided extremely well for me. I attended private school. They paid for college."

She gestured around the building; her hands open with palms up. "The inheritance I received from them has helped me with all this."

Brett looked up from the journal, "But it seems like they had a bit of a sterile attitude towards you, at least, clinically speaking."

She met his words with a sad smile. "They were kind people, but not demonstrably warm or affectionate, at least not with me. I remain incredibly grateful to them."

While Brett was listening, the journal held his attention.

Jed was a bit wide-eyed and antsy for her to continue.

Glancing at Zeke, he had a tense and pained expression across his face. His eyes held nothing but concern for her.

Without looking up, Brett queried "Do you remember anything prior to the surrender?"

"No."

"Do you still have nightmares?"

"Yes."

"How often?"

"I would rather not think about it."

Brett looked up. "Are they the same as described here?"

Her eyes shifted upwards and toward her left, as she tried to remember what was immortalized in the journal. "I think so… let's just say that they have rarely deviated in the last decade or two."

Brett paused and studied her with compassion. "I am sorry."

She took another sip and tried to smile brightly. "I am not sharing for pity's sake. I actually like who I am, and I am proud of what I have managed to accomplish thus far." Casting a glance at Jed with another smile, "one failed marriage, notwithstanding."

Defensively, Jed apologized. "I did not mean to upset you, Bree."

"I am not upset. Truly." She continued to assure him. "I share this to fully answer your question."

He seemed relieved but dared not look at his older brother. He was certain, he would hear from him later.

"So," she returned to the prep, "by the time I entered college, I was an extremely shy, introverted, and emotionally starved and stunted individual. I excelled at books and school but failed horribly at friends and socializing until a really good-looking frat boy in one of my classes asked me for my notes one day."

As her explanation became more wistful at the memories, Zeke began to feel some of the tension fade, although there was a pang of jealousy.

"Over the semester, we got to know one another, and eventually began dating, which was a whole new experience for me."

"Wait," Jed interrupted, "you didn't date before college?"

"No," she laughed, "I was the weird, nerdy, egghead kid no one bothered to notice, much less speak to."

Jed was unconvinced. "I mean, Bree, look at you. How could no one notice you, you're beautiful?"

Her heart swelled at his earnestness and tears sprang to her eyes. She reached across the counter and squeezed his hand before wiping them away. "Bless you, Jed, that may be one of the nicest things anyone has ever said to me. Thank you."

Zeke was amazed, not only at how someone like Bree could be so easily overlooked, but how completely open and unguarded she was to allow her emotions to freely express themselves.

"Clint was golden. He never met a stranger. Everyone loved him and wanted to be around him. He enjoyed the attention and everything social seemed to come naturally to him."

Brett finally returned to the conversation, slowly closing the journal, and returning it to the counter. Curiously, he kept one hand on it. "He cannot be perfect, though, he let you get away."

Bree shrugged. "For the first time, I felt less isolated and began to feel almost like I belonged somewhere." She pursed her lips and scrunched her face, searching for the words to best articulate the feelings at the time.

"As Clint's girlfriend, I finally had an identity, as stupid and shallow as that sounds. When I was with him, we had fun. Life was not about books and grades or hiding from the world."

Jed smiled. "I totally get that, but what happened?"

"Well, as we were preparing to graduate from college, Clint knew he wanted to go to law school. I had considered it, even before we met. Truly." She emphasized. "He was originally from Austin and UT had an excellent law school. We both applied and were accepted."

Zeke was motivated to inquire. "Let me guess. Your grades and test scores were probably high enough to get you in, but why do I doubt he could get in on his own?"

Once again, she was struck by how shrewd Zeke was. He had the ability to see through most things.

"Yes, I was the stronger student, but I did not have a full social life to distract me, and..."

Zeke interrupted: "And, his family had the money and connections..."

Brett added: "Is there an endowment in the family name?"

"Geez," she laughed, "you guys are tough. I do not know what, if anything, was involved, but his GPA and LSAT scores were below the admissions average."

"Bree," Jed quietly inquired, all too aware his brother's wrath was in striking distance, "was it possible he was just using you for your smarts?" He braced himself for another slap, but none came.

Instead of taking offense, Bree smiled. "You have not met my friend and boss Donovan? We met in law school. According to Donovan, the only reason Clint wanted me was because I mothered him. I made sure everything in his life ran smoothly and was taken care of. I managed his schedule and his calendar. I reminded him when papers were due. I made outlines for his classes and basically laid out everything he needed to know for each exam. I proofread his assignments and typed his term papers. I did a lot. So, based on the facts, I think there is a very compelling argument that I basically outlived my usefulness. He became bored with me and moved onto someone far more exciting and socially adept at being the wife of a politician. I served my purpose and that was the end of that."

Brett looked at her intently. "I may have missed it, but I failed to detect even a hint of bitterness in anything you just said."

She considered his observation and asked herself. "Am I bitter?"

She pondered it for several moments, then said: "You know," she half-laughed, "Donovan told me more than once not to marry him. He flat out said 'He's using you, he's not who you think he is, don't do it.'"

Jed spoke, stating the obvious, yet again. "But you did it anyway?"

"Donovan is the one person on this earth who is the closest thing to family I have. He has believed in me since day one." Glancing at Zeke, she pleaded with a smile, "Please do not tell him because it will make him completely insufferable, but I have the utmost respect and affection for him. I would actually be lost without him, but yes, I married Clint anyway. Moreover, and despite everything, I do not regret it. Even knowing exactly what I know now, I would do it again."

"But Bree," Jed struggled to understand, "he hurt you."

"Jed, I am not unhappy with how things have transpired. Actually, I said that wrong. If I had never met or married Clint, I would not have this place, and I certainly would not be here with each of you right now. Saying I am not happy is a gross understatement. At this very moment, I can honestly say I am happy. I love this building."

She looked directly at Zeke, "I so appreciate every single thing you have done to turn this into a home for me."

Zeke smiled and nodded.

"I have CoalBear," she reached to pluck him from the floor at her feet. "My reason for living in one neat little ten-pound package. Although, I do admit, when I asked God for a nice warm body in my bed, this is not what I had in mind."

They laughed with her.

She looked at Brett. "I have new friends."

"When I look around, I am overwhelmed by the potential and promise of this place and the direction my life has taken. I am so profoundly grateful for what life has given me."

A silence fell upon them.

Suddenly embarrassed, Bree struggled to find the appropriate words for oversharing when Jed spoke.

"I am glad you are happy, Bree. I really am. What I really wanted to know is whether your ex liked your cooking?"

Chapter 34

At breakfast Saturday morning, Bree's phone dinged, indicating she had received a text. Retrieving it from the island, she sat back down with Zeke at the table.

He watched as a delicious smile enveloped her face, raising an eyebrow in askance.

"Would you mind if Pris came by for a little while this afternoon?"

"Not at all. Shall we pick up burgers and christen that new grill?"

"Good idea, but I have no desire to grill."

He grinned, "I am actually interested in seeing how it works, I have been doing a little research."

Remembering Donovan's words, he thought about teasing her regarding learning to grill to find a husband but decided that hit a little too close for his comfort.

"I need to pick up a few things from the market, anyway. I will go shortly."

He cleared the table as Bree texted her friend.

∞∞∞

When Priscilla arrived, she was dressed in a chic business casual outfit, shift dress and jacket with hose and heels. She appeared she had just gotten off work, and she had.

Bree gave her a hug and searched her face.

Pris presented her with a basket of goodies and warm smile.

Zeke offered her a hug as well, and she gladly accepted.

With an excited "May I?" Bree dug into the basket and pulled out homemade tortillas, banana bread, and jar of Whipped Honey Amaretto. Holding it up, she asked "What manner of sinful goodness is this?"

Grinning, Pris encouraged her, "Try it on one of those tortillas."

Grabbing a spoon, she handed the jar to Zeke to open, as she put a tortilla on a napkin. With the spoon, she extracted some of the gooey goodness and smoothed it out before rolling it and on the flat bread, breaking it in half for Zeke.

He watched as she took a bite. Ecstasy covered her face as she allowed her eyes to roll back as she chewed. He recognized that look and watched with pleasure as she devoured what was in her hand.

"Oh, gosh, Pris, that is one of the best things I have ever put in my mouth."

"It is heaven on a tortilla." Her friend agreed.

They both turned to Zeke who was licking his fingers. He groaned in satisfaction.

"Not only is that the best tortilla I have ever had, that stuff is amazing." He agreed.

Delighted her gift was a success, she was about to ask if she could excuse herself to change when Brett knocked at the door. They could see him through the window.

Zeke was washing his hands, so Bree let him in.

He gave her a quick hug with a nod to Zeke, but his eyes remained on Priscilla.

He walked directly over to her, "Good afternoon, Gorgeous. How are you today?"

Bree noticed the smile on her friend's face was genuine, but if she were the least bit surprised at his presence, she hid it well.

Her eyes never leaving Brett's, she picked up her large handbag and excused herself.

Brett's gaze followed her across the room.

Bree looked at Zeke and they exchanged a glance, certain

neither of the other two had any idea they were still standing there.

Zeke winked at her. She grinned back.

Zeke spoke first, "Have you had a chance to think about our proposal?"

There was no response.

Bree reached out and tapped him on the shoulder. It was several seconds before he turned and had to blink twice to focus on her face.

She looked at Zeke, who repeated his question: "Have you had a chance to think about our proposal?"

He finally seemed to snap out of his daze. "Yes!" He smiled. "I have spoken with my financial planner and a banker. I am confident I will be ready to proceed in the next week or two."

Zeke was pleased. "Outstanding."

"As soon as I have been approved, I will make an offer on the property."

Any further conversation was interrupted by Priscilla's return, she had changed into a simple black tee shirt and jeans with strappy sandals, the simple ensemble accentuating her curves. She had the undivided attention of both men.

Even Bree had to admit, her sweet friend exuded sensuality, even when she was trying not to. It was just who she was.

It was an hour before she was able to shoo the men to carry their conversation outside and start a fire in the grill, leaving her a moment alone with her friend.

"Okay, spill, what is going on here?"

Sheepishly, she grinned back. "He seems so nice, Bree."

"He is."

"I was a little disappointed when I left last week that he did not ask me for my number or attempt to get it from you."

Bree had also wondered about that.

"But a few days later, he walked into the bank with a bouquet of flowers and asked if he could call on me."

Bree was stunned. "How on earth did he find you?"

"I asked the same thing. He said I told him which bank I

worked for, and he pulled out a phone book and started calling each of our branches in town asking for Priscilla. When he found one, he described me, and continued until he found the right one."

"He could have asked me."

"I know, right?" she marveled. "He said he did not want to involve you."

She laughed. "That is insanely romantic."

"I gave him my number, and he has been calling every evening, after I put the boys to bed."

Bree smiled, urging her to continue.

"He asked me to dinner, but I told him I was not quite ready yet. He said he understood and asked if he could continue to phone me."

"And..."

"Of course, I said yes. I was not supposed to work this weekend, but I had a sick employee and no one to cover. The Ex wanted to take the boys to a family reunion. I mentioned I would like to see you, but we had not planned anything. After I slept on it, I decided to text you this morning, kind of hoping he might be around."

Bree hugged her. "I like him a lot, so does Zeke."

"By the way, I envy how Zeke looks at you. He is crazy about you."

Bree dropped her gaze.

Priscilla squeezed her hand. "Honey, what is wrong? I thought you guys were doing great."

"We are," she insisted, "but he leaves early Monday for Florida, and I am insecure about the whole thing. I know he needs to go through with what he started a year ago, but I do not want to lose him."

"Shush," she admonished her, "I assure you that man is not going to let you go. Smart money says there is nothing in Florida for him without you."

With shining eyes, Bree admitted, "I hope so."

The couples spent a relaxing evening together. Bree tried to maintain Zeke's attention, which was not difficult, but to give the other couple a bit of time and space to get to know one another. Zeke was a willing accomplice.

As Zeke helped Bree clear the table and clean up, Brett invited Priscilla for a stroll. He was keen to share his plans for the clinic.

Bree was not surprised Priscilla accepted the hand he offered and joined him.

They promised to return shortly.

An instant after the door closed behind them, Zeke cast a knowing look toward Bree.

"Which of us is playing matchmaker here?" She asked.

"I am just the wingman..."

"And just what exactly is the role of the wingman?"

He chuckled, "There is an unspoken commitment to support your buddy in whatever endeavor or situation he finds himself."

"So, if he gets into a fight..."

"The wingman protects him."

"Okay, if he is interested in a woman?"

"The wingman makes him look good and builds him up."

"You seem to have a lot of wingman experience."

"Always the bridesmaid and never the bride, it seems."

"Who is your wingman, Zeke?"

"I do not need one, I have the girl of my dreams."

He drew her in and kissed her deeply.

When Priscilla and Brett returned an hour later, her face was flushed, he was smiling, and their fingers were intertwined.

Priscilla announced she had had a long day and began to excuse herself. She thanked her hosts for a lovely evening.

Brett quickly followed, and they walked out together.

Bree cut the lights to give them a bit of privacy.

She turned to Zeke, "I have a good feeling about them."

He placed his hands on her hips and pulled her close to him, "I have a good feeling about us."

Chapter 35

All too soon, it was early Monday morning. Zeke was packed and ready to leave for the airport. She had offered to drive him, but he had insisted it was too far. He wanted her home, safe and sound. After promising her he would call when he landed and keep her apprised of his activities, he kissed her one last time and was gone.

Despite CoalBear for company, when she looked around the warehouse, she felt empty and alone.

The clock on the microwave read 7:58. The groomers opened in an hour and CoalBear had an appointment.

She decided she would shower, change, drop the dog for his appointment, and devote herself to dressing her looms when she returned.

As weaving had given her comfort and solace in recent years as her marriage to Clint fell apart, she knew it would get her through the next few days until Zeke returned.

Then, together they would decide in which direction life would take them.

∞∞∞

Zeke had always trusted his gut.

The closer to the San Antonio airport he got, the more the gnawing feeling in the pit of his stomach told him to turn around.

When he arrived at his gate and checked his flight, he saw that it was delayed by two hours due to an engine problem.

He pulled his laptop from his carry on and checked his itinerary. With the delay, he would be cutting it close, but he should still have an hour and a half between landing and the first interview. Instead of picking up a rental, he may have to take a cab.

He caught up on his emails and decided to see what Bree was up to. The tracking app showed she had left for the groomers but was already back at the warehouse. He smiled.

He scrolled through his texts to ensure he had responded to everyone.

His sister had sent him a message the day before, advising their parents had returned from Africa.

Reflecting on his unease with this particular adventure and having missed his father, he called him.

After a lengthy discussion, Zeke was secure in his decision and grateful to have the wisdom and guidance his father offered.

He checked the status of his flight. It was delayed another two hours.

He took it as a sign.

He called his contact in Florida, explained the delays, and regretfully withdrew his name from consideration.

Checking his watch, it was a quarter past noon.

He thought about calling Bree, but this was not a conversation he wanted to have over the phone.

Sliding his laptop into his bag, his phone rang, it was Jed.

"Yeah."

"Zee, where's Bree?"

"At the warehouse?"

"She's not here, Zee. I am standing at her SUV, the door is open, her bag and phone are inside, but there is no Bree."

Zeke's heart stopped. His head was spinning, and he was fighting to think clearly. Forcing himself to breathe, he instructed his brother to gather her things and check the laptop in the office upstairs.

Fortunately, Jed had a key to the door and was able to get in. He was also savvy about computers.

By the time Zeke reached his truck, Jed was replaying the footage from the camera closest to where she parked. Zeke had him zero in on the time period between 8 and noon.

According to Jed, at 9:19 Bree drove up and opened her door, as she stepped down and prepared to reach in to gather her things, someone came up behind her, struck her in the head with an object and dragged her away. He said it took 11 seconds.

Stunned and sick, Zeke could not see straight. He was uncertain he had heard Jed correctly. He fought waves of nausea.

Again, he forced himself to breathe and his mind began to clear.

"Okay, Jed, listen to me. I am on my way. Call the sheriff's office. Tell them she is missing. Look through the camera on the back to determine whether we can identify who did this."

"On it, Zee. It looks like Mr. Miller."

Zeke swore.

"Call the sheriff's office NOW. I am on my way."

Starting his truck, he backed out of the parking space and called Donovan.

Chapter 36

Images swirled around her. Voices shouted, both near and distant.

He was yelling again, this time at her. One moment, he called her Lila, the next it was Lily, but the other words were all the same, usually a variation of slut or whore and almost always followed by a slap, kick, or other blow.

In the distance, she thought she heard a woman's soft voice, whimpering and pleading for him to stop. The man's varied from screaming rage calling her names to pitiful mewling telling her he did not mean to hurt her.

The face was the same or nearly so from the one in her dreams just older, more bloated, and wrinkled with age. The fury and rage, though, those had intensified.

She recognized his was a tormented and unrepentant soul focused on sharing every wrong, perceived or imagined, he had ever experienced.

The blow to the head, the pain, his voice, his face, or the combination of them all released the memories of her childhood. She remembered her name, the house in which they had lived, her mother's face.

The horror of those memories sent her scurrying deep within herself. The experience far too traumatic to relive.

Chapter 37

Jed was at the hospital when he arrived.

Zeke quizzed him: “Any news?”

“Nothing.”

Zeke asked if Dr. Parker were on duty. He was not.

Zeke called him. He answered groggily; however, when Zeke explained, he was fully alert and promised to be on his way.

Within twenty minutes, Brett arrived. He pulled Zeke aside, “Have you heard anything?”

Zeke shook his head.

“I will be right back.”

Another fifteen minutes and Brett returned, grim faced.

“She’s alive, but unconscious. Blunt force trauma injury to the back of the head. Ruptured ear drum. They are taking her up for an MRI. She has broken ribs, a collapsed lung, and one of the bones in her left forearm is fractured. That is all they know right now.”

Zeke closed his eyes. Bile rose in his throat. He felt as though he had been kicked in the stomach and the life was being squeezed out his heart. He ground out. “I want to see her now.”

Brett understood. “As soon as she is stable and moved to a room, I will get you in to see her. Right now, we need to determine the extent of her injuries so we can treat her.”

Zeke knew he was right.

“I am going up to find her. I will try to stay with her until she is moved to a room. I will text you with any new information.”

Zeke nodded.

An hour later, Donovan walked past both of them and asked for the charge nurse. Once she appeared, he pulled her aside and spoke quietly with her for a few moments. She nodded before walking away.

Addressing the brothers quietly, he explained: “I had the office fax over a copy of Bree’s Medical Power of Attorney, which allows me to act on her behalf.”

He glanced at Zeke, “I never trusted that twit she was married to and insisted.”

Zeke nodded, filling him in, almost verbatim what Brett had told him. “Bree has blunt force trauma injury to the back of the head. Her eardrum is ruptured. They were supposed to take her for an MRI. She has broken ribs, a collapsed lung, and one of the bones in her left forearm is fractured. She is unconscious. A friend of ours is a doctor here, he is with her now.”

Turning toward Jed, Donovan asked: “Where’s Miller?”

His younger brother clenched and released his jaw. “When the deputies broke down the door, he reached for a shot gun. He was still in surgery an hour ago.”

Zeke spoke first, “She was afraid of him.”

Donovan probed, “Other than the Tavern, was there any other contact?”

“She said she saw him one other time when she was leaving the market. He was standing in the parking lot, but he did not approach or accost her in any way.”

“What do we know about this guy?”

Zeke looked at Jed: “He owns land adjacent to our parents’ place. He used to farm and raise goats at one time, but word is, he fell off the wagon and his wife left him years ago. Since then, he leased the land to others. Likely his only income.”

“That’s consistent with what George dug up” Donovan revealed.

“Call Pop.” Zeke directed.

Jed returned with a phone to his ear: “Wife was Lila, they had a daughter named Lily. Pop said she would be around thirty-three.”

Donovan got on his phone. Zeke could hear him instruct George to get him the birth certificate of one Lily Miller and search nationally for the location of Lily Miller and Lila Miller and anything else that could be found.

Zeke turned to Jed: "What else did Pop say?"

"They are booking a flight as soon as they can."

Zeke nodded absently, numb with worry.

"Zee..."

"Yeah."

"Pop said you may remember Lila and Lily, they used to visit before I was born."

Zeke wracked his brain; he was unable to conjure a single image of either of them. His father was a preacher, and there were always people in and out of their home.

Carefully eyeing his little brother, Zeke noted the worry on his face, as well as the dark circles under his eyes. Normally, he was not outwardly or physically affectionate with either of his brothers, but he clasped Jed's upper arm. "Good job today. I owe you."

He could see the younger man shake his head and fight back the emotion. Zeke tightened his grip.

"I was so afraid we would be too late." Jed shared.

Zeke nodded; he had shared the same fear.

"When you watch the tape, Zee, you will see. He came at her with a vengeance. She never stood a chance."

"Go home, Jed. Hug your wife for me."

"No, man. I am here for you."

"There is nothing you or anyone else can do for me right now. She is going to be fine. She has to be."

Long after Jed left, Donovan came back around. Zeke noted he was a pacer and almost always on his phone.

George, he reported, could find no trace of a Lila or Lily Miller, but he added it would not be uncommon for people to take another name or marry, especially if they were running scared.

When Donovan was not pacing or on the phone, the men hypothesized different motives for the attack, but the only one that made any sense to either of them was that Miller, in his alcohol addled brain, confused Bree with the wife who had left him long ago.

Donovan even suggested Bree might be the long-lost daughter, but neither could understand why Lila would have left Miller, then abandoned her child to foster care.

While he paced, Donovan kept a close watch on Zeke, never allowing him more than a few strides away.

When Zeke walked down the hall, Donovan fell into step alongside him.

Annoyed, Zeke glared at him.

Donovan put a hand on his arm and leaned in. "I am your alibi should something happen to Miller. Do not forget that."

Zeke nodded, as his phone vibrated.

It was a text from Brett: "Moving Bree to a room. No further injuries noted."

Zeke shared it with Donovan.

It was well into the evening when a man in scrubs identified himself as Dr. Banks. After he confirmed Donovan's identity, he reported Bree had a hairline fracture to the back of her skull, contusion with swelling to the brain, but with steroids, they had already seen a positive response. She sustained a ruptured eardrum on the left and a non-displaced fracture to the ulna, also on the left, likely resulting from blocking a downward blow. She had fractures to three ribs on the left side with puncture and subsequent collapse of the lower lobe, which he called pneumothorax. Dr. Banks stated the injuries would be consistent with blows or kicks. In all, she had suffered a severe beating, but was expected to make a full recovery. He added, while conscious, she was not speaking. In fact, he noted she was awake, but completely unresponsive.

As her appointed agent, Donovan was allowed to go in and see her, but he promised Zeke, he would be next.

∞∞∞

Zeke had adopted pacing outside Bree's room when he noticed the sheriff and a deputy approaching. The men shook hands before the sheriff asked: “How is she doing?”

“Not great. She took quite a beating. I understand she’s awake, but not ready to give a statement.” Zeke explained.

The sheriff kindly responded: “Yeah. The hospital called when she woke up. The suspect did not survive the surgery and is now deceased. There is no immediate hurry to get her statement, but we will need to speak with her.”

Donovan emerged and caught the last of the conversation. Zeke introduced them. As Donovan took over the discussion, Zeke searched his face for an indication of Bree’s condition.

He observed the usually relaxed and confident Donovan looked much like he felt. There was no amusement in his eyes, in fact, he had a grim expression in them. His lips were drawn thin and tight. There was a sharpness to his words and impatience in his tone. Zeke knew his concern for Bree was nearly as great as his own.

Although it was only a few minutes, it felt like an hour before the sheriff departed. As soon as they were out of earshot, Zeke’s eyes bored into Donovan.

He shook his head and admitted: “I could not reach her.”

Confused, Zeke implored “What do you mean?”

“Her eyes are open, but there’s nothing but a blank stare. There is no emotion, no reaction, no response.”

“You do know, when she was five and surrendered to foster care, she was non-verbal for about a year?”

“No,” Donovan knitted his brows, “I did not know. She told you that?”

“Yes. She said the only thing she spoke during that time was ‘Bree’ or ‘Breezy’ when they tried to call her by any other name.”

“Interesting.”

“There is also a journal, clinical notes, really, from Dr. Lancaster.”

“She shared that with you?”

Zeke nodded, he was surprised, as well, he had assumed

Donovan would know at least as much as he did.

"She specifically allowed you to read those notes."

"Yes"

Donovan's raised eyebrows were one thing, but his smile was another.

"Then YOU are exactly what she needs, but before you go in, brace yourself, he did a number on her. She does not look like our girl."

Chapter 38

He found her curled on her right side, facing away from the door. She already had a cast on her left arm. The top of the bed was set on an angle, forcing her almost upright, but on her side.

To let her know he was there, he whispered "Hey, love. It is me, Zeke," and placed a gentle hand on what he thought was her ankle, buried beneath the covers.

She did not move.

As he came around the foot of the bed, he noted her left eye and temple were swollen and deeply bruised purple and black. He pulled the chair closer, so he could face her. The veins in her eyes had burst. Despite his face squarely in front of her, she simply stared through him. She had a nasal cannula for oxygen. He looked past her injuries, knowing she would heal physically. His greater concern was what it would take to heal her mentally and emotionally.

Once settled a mere few inches from her face, he gently smoothed the stray hairs behind her ear. He briefly touched his lips to the edge of her mouth. She seemed to flinch, but he was certain the contact did not pain her.

He was profoundly grateful she was alive and safe with him, but his heart was twisted and heavy at all she had had to endure.

Uncertain how to help, he began whispering to her. He told her of his aborted trip and how hard he found it to leave her. He revealed he knew he no longer wanted the flight instructor position and he certainly did not want to leave Texas or her for Florida. He said the entire time he was away; all he could think about was the life they had before them. He wanted to renovate the buildings for Brett's clinic and start a business of his own, designing container homes. He explained the warehouse garage was certainly large enough for a workshop and center to fabricate them. He confided he hoped they would marry and looked forward to having a child or two of their own with her beautiful dark eyes and sharp intellect.

This last admission actually surprised him because after the demise of his first brief union, he had carefully guarded himself from that particular dream.

Now, he smiled and embraced it because he had found a special someone with whom to share it.

Suddenly shy and vulnerable, he refocused on Bree's battered visage. Her eyes were closed as single tear threatening to escape one corner.

Ever so gently, he moved to wipe it away.

"Rest, my love. We will talk more tomorrow."

He pulled the covers up around her and kissed the air above her forehead. Looking down on her bruised and broken body, his eyes burned, and his heart ached.

When he finally emerged from her room, he found Donovan in a chair across from the door. His head was tilted back and resting on the wall behind him. His eyes were closed and both hands were around CoalBear sitting in his lap.

CoalBear became animated at the sight of Zeke. His movement triggered Donovan to jump awake.

Zeke reached for the dog.

Donovan yawned as he gained his feet.

"Your brother came by with the Hell Hound. He thought he might possess the magic to bring her back."

Zeke pet the dog.

"How is she?"

"No change, although she seems to be sleeping."

Zeke checked his watch. It was well after midnight.

"Are you headed to Austin tonight?"

Donovan shook his head.

Zeke reached into his pocket and pulled the warehouse key

from his fob. He handed it to Donovan. “There’s a Murphy bed in the office upstairs. Get some rest. I am sure there is food in the fridge.”

“You staying?”

Zeke nodded.

“Thanks. I will be back first thing.”

“There’s dog food in the utility room to the left of the sink. Bring some back.”

Donovan cracked a smile. “Thank goodness. I was scared you were going to send him back with me.”

Zeke walked him out and grabbed his pack from the truck. He gave CoalBear a chance to relieve himself, and they returned to Bree’s room. She did not appear to have moved.

He placed the dog on the bed and watched him immediately dip a nose under the fingers of her broken arm. He started to reach for him, concerned the movement would cause her pain, but even in her sleep, she lifted that arm slightly and the dog wormed his way under it.

“Maybe that dog is magic,” Zeke pondered as he tucked into the attached restroom.

Chapter 39

Her head throbbed and she could hear the rhythmic whooshing of the blood running through her veins every time her heart beat.

The sharp pain in her chest made anything more than a slight breath impossible. Her whole body ached. She struggled to open her eyes but felt the familiar silky fur of her beloved companion under her fingers. She moved them slightly and almost smiled when he licked them.

If he were near, she knew Zeke must be close by and she was safe.

When the lids of her eyes finally opened, she found him hunched over in a chair, his arms folded on the side of the bed, near her feet, his head resting on his arms. His position looked uncomfortable, but he seemed to sleep.

Her heart torn, as it wanted to swell with the softest emotions, but she clenched it in anguish. If the man had spoken the truth, then they were the most unnatural of couples and a life together would never be theirs.

CoalBear stretched, moving her arm, which sent a gasp of pain through her.

Zeke awoke instantly, his head up, his bleary gaze immediately locked on hers.

He rose stiffly.

"Bree, are you okay?"

She stared at him mutely, fighting the urge to retreat within herself.

"Stay with me," he pleaded.

Her eyes filled with emotion and began to overflow.

"It is okay, baby. You are going to be okay."

Very gently he placed his hands on her, their warmth reaching her beneath the covers, his cheek next to hers.

"You are okay, just stay with me, please."

He heard the door open and shifted slightly. Donovan was there. He reached for the dog and retreated silently.

Zeke let her quietly cry, murmuring words of encouragement and support.

When she finally spoke, her voice was so weak and slight, he almost missed her words. "I am sorry."

"No, baby, I am sorry. I am so sorry this happened."

"No."

He pulled away to look at her face. "No?"

She shook her head.

"I am sorry," she whispered urgently, "because we cannot be together."

He blinked several times; certain he had misunderstood. He searched her face for some sign, of what, he did not know. All he found was anguish and pain staring back at him.

"Bree, you have been through a lot. I know you are hurting and probably confused. You will get better. You will be fine. We have our whole lives together."

She shook her head again.

"Yes, Bree," he insisted. "I am sorry I was not there to protect you."

"Stop!" she choked before coughing and gasping for breath, the exertion shooting pain across her whole body.

He poured water into a cup and helped her take the slightest of sips.

He pulled the chair back over to face her at eye level.

"Why?" He asked, pain etched on his features. "Why can we not be together?"

"He said," she stammered weakly, "we share a father."

The statement dropped like an anvil on his head.

"Miller was nuts, Bree. What he did to you is proof of that."

"He was married to my mother," she choked. "He said my mother was a whore who had an affair with your father."

"No," Zeke was adamant. "My father would not have done that. Miller was lying, Bree."

"What if it is true?" She whispered urgently.

"We will take DNA tests. No problem. We will do it now."

She closed her eyes. The physical pain and emotional pain were too much. Her head was spinning, it was difficult to breathe, and her heart was hurting.

She heard him whisper, "Stay with me, Bree. Please do not leave me. I cannot do this without you."

"Just let me go, Zeke. I just want to die..."

She continued to hear his pleas, but she was too exhausted, she let go and allowed the darkness to crowd her mind, muffle the pain, and quiet her racing thoughts...

∞∞∞

Zeke was pacing when Donovan returned. He glanced at Bree's motionless body before taking in the near panic in Zeke's face. He placed a hand on Bree's back and waited. He had not realized he held his breath until he released it as he felt her exhale.

He returned the dog to the bed and motioned for Zeke to follow him outside the room.

He turned to Zeke and waited.

Fighting to remain calm, Zeke demanded: "I need you to order a DNA test on Bree."

"Okay," Donovan agreed, "why?"

"Miller told her we share the same father."

Caught completely off guard, Donovan released a long, low whistle.

"What color are your father's eyes?"

"Blue, like mine."

"Light colored eyes require two sets of recessive genes."

"I know. Bree has brown eyes."

"And Miller?"

Zeke's eyes moved to his upper left, as he conjured an image of the man. "I am thinking dark hair, dark eyes, like Bree."

"Not scientific, but a start." Donovan paused. "Tests on her and Miller."

Before Zeke could agree, Donovan leaned in and whispered. "This is a small town. We want no hint of a scandal. If Miller is not her father, we have private tests done."

Zeke wanted immediate answers, but he could not fault the man's logic.

"Now," Donovan continued, "I will stay with her. You need to shower and change."

As Zeke began to argue, he added "Your friend, the sheriff, needs a statement this afternoon. We have to be on and at the top of our game to wrap up this investigation up quickly and successfully. Leave Bree to me."

Zeke reluctantly agreed.

Chapter 40

When she awoke, she found Donovan scowling at his phone. CoalBear had moved to lay along her chest, his nose inches from her chin. She could feel him breathing on her. Her head felt huge, but it was less fuzzy than it had been. Without moving it, she scanned what was in her field of vision.

"Fly Boy needed a shower; he was beginning to stink up the place."

Her eyes returned to her old friend. He rewarded her with a wink.

"When I said you needed to take some time off, Sweetheart, this is not what I had in mind."

She raised an eyebrow in agreement.

CoalBear yawned, stretched, and moved closer to her face.

"By the way, if anyone asks, the Hell Hound is an emotional support animal."

She questioned him with her eyes.

"You deposed Dr. Bauer last year." She nodded. "He signed off on a letter suggesting it was paramount to your emotional health and recovery to have him with you at all times. Judge Armstrong signed an order to that effect, as well."

She shook her head slowly and mouthed the words "No jurisdiction."

He smiled. "They don't know that."

Tears of gratitude swelled in her eyes. "I am sorry." She whispered.

"No, Sweetheart," he choked back his own emotions, "you have done nothing wrong."

"Too much trouble..."

"Well," he chided her, "you have always been trouble..."

Chapter 41

Zeke checked the security footage as soon as he arrived at the warehouse. He knew the authorities would want to view it. In the event they took the original, he made a backup. While grainy and fish-eyed, the image of Miller striking Bree, her collapse, and being dragged beyond the scope of the camera would haunt him the rest of his days.

Guilt, fear, and despair threatened to overwhelm him, but he firmly forced them down to be addressed much later.

Following Donovan's advice, he shaved, showered, and dressed, anxious to return to Bree, but his stomach continued to growl, and he realized it had been a solid day since he had last eaten anything.

Chapter 42

By mid-morning, Donovan had fully briefed Bree. Processing the information he provided exhausted her.

Despite refusing all pain medication, she was sleeping once again when Zeke returned.

Donovan collected the dog for a bit of fresh air, while Zeke settled in.

He was able to rouse her around one for lunch, but after a sip of broth and two sips of apple juice, she was done.

A brief visit from Dr. Banks advised she would not be released until she was mobile and able to move about without assistance. He also sought her permission to allow the sheriff to speak with her. She agreed.

Brett continued to check in with Zeke via text.

He had been in and out all night, hovering, but he did not wish to disturb them.

Once he knew Bree was stable, he had called Priscilla.

It was mid-afternoon before she asked Zeke to help her to the restroom to freshen up. She hardly recognized the image which stared back at her when she washed her face. The bruising and swelling were less of a shock, than her sunken, blood shot eyes and hollow expression.

Her head still felt huge and throbbed. Her body hurt, every inch of it, and each breath sent sharp pains through her chest, but she pushed herself to hobble back to the room.

Zeke remained a hand's width away from her at all times, ready to catch her, if needed. He was gentle and attentive, but they had fallen into a silence, as neither had really spoken since he had returned.

Donovan was in and out, pacing and on the phone. She expected him to return to Austin following the session with the sheriff.

Zeke was surprised when Bree shuffled past the bed and moved toward the chair. Before she turned to sit down, he covered her with a light blanket from the bed. Clad only in a thin hospital gown, completely open in the back, she was too exposed for visitors.

He knew she was in excruciating pain and completely exhausted, but she pushed on, like the stalwart trooper she was.

CoalBear, perched on the edge of bed, whined once, and looked as though he might leap.

Zeke issued a firm, but quiet "No" in his direction.

It was enough, and the dog moved to the middle of the bed, turned around three times, and settled down for another nap.

Bree smiled at them. She knew Zeke was as attached to the animal as she was.

Donovan returned minutes later and announced the sheriff was *en route*. If he were surprised, she was up and seated, he kept it to himself.

The sheriff was, once again, accompanied by a deputy. After the brief formalities, he asked Bree to describe what happened yesterday, in her own words.

With Zeke and Donovan flanking her, she began slowly, carefully, and very quietly to tell her story.

She relayed she had taken the dog to the groomer and returned home. She parked in her usual spot, along the back area of the building. Her intent was to enter from the patio.

She parked, exited the vehicle, and before she could grab her pack or close the door, she blacked out.

She indicated when she came to, she was lying on the floor in a house with Miller standing over her, agitated, pacing, and mumbling to himself.

Her head hurt, and she had difficulty focusing at first, but she was able to positively identify Miller from photos provided by the sheriff.

After some time, she reported Miller noticed she was awake

and began talking to her, calling her Lila. She did not respond or engage him, which seemed to further enrage him.

He pulled her into a sitting position and asked her something about someone, but nothing he said made sense.

When she failed to answer him, he moved to strike her and she attempted to fight him off, but he was so big and so much stronger than she was. She thought this may have been when she broke her arm.

She stated she was hazy after that, as he continued to slap and hit her. She remembered curling into a ball and him kicking her again and again. She thought at that point, she may have faded out.

The next thing she recalled were voices outside shouting his name. She heard a crash, more voices yelling, and a gunshot.

She had no memory of seeing a gun of any kind.

She had a vague recollection of being lifted and hearing someone who kept telling her she was going to be okay.

Once she was done, no one moved or spoke.

Both Zeke and Donovan were stone faced. A muscle twitched along Zeke's jawline, the only hint of the storm brewing within him.

The sheriff cleared his throat and asked Bree if she was acquainted with Miller prior to the attack.

She stared straight at the bed. Her dog was on his feet and equally intent and fixated on her.

Donovan stepped forward to retrieve him and gently placed him in her arms.

She looked down at him, absently running a light hand along his body. When she finally spoke, her words were barely a whisper.

The sheriff brought a chair closer and sat down before her.

"Prior to yesterday, I saw him once at the Tavern and another time outside the market."

He nodded and concluded "Well, we may never know his motive..."

"Since yesterday," she interrupted, "I remembered who he

was."

He studied her face, as though he were seeing her for the first time. He looked past the bruises and noted a haunted, vacant quality about her eyes and the sound of her voice.

"Go on, please." He urged.

"I was surrendered to foster care in St. Louis at the age of five. As of yesterday morning, I had no memories prior to foster care."

She closed her eyes, as the images from the past flooded her senses.

She felt the warmth from Zeke's hand on her shoulder fill her with the courage to continue.

"I was born Lily Miller on June 28th. My address is Route 2, Box 485. My phone number is 463-7021. My mother's name is Lila Miller." Her voice cracked, but she continued. "My father's name is Henry Miller."

The sheriff shook his head in disbelief. "Your mother left and surrendered you to foster care in another state?"

Slowly she opened her eyes and stared directly at him.

"No," she ground out, "my father beat her to death. Then he drove us all night and the next day. He gave me to foster care a day or two after that."

When she trembled, Zeke looked at Donovan who spoke first, "That's enough."

The officer continued to study Bree's face several more minutes before nodding. He knew Donovan was an attorney and held her Medical Power of Attorney. Standing he faced him: "Would you and your client agree to a DNA test to compare it to Miller's to verify her statements?"

Donovan paused, taking his time, as though he were seriously pondering the request. "We are amenable."

The sheriff nodded in agreement. "We will get an order to search the house, surrounding buildings and grounds."

Bree startled everyone when she looked up at him. "There are two doors to the kitchen, one from the outside, the other from the living room. As you walk in from outside, the stove, sink, and fridge are along the left wall. There was a table against the wall opposite the outside door. Under that table was the opening in the floor. One slat will slide forward toward and under the fridge. There is a ring under it to pull the floor up. It should not be very deep. I could stand in it with the top closed, and I could still touch it..."

Donovan walked out with the officers.

Zeke knelt beside Bree.

"Hey," he smoothed the hair from her face. "How are you doing?"

Without looking at him, she shook her head. "I cannot escape the images in my head of him beating her or the sound of her screams."

He wanted to hold her and make them stop, but he was afraid touching her would cause her more pain.

"It is not your fault, Bree. There was nothing you could have done. You were five years old."

"I should have gone for help. I should have tried."

"Excuse me, son."

Neither had heard the door open.

Zeke rose.

Bree looked up and met the blue eyes of an older version of Zeke.

"Pop."

The older man briefly acknowledged his firstborn son but focused intently on Bree. He slowly approached and placed a hand on the chair in front of her. "May I?"

She nodded.

He sat down and reached for her right hand, lightly rubbing it between his weathered hands.

"Do you remember me, child?"

She chewed the bottom of her lip with her brows knitted as she studied him. There was an obvious and undeniable resemblance to Zeke, but she shook her head no.

He smiled at her warmly. "It has been a long time."

"Please," she asked, "I can see my mother's face, but I am not sure, can you tell me, what color were her eyes?"

Zeke clenched his jaws and flexed his hands to keep from also clenching his fists.

The older man's warmth and smile never changed.

"Your mother had blue eyes, Bree."

Pulling her hand from his, she wrapped her arms around the little dog and folded over, the tears flowed, and she gasped for breath, her body screaming in pain.

She had not cared about anything else, just some sign she and Zeke were not siblings, half or otherwise.

Zeke's father leaned forward and wrapped his arms around her as she cried.

"Your mother was a sweet, faithful woman, young lady. I am not your father."

Overcome, Zeke hugged them both, allowing his own tears to join theirs.

Chapter 43

The sun had barely broken the horizon when his phone alerted to an incoming call. In the days since her discharge from the hospital, Donovan's check-ins had become habit. Zeke suspected they were as much for his benefit, as they were for updates on Bree, and for that, he was profoundly grateful to the man he had come to rely on as friend.

"Morning," Donovan greeted him.

"Morning."

"How's our girl?"

"She is okay. I think she is resting better at night, not quite so fitful."

"Excellent. Perhaps, she is not in so much pain."

"Yeah. She prefers not to take the pain medications. She still naps on and off throughout the day."

"Eating any better?"

"No. A few bites here and there, but she drinks water."

"And you?"

"I am fine. Grateful to have her home."

"Seriously, what do you need?"

"I need for her to get better."

"We are not two weeks out..."

"I know, I know. Her balance is off with the eardrum rupture. I worry about her on the stairs. Physically, I know it will take weeks more to heal. What gets to me is she is a shell of herself."

"Yeah."

"I know she is in there. I know she is a fighter, but this whole thing has robbed her of something vital. For a while, I thought it may be her will to live."

"Bree has always struggled with her identity, as well as abandonment. She literally believed her parents threw her away because they did not want her. The Lancasters were good people, although eccentric in their 'new age' psychobabble crap. From what I have gathered, they were sterile, clinical, and not warm or affectionate. They provided a home and stability. I have no doubt they loved her, but they probably did not show her affection at all, for fear of spoiling her."

"My impression tracks that."

"Furthermore, when that twit came along…"

Zeke smiled at Donovan's reference to Clint.

Donovan continued, "he was like a puppy, all sloppy and drooling, following her all over the place. The attraction there was he showered her with attention, the likes of which, she had never known. At first, she shined and really grew into herself. But that was short-lived. She soon outgrew the mama's boy."

As he listened, Zeke nodded.

"The Bree you met had finally come to terms with who and what she was. She was comfortable in her own skin. She was actually okay with what she believed to be her history."

Zeke added "And now, she thinks she does not know who she is because that history has been drastically altered."

"Exactly," Donovan agreed. "She needs time to come back around to realize that while all this has deeply affected her, it has not changed her character or the person she is at her core."

Zeke's heavy sigh was audible.

"I know. It is tough. It's eating at me, too." Donovan conceded. "But you are exactly what she needs."

"It may take more than me, but I have an idea."

Chapter 44

Zeke rode with Donovan in his suburban to the Miller place. As a courtesy, the sheriff's office let Donovan know a search warrant had been secured.

Donovan knew well enough not to inquire whether anyone could be present. He preferred to ask forgiveness, if necessary, rather than request permission. He had texted Zeke and invited him to join him to observe.

Zeke met him outside the warehouse early on a Tuesday morning. They drove in silence, each lost in his own thoughts. Zeke merely pointing out the turns to the property.

Once they left the highway, the roads were dirt and gravel. Once a year or so, the county came through with a grader, followed by dump truck to add another layer of gravel, in an attempt to smooth out the worst of the ruts. By all accounts, it was a rough ride, even at walking speed.

From the public road, there was a right turn over a metal cattle guard down a drive identified by no more than two dirt ruts with a mound of grass growing between them the length and a half of a football field. A sad fence line along either side marked the end of the lane and fields beyond. At the end of the drive was a copse of trees, mostly live oak. There was a farmhouse on the right with a barn and workshop off to the left. The buildings were in various states of disrepair. The upright support on one corner of the barn had given way, which caused the roofline above it to sag, taking one of the trusses with it.

The house had once been painted a bright yellow with dark green shutters, but greyed wood peeked out across most of the bottom third of one side, where the paint had given up and flaked away.

Despite the bright sunlight and fresh breeze blowing from the south, everything had a decrepit and decaying feel to it. Even the weeds, which had sprung up along the paths to the front and side doors of the house, seemed tired and worn.

Zeke thought the place seemed vaguely familiar to him, but he had no specific recollection of ever having been there.

Neither of the men had taken two steps, when a cloud of dust along the road alerted them to company.

Within minutes, three marked county vehicles joined them.

The sheriff was the first to greet them, albeit it was nothing more than a slight nod, as he walked past them to the house.

The front door was boarded up, as the officers had kicked it in to liberate Bree from her captor.

Brandishing a hammer and a crowbar, two of the sheriff's men quickly removed the boards.

Donovan waited until the peace officers had entered before approaching the threshold, Zeke one step behind him.

They chose a spot in the living room, which looked directly into the kitchen.

Donovan noted the cabinets were along the wall across from him with a sink, stove, and refrigerator, just as Bree had described. There was a small table along the wall perpendicular to the refrigerator, which was moved immediately. One man ran his hands along the floor just under the fridge. Within moments, he found a slat which moved and popped open the panel on the floor.

Zeke knew in his heart what the men would find. He had not doubted a single word or memory Bree had shared. His focus was on the floor to his far right where the dust on the floor was disturbed. Stepping over and kneeling before it to inspect it more closely, he could make out the outline of a body laid over on its side. There were round and oval shaped stains on the wood floor. He reached out and ran his index finger over them. Examining his fingers, he knew the ruddy brown residue was blood, Bree's blood. Anger welled within him.

Glancing at his friend, Donovan instinctively knew what he

had discovered. For not the first time, he said a blessing Miller was already dead.

The officers worked in silence, the noise of their tools and efforts the only sounds; however, within minutes of opening the panel, everything stilled.

Several of them removed their headgear, as their heads bowed for a moment.

Turning toward Donovan, the sheriff made a slight movement with his head, motioning toward the door.

Both Donovan and Zeke stepped outside.

The sheriff joined them; his face grim. “The remains are right where she said they would be.”

Donovan nodded.

The sheriff continued, “We are tracking down dental records for identification, but our best bet is to compare it to Ms. Lancaster’s DNA. Those will take a week or so, as the lab is backlogged, and our suspect is deceased.”

“Please keep me posted,” Donovan requested.

He nodded. “I would appreciate if both of you would leave before we remove the remains. Trust me, it is not something you can unsee.”

Chapter 45

Putting his coffee down and reaching for his phone, Zeke answered "Hello."

"How's our girl?" Donovan inquired.

"We are okay. You?"

"Nightmares?"

"She does not seem to be having any; however, every time I close my eyes, I replay those images of Miller getting the drop on her, beating her, and all those horrible things she lived through as a child."

"I know. I close my eyes and dream about that Hell Hound standing on my chest, licking my face after I know darn well, he has been licking other things, if you know what I mean."

Zeke chuckled. He had grown well accustomed to his friend's manner of diffusing situations. He knew he was trying to instill a different set of images with his comments.

"I have your favorite furry friend in my lap right now."

"Give him a pound of bacon and a scritch from me. That dog is gold."

Petting him lovingly, Zeke agreed. CoalBear was Bree's comfort and joy. He was almost jealous of the affection and attention she lavished upon him. Almost, but he knew the dog provided a much-needed outlet for her.

The only reason he had him now was to give her a chance to sleep in a bit.

She was exhausted physically, mentally, and emotionally.

They were well past three weeks since the incident, but he knew she still had a way to go before she was fully healed.

The DNA results confirmed the remains belonged to Lila Miller.

He still tried to fathom how she had been able to reveal so calmly what she had witnessed as such a young child.

The horror of it all stunned him. As difficult as it was for him to process, he simply could not imagine how Bree was coping with it.

They were existing together in some kind of weird stasis. There was comfort and familiarity between them. She leaned into him physically throughout the day, and they hugged often. At night, they spooned, or she curled into him.

He knew physically, she was not well enough for intimacy, and he understood, of course. What troubled him was how quiet she was and how closed off she had become emotionally. She had withdrawn deep within herself. He felt, more than he knew, she was struggling with redefining herself based on what had been revealed about her past in recent days.

He believed her feelings for him had not changed, but neither of them was where they could express themselves verbally.

Patience, he told himself. She needed the space and time to heal.

The moment CoalBear alighted from his lap, he knew she was awake and stirring. He grabbed his mug and followed the dog back inside.

He found Bree gingerly making her way down the stairs.

"Morning, beautiful!" He grinned.

Her hair was down past her shoulders. She had a tee shirt on with a sarong tied around her waist.

Her left arm was still in a cast, but the bruises had nearly faded. He knew her ribs ached when she breathed deeply, coughed, or sneezed, but she was moving much better.

She returned a smile, then walked over and into his arms. She leaned heavily into him, inhaling his scent, and allowing his warmth to seep into and soothe her body.

For the hundredth time in the prior weeks, she thanked the universe for this man.

She felt him kiss her forehead. She melted more into him.

This was how they had been communicating. There were few words, but plenty of contact and affection.

"Why are you so good to me?" She asked against his chest.

"Because I love you, lady. You are my one and only."

He felt her shake her head against him.

"No?" He asked, pulling back to see her face.

He had to raise her chin. Her eyes remained drawn and haunted. The pain in them chipped away at his soul.

"I do love you." He insisted.

"I am not worthy."

He had sensed this was part of her struggle. He was unsure whether to pursue it, but feared if he let it be, those feelings would take a stronger hold.

"You are the bravest and most courageous human I have ever met."

She backed away from him, shaking her head.

"How can you say that? My mother was beaten to death, and I did nothing."

"The twins are seven. If they were faced with that, tell me, just what would you expect them to do?"

"It is not the same."

"How is it different?"

"I should have run for help."

"'Where would you have gone?"

"Your parents' house."

"Yes, the properties adjoin along one side, but that is, at least, a two-mile drive."

"What about through the pasture?"

"There is a wooded area on the other side of the fence line. There are cactus and mesquite everywhere and one heck of a hike in broad daylight. I would not attempt it in the dark at my age." He paused, hating to argue with her. "You expect far too much from the five-year-old you."

"Zeke, I let her down."

"No, Bree, she wanted you to live and you have done just that. Despite everything you have been through, you have lived and given every bit of your best self to others. Baby, I have no doubt, if she were here right now, she could not have been prouder of you."

"She is not here, Zeke."

"I know, and I am so sorry."

Spent, she turned toward the kitchen and set the kettle to boil before easing herself into a chair, CoalBear at her heels. She lay her casted arm on the table and stared out the window.

He poured another cup of coffee and pulled down a mug for her tea. He added a spoon of sugar and a tea bag to her cup. He poured the hot water and carried it to her with cream and the spoon.

He heard her quiet "Thank you," as he retreated to collect his coffee.

Sitting across from her, he asked: "What are your plans today?"

She blinked twice before she was certain she heard him correctly.

The question was innocent enough, she realized, just unexpected. He usually inquired as to how she was feeling or whether she was okay. Inquiring as to her plans seemed to imply, she had something to do or something was expected of her.

She further realized she had expected him to continue to coddle her. Partly ashamed of herself, but mostly amused, she asked "Have you been receiving tips from Donovan?"

He grinned. "He is effective."

"Hmmm," she hemmed, "I thought I might mope around a while, continue to feel sorry for myself, then take a nap. Self-indulgence is taxing, you know."

He chuckled, "Well, if you can spare a few minutes, I actually need your help with something."

Her brow furrowed. "My help?" She was confused.

Physically, she could barely lift her head and shuffle her feet from upstairs to downstairs. How on earth could she assist him with anything.

"Yes, Ma'am."

"Sure."

"Okay," he rose from the table. "Let me know when you are available."

Bewildered, she watched him walk away.

"How about now?"

He stopped, and she rose to her feet.

He extended his hand. She closed the distance between them and took it.

He led her to the metal door to the storefront.

He turned the bolt and lifted the lock and opened the door, releasing her hand, and stepping back to allow her to pass first.

The front of the building faced South but caught a lot of light from the east. While early, the sun was bright and blinding. It took her eyes a moment to adjust.

Her hand flew to her mouth as she gasped in surprise and delight.

Before her stood the barn loom, complete and fully erected.

She blinked and blinked again, so total was her shock.

She had only ever seen it in pieces, some of which she knew were eight feet long, but could have hardly imagined how massive it would actually stand.

She was speechless.

When she turned to him, her eyes radiated her joy, and she threw herself into his arms, a painful decision, but she pushed her discomfort aside, and with her good hand, pulled his head down, and kissed him deeply and thoroughly.

Carefully caressing her body with his hands, he reluctantly pulled away from her. Running his tongue over his lips, he caught his breath and smiled down at her. "Lady, kiss me like that again, and we may have to christen this room, here and now, passersby be damned."

She buried her smile in his chest.

He lowered his voice. "Seriously," he asked, "are you pleased?"

She looked up and graced him with the most beautiful luminous brown eyes. “I am beyond thrilled. I never really expected to see it assembled.”

Cupping one side of her face, he tenderly moved his thumb over her lips. “The only thing I want to do in this life is make you happy.”

She kissed him again. This time, she made sure it was soft and sweet.

Admiring the loom again, she gushed “When did you do this?”

“You have been resting lately.”

“How did you know how to fit it together?”

“It was a puzzle at first, but when I studied the mortise and tenon joints, there were no bolts or screws. There was only one way each of the pieces fit because they were chiseled and carved by hand.”

“You are amazing.”

“It was fun, actually.”

She leaned into him, wrapping her good arm around him.

“When you feel better, we will get it warped and weaving. “

She hugged him tighter, until she hurt.

Chapter 46

Zeke's parents had hovered about, bringing food early in the mornings as not to disturb Bree, but inquiring about her. Zeke knew they had memories and information to share. He also knew his mother dearly wanted to meet and hug her, but they understood she was struggling, as was he.

Two days after her mother's remains were positively identified, Bree had finally agreed to see his parents; however, she had insisted they go to their house and not entertain them at the warehouse. He understood her need to control the length of the visit. He also recognized it would be easier for her to disengage and retreat when needed.

As she rarely ate much of anything, they decided the best time was early afternoon.

While neither of them had rested well the night before, Bree anxious about the meeting and sleeping fitfully, Zeke completely in tune to her and still only lightly dozing, as he remained on high alert, they were up early.

With the cast on her arm, she preferred to bathe in the tub, rather than the shower.

This arrangement delighted Zeke, as he enjoyed washing her hair, rinsing it with the handheld sprayer, and bathing her. She was now wholly at ease with her nakedness in front of him. He had no doubt she trusted him completely, and it showed in how she responded to his ministrations while he attended her.

She took extra care in her appearance, carefully applying just a hint of makeup.

She chose a sleeveless sundress in a deep burgundy, which

was supposed to be fitted through the waist while the skirt was loose and full, hem almost to her ankles.

Zeke found she looked lovely, but noted it hung on her, as her frame had become more skeletal in recent weeks

He knew she was exhausted but vowed to encourage her to eat better for healing and energy.

He was seated on the sofa with his laptop when she presented herself to him. He set it on the ottoman and stood up, extending a hand to her. "You are so beautiful."

Suddenly shy, knowing she had put no effort into her appearance in weeks, she gave him a half smile and offered her lips to him.

He kissed her, running his hands along her back, as he pulled her to him. "Nervous?"

She squeezed him in a hug and shook her head. "I do not think I have the energy to be nervous."

"Hungry?"

Lifting her face to his, her brows furrowed a bit. "Actually, I think I am."

"I am not talking about hunger for me, lady…" He teased.

Her smiled reached her eyes. "I am hungry for you, too."

"I am at your disposal, my lady love."

"Hold that thought."

"What would you like for lunch?"

"Fish tacos?"

"Lupita's?"

"Yes, please. They have the most romantic table, just off the parking lot…"

Enjoying the life dancing in her eyes, he cupped her face, kissed her, and allowed the contact to deepen, letting her know his hunger for her had not waned.

Leaving CoalBear to roam free in their absence, they had lunch at Lupita's before heading to his parents' home.

∞∞∞

Zeke followed the same route he had taken with Donovan; however, instead of turning down the Miller lane, he drove another two miles and took a right across a cattle guard made of rail ties. Thirty feet after the turn, there was a wide gate with a box on a curved metal pole. Zeke rolled down his window, reached out, and pressed a few buttons. The gate began to open.

He rolled his window up and turned to her as they passed the entrance, "3285."

"Does it ever change?"

"Not in the last twenty years."

Unlike the public road, the driveway was paved. When Bree made note of it, Zeke responded with "Chip and seal."

"Is that like asphalt?"

"They both use the same ingredients, but asphalt is applied as a hot mixture, laid down, and compacted. Chip and seal is a thin film of asphalt that is sprayed on as a liquid. The chips are aggregates, which are applied over the liquid. They stick when rolled around in it. Not as durable, but a lot less expensive."

"I like it, much better than dirt and gravel."

As they drove, the pastureland receded, and they were surrounded by more trees. Coming out of a gentle curve, the tree line opened up a bit to reveal a white two-story house with dark grey, almost black roof and shutters. Huge oak trees shaded the house from either side. A freshly painted picket fence stood along the front.

She recognized Pastor Abraham Buchanan sitting on the expansive porch in a rocking chair. Next to him was a slim and athletic looking woman in a red top tucked into a pair of jeans and white sneakers. Her platinum blond hair was pulled up in a high ponytail. Bree could see her blue eyes sparkling from across the front yard. She marveled at how youthful and energetic she looked.

Mouth agape, she turned to Zeke. "That is your mother?"

He grinned knowingly. "Hard to believe she's sixty-two."

"How old is your father?"

"Sixty-seven."

Before Zeke could help her from the vehicle, both of his parents were there to greet them. Her feet had barely reached the ground before his mother wrapped her arms around her. "Bree, darling, how are you feeling?"

"Hi. I am much better, thank you."

His mother was beautiful. She had high cheek bones, bright blue eyes, a dainty nose, and lovely smile with perfect teeth. She stood at least five feet, ten inches tall, and even with her wedge sandals, Bree had to look up to her. Her warmth and graciousness were almost overwhelming.

"Please call me Rachael." She insisted.

Slipping her good arm through her own, she would have led Bree to the house, but for the good pastor standing before them.

"Hang on, Rach," he beamed, "Allow me a hug, as well."

She stepped back, as her husband pulled Bree into his arms, careful of her cast, and hugged her tenderly. "I am so happy to see you, child. Are you well?"

When he moved back, he cupped her face between his weathered hands and with a gentle smile, he looked deeply into her eyes, willing her soul to reveal itself.

Comfortable and safe, she allowed him to gaze intensely, revealing herself openly.

"You are going to be just fine, Bree. I know it."

Zeke offered his mother his arm to allow his father to escort Bree inside.

Despite insisting they had just eaten, his mother led them to a sunroom off the kitchen where a large table fought the sun light for dominance. She had a tray with lemonade, glasses filled with ice, cookies, and cloth napkins waiting for them.

Zeke's face lit up, "Shortbread?"

Bree watched as he reached for one and his mother slapped his hand in gest. She was in awe of how childlike and boyish he appeared at that moment. A pang of guilt struck her heart as she realized he had been consumed with worry for her the past few weeks, he had not had the benefit of love and levity to allow him to lower his guard.

Observing her closely, Pastor Buchanan wrapped a loose arm around her shoulders and lowered his head to whisper in her ear, "In due time, my dear, all will be right. It is a journey, and you are almost home."

Without giving her a chance to respond, he guided her to one of the chairs and pulled it out for her to sit.

To her left, at the head of the table, he offered the seat to his wife.

He took the one opposite Bree, with Zeke sitting to her right.

Rachael served each of them.

As Bree took a bite, Pastor Buchanan smiled at her. "Bree, I want to tell you a story. You probably have questions, but my heart says you need to hear this."

From under the table, she felt Zeke's hand squeeze then rest on her thigh. She braced herself.

Like his son, Paster Buchanan reached for his wife's hand and held it while he spoke. "We came to Texas while I was a chaplain with the Air Force. The big boys, Ezekiel and Samuel were six and four at the time. We were expecting Rebecca. We fell in love with this area, there was a need for a pastor in this community, and we decided to stay. We bought this land and began renovating this old house, a little bit at a time, as the budget and time would allow."

Bree looked around them while he spoke. The house was beautiful with careful attention to detail. The sills in the windows, along with the countertops, were creamy marble. The handles on the cabinet doors were antique glass in various shades of green. The millwork was extraordinary. The thought she had when first stepped into the home, which returned to her now, was modern country. The entire place looked as though it belonged in a home and garden magazine, so lovely were the finishes and workmanship around her.

"Our neighbors to the south were a young couple. Henry and Lila Miller. Henry was born here. His grandparents and great-grandparents on his father's side immigrated from Germany in the late 1800's. His wife Lila's people came from back east about the same time; however, she grew up in a little town to the southwest of San Antonio called Devine. I believe her maiden name was Fischer. They met at the livestock show and rodeo in San Antonio one February."

Zeke felt Bree's muscles contract. From the corner of his eye, he saw her arms cross and a storm settle in along her brow.

"Your mother was a beautiful woman. You share her bone structure and eyes, although yours are brown. She was about your size, as well." He took a sip of his lemonade. "Your father was good to us. That first winter, he shared several cords of wood to keep us warm, as we moved in late September. I had not been able to put enough away between my duties on base and at the pulpit on weekends."

Rachael added, "Your mother was a dream. There were many days, when I was heavy with Rebecca and unable to keep up with the boys, she would come over and take them for the afternoon to give me a break, when Abraham was on base. You were just a sweet, little thing at the time."

Bree shook her head. The images their words conjured were alien to her. She could not imagine she knew Zeke in this other life they presented.

Looking to his wife, Zeke's father made a motion with his head.

Rachael stood and disappeared momentarily into another room while he moved the tray off the table and into the kitchen.

When she returned, she had a box of photos.

She presented one to Bree and softly explained, "This is a photo of you, Zeke, and Samuel."

Taking it from her hand, Bree examined it closely. Although grainy, she saw the profile of a little girl, probably two or three years old in a white sundress and sandals. There was a boy standing behind her with a popsicle and one standing in front of her holding two of them. Both boys were looking at the camera. The girl was looking at the treat closest to her, her chubby hand on the boy's arm. Studying the faces, she could not tell which of the boys was Zeke. She guessed because he was older, he must be the taller of the two.

"That cannot be me." She said quietly.

Zeke took the photo from her, turned it over, and read: "Sam and Z with Breezy."

"Cool Breeze or Breezy," his father relayed, "was Henry's nickname for you because you liked nothing better than running around with the wind in your hair."

Zeke smiled at the image in his mind, as well as in the photo. He was as amazed as Bree. "I have no memory of this."

His father smiled. "You two have known one another for a very long time."

His mother added, "Bree, Zeke adored you the very first time he saw you. No matter what he was doing, playing ball in the yard or helping his dad in the shop, as soon as he knew you were around, he would come over to see you. He would do anything to make you laugh. Make weird faces or noises, stand on his head, whatever. He loved to hear you laugh."

Bree shook her head, her eyes full of tears, ready to spill, but she said nothing.

They lay more photos in front of her.

There was one of a young couple standing before a car. The woman wore a nice dress, her hair pulled in a fancy do high on the back of her head. In a suit, the man stood proudly beside her holding an infant. They were both smiling. She turned the photo over. It read: "Lila and Henry with sweet Lily."

The date indicated she would have been about six months old.

"When we first met them, life was good. Henry's crops did well, and he had a few cows he had invested in. He was proud to have them. His plan was to raise them for your college."

The older man watched Bree carefully, gauging how far he should push her.

She remained silent, so he continued. "Unfortunately, when

you were about three, a drought hit and lasted almost four years. Everything around here dried up completely, the creeks, the wells, the cattle ponds, everything. No one harvested much of any crops. Henry sold the cows because he could no longer afford to feed them. He quit farming and started working on a highway construction crew, which made for long, grueling days for little money."

Rachael shared, "Your mother looked for work, and you came over a few days a week while she cleaned houses to make ends meet."

"They were doing okay for a while," Abraham said, "but I suppose the stress got to him, and your father began drinking."

Rachael lowered her head, guilt laced her words, "That was when we stopped seeing you and your mother."

He squeezed his wife's hand again and held it tightly. "We should have known there was a storm brewing, but life was hard on everyone at that time."

She nodded at her husband's words, "Time seemed to fly with three kids and Abraham gone so much, when I look back, my memories are such a blur, but we should have done more to check on you and your mother."

She looked directly at Bree, tears in her eyes, "I will forever regret not doing more to protect you both."

Zeke felt a tremor run through her. He shifted in his chair and moved closer to her, his leg brushing against her, his arm around her.

When he next spoke, the older Buchanan's voice was thick with regret. "By the time she came to us for help, your mother was a shell of her former self. She had lost weight and the evidence of his demons was evident. Her body was bruised, her spirit broken. All she said is that she tried, but simply could not do it anymore. She asked for assistance to leave him."

Zeke's mother nodded. "We made arrangements to get both of you to Montana where we have family. There was a job lined up for your mother. We just needed Henry to return to work for a day or two, to whisk you both away."

Rachael rose again and returned with a small piece of luggage.

The photos were returned to the box and placed at the far end of the table.

She put the suitcase on the table and unzipped it, opening it before Bree.

On top was a small, blond doll dressed in a white seersucker dress with pale pink ribbons in her hair and darker pink rickrack along the hem and around the edges of the sleeves.

Bree breathed, “Penny.”

Zeke picked it up and handed it to her.

She was reluctant to take it, but the instant she did, she was flooded with images of the doll and her mother, even her father, in happier times. Hot tears streaked her face as she buried her face in the folds of the doll’s dress.

Pastor Buchanan stood next to his wife, his arm around her, their fingers intertwined, as Bree’s grief washed over.

Helpless, Zeke rested his forehead on Bree’s temple and held her as she cried.

Several minutes passed before the emotional tempest subsided, and Bree was able to wipe her eyes and quietly inquire: “What happened?”

Abraham sat again. “Your mother first came to us late on a Friday night, after your father left for town, presumably in search of additional drink. We settled on a plan. She left this suitcase with us; afraid he would find it. The following Monday, once Henry left for work, she was going to make her way here with you, and we would put you both on a bus for Montana.”

With hollow eyes, Bree’s voice was flat, “Let me guess, he discovered her returning in the dark from your house, accused her of having an affair with you, and beat her to death…”

“I do not know what transpired. That was the last time we saw Lila. When I went over there on that Monday, the house was locked up, both vehicles were gone. A few weeks after that, I ran into Henry in town. He was hostile, but when I pressed him, he said Lila had left him and taken you with her to parts unknown."

Chapter 47

Carrying the glass in her good hand, she carefully negotiated the stairs to the office. She found him on the phone, facing the window with his back to her. Hesitant to interrupt, she paused, enjoying his presence and the sound of his authoritative voice.

Sensing he was not alone, he slowed turned his chair to find her just outside the doorway, glass in hand, bright eyes, and a pensive expression on her face.

As the sight of her so often did, he lost his train of thought, as he greeted her with a warm smile. "Roger," he interrupted, "allow me to get back to you on that later this afternoon… thanks."

"I apologize for interrupting."

Continuing to drink in her appearance, he noted the oversized tee, sarong, and bare feet, which had become her default uniform in recent weeks, were replaced with a black fitted V-neck tee, jeans, and sandals. She displayed a hint of mascara on her lashes, as well as the briefest spot of her color on her lips. Instead of a messy bun or careless ponytail, her thick locks cascaded down her shoulders, which bounced as she approached.

Struggling to find his voice, he finally uttered "no interruption."

"Sweet tea?" she offered.

Dropping the phone on the desk, he reached for the tea with one hand and for her with the other. He took a quick sip before placing it on the desk and exclaiming "You make the best iced tea. Thank you."

She tucked her head, knowing it had been almost a month since she had last made any. With one hand behind her back and the other moving behind her knees, he easily lifted her onto his lap.

She did not resist and allowed him to cradle her, her head nestled between the crux of his shoulder and chin. His strength and warmth infused her with life. She counted fifteen steady beats of his heart before she shifted to see his face.

"May I speak with you about something, please?"

His eyes narrowed slightly, but his smile remained. "Of course."

She attempted to pull free and stand, but he resisted. At best, she could straighten and sit taller in his lap. She looked past his intense gaze and trained her focus on the window.

"Donovan called this morning."

He had heard her speaking with someone earlier. As Donovan was one of the few people in her circle, he had assumed it was him.

"What's he up to?" he asked cheerfully, but cautiously.

"Apparently," she sighed, "he has been delving into estate law."

His brow furrowed. He had nothing to offer, so he waited, noting her body had stiffened.

The nod of her head was ever so slight, he almost missed it.

"Yeah."

Silenced echoed between them for several more minutes.

"Did your parents have property?" he gently whispered.

Grateful his agile and rational mind was able to connect the meager dots she had provided. She nodded again, before inhaling deeply, exhaling, and returning her attention to the concern deeply etched in his face.

"With death certificates for each of my parents, he has asserted succession rights on my behalf. Thirty-something years ago, they bought that 500 acres west of town. The mortgage was paid a few years ago, and the taxes are current."

"Nice," he offered, while continuing to gauge her emotions. He noted she did not seem upset, just sad. In an attempt to cloak the narrative with positivity, he added "You are sitting on a pretty penny there, lady. What are you thinking?"

Her expression hardened with lines appearing across her forehead and her lips tightened into a thin line. Again, she attempted to disengage from his arms, but he persisted.

Locking eyes with him, she asked, "Would you think less of me, if the first thing I do is burn that house to the ground?"

His heart swelled as he sensed the closure and strength rising within her.

"I will pour the gasoline and hand you a match."

She studied him for several long moments, searching for the best way to continue.

He could see the struggle within her, but her expression relaxed only slightly.

"Once that is done, I would like a survey of the land. What is it called, the map thing, that shows grade changes?"

"Topography with elevations."

"Don't you or your brother have a drone where we can get aerial photos and superimpose them on a map?"

"Yes, but if you are going to sell the land, why go to the trouble?"

"Sell?" She asked. "Why would I sell? I'd like to see all that to determine the best place to build a house."

"Build a house?" His confusion was evident.

She shared a big, warm smile that revealed her porcelain and reached all the way to her eyes. "It's the perfect place to live and raise children, that is, if you will have me."

He blinked twice, trying to make sense of what he thought he just heard.

Suddenly shy and insecure, she bit her lip and looked down, toying with the buttons on his shirt.

He kept his expression even, almost stern, as he shifted and rolled them closer to the desk. Reaching into the right upper drawer, he withdrew a small square box and flipped it open with one motion to reveal a raised sparkling marquise diamond set in a platinum band with rows of smaller diamonds along the front and back of the large center one and down the sides of the band. It was unique and breathtaking. Instead of the diamond being set parallel with the length of her finger, it was perpendicular. She had never seen anything like it.

She stared at it in disbelief.

His voice was low and husky when he explained: "I bought this the Monday after our first 'date,' when we visited the architectural salvage auction in Georgetown. I knew I had found my forever. I knew you were the woman of my dreams."

He watched a single, fat tear escape and roll down her face, as he asked: "Will you marry me?"

She slowly nodded, as she cupped his face in her hands and kissed him as deeply and thoroughly, as she possibly could.

Bandera Bound

Book Two: Love in the Texas Hill Country

Coming Summer 2021

Chapter 1

The Gambia, a former British colony in West Africa, comprised scarcely more than a long, flat, and skinny country flanking the River Gambie. On the map, it appeared as though someone had stuck a crooked finger into Senegal, which maintained borders to the north, east, and south. The Atlantic Ocean to the west, was its only escape from the much larger country.

It had taken him eight days to travel almost forty-eight hundred miles. The first two were spent on various buses and open trucks covering the one hundred and forty miles from Cankuzo, Burundi to Kilgali, Rwanda. A flight from Kilgali to Dakar, Senegal ate most of the miles, but with two long layovers, it was another day and a half.

Dakar was a major port established on a sharp point extending into the Atlantic and home to almost 2.5 million people. He found the infrastructure well laid out, although the traffic and number of high-rise concrete buildings were vastly different from the mud block buildings he had been constructing in various locations between Tanzania and Rwanda.

From the airport of Senegal's capital city, he hired a taxi and headed to the Ngor area of the city, which comprised the westernmost point of the African continent. As they drove, he caught glimpses of beach and water as they wound their way west. When they finally stopped, he stepped from the vehicle with a sense of wonder. The ocean before him was a far cry from the land-locked and arrowhead-shaped Burundi, the poor nation just south of Rwanda where he had spent most of the prior year.

Grabbing his duffle and backpack, he paid the driver and

walked toward the beach in search of meal with a view. Within fifty yards, he was rewarded with both. Dropping his pack in an empty chair and kicking the duffle under the table, he sat down and inhaled the salt air as the cool breeze washed over him, grateful for the sound of waves crashing before him, which quieted the constant storm raging in his head.

∞∞∞

After two days enjoying the hospitality of a larger city and the comforts of a hotel room with actual hot running water, he ultimately decided to purchase a ten-year-old dirt bike large enough to carry him, his duffle bag, and backpack for 250,000 West African CFA Francs, the currency of Senegal and the equivalent of $450 greenbacks. He could have found a scooter or moped for a third of that, but he could not bring himself to do it.

The bike was nothing like the touring one he had in Texas, but he was grateful for the independence and freedom it promised. He was aware of the dangers of traveling alone; however, a year in country had drastically altered his appearance, as well as his mind set. He knew he continued to appear as a foreigner, but there was nothing about him which screamed tourist.

The 200 miles from Dakar into The Gambia was difficult with rough red dirt roads, potholes the size of a wildebeest, and several crowded ferries, but he had missed the joy in traveling as his own master.

Prudence had dictated a helmet with a full screen, despite the heat and his preference to ride without it. Once he was underway, he was pleased to have it, if only to protect the grin he had no desire to wipe from his face.

It was late afternoon when he finally arrived in Lamin, a village along the west division of the River Gambie, closest to his new missionary assignment. While stiff from the bone beating ride with such tight suspension, even at relatively slow speeds, he decided he had enough daylight remaining to get a feel for the area and secure lodging before he called it a night.

Following a cool night and gentle dawn, he woke restored and well rested. The accommodations near the river serenaded him throughout the night with the soothing sounds of gentle lapping of water through an open window. He was grateful for the sense of calm it had provided. Tossing the sheets off, he padded naked to the bathroom, catching a glimpse of a wild man in the mirror as he walked by. Turning, he returned to the sink and peered more closely at the reflection.

Other than the sharp blue eyes which stared back at him, he hardly recognized the image before him. He had not shaved since his last debriefing in Germany, after he left Afghanistan for the last time, which had been at least thirteen months ago. Neither had he bothered to cut his hair. Pulling on the ends of his beard, he realized it was three or four inches below his chin. His dirty blond hair once kept neatly cropped, high and tight, was at his shoulders in a thick, wavy mane. He had not yet resorted to a man bun or a ponytail, but if allowed to go unchecked much longer, he would have to do to something.

Checking his watch for the date, as well as the time, he confirmed he was well within the period he was expected to arrive, at least by western standards. He almost chuckled, on African time, he had another few weeks to show.

Chapter 2

She rose with the first light, although thanks to the anticipatory predawn crowing of the resident roosters across the yard, she had been awake for an hour. She did not mind, though, it gave her a chance to set her intentions for the day.

Making her bed as soon as her feet graced the floor, she retrieved the old sweatshirt from the chair in the corner and pulled it over her head. It was late January and still a cool 66 degrees at night and into the morning. She slipped her feet into her sandals and shuffled to the front of the building, which housed the clinic and the only proper bathroom in miles.

Relieved, she exited the front door, turned toward the east, and bowed, before inhaling and beginning her daily Tai Chi.

Half an hour later, she returned to the back of the building, plugged her kettle into the only electrical outlet in the makeshift common kitchen, and poured water from a jug into it. Dropping a tea bag into a mug, she exited the side door, and began searching out an egg or two from under one of the several laying chickens who perched in the yard.

She knew none of the chickens actually belonged to her, but there were chickens everywhere and few ever collected all the eggs, which probably explained why there were so many chickens...

Once her water boiled, she waited for her tea to steep, unplugged the kettle, and plugged in the hot plate to cook her eggs, pulling a piece of flat bread from a linen bag hanging next to the sink.

Her breakfast complete, she carried it over to the small table in front of the frameless window, sat down with her fork in one hand, and opened her journal. The calendar within it showed it was a new moon, which signaled the Lunar New Year.

Returning the fork to her plate, she closed her eyes, allowing her homesickness and the pain of separation wash over her. She gave up fighting it long ago, having learned to acknowledge it and allow it run through her without resistance. It did not mean she was immune to the pain, but it passed more quickly and with less effort.

Struggling to channel the energy and morph it into something positive, she asked the deities, as well as her ancestors to grace her with a fresh start and hoped for good things to come.

Closing the journal, she finished her breakfast, cleaned up her dishes, and prepared to shower.

When she emerged, fresh faced and wet hair plastered to her. She removed the towel from her shoulder and quickly ran it over her head. Using her fingers, she pulled them through her rather short crop, at least for a woman, and allowed it to finish drying on its own.

Donning one of her two pairs of cotton trousers, she pulled her arms through her bra and pulled it down around her, never bothering with the clasps. Selecting a long-sleeved linen blouse in tan, she slipped her arms in the sleeves and quickly buttoned it up the front, smoothing the wrinkles with her hands. She had not owned an iron in years. Checking her reflection in a hand mirror propped on the desk in her room, she consoled herself that the beauty of linen was that it looked better as the day wore on.

Smiling, she grabbed the pair of small pearl stud earrings from the bedside table and put them on. Her only other adornment was a single jade bangle she had worn continuously since she was fourteen, a gift from her paternal grandfather on her one visit to Taiwan.

Moving into the clinic, she tidied up. The open windows meant dust constantly blew in and coated everything with a thin, fine film. It was her routine to dust first thing in the morning, then again after noon. She was the only nurse at the clinic at the moment, but she strove to maintain some semblance of cleanliness, sterility was an impossibility in the clinic as a whole, although she kept her tools pristine.

Collecting the key to the supply cabinet, she opened it up and did a quick inventory. She hoped new supplies would arrive soon. She was completely out of vaccine and had precious few doses of antibiotics; however, she had plenty of material to treat superficial lacerations, malaria, and diarrhea. Anything more serious would require transport to a much larger facility. God help her if someone presented with a complicated delivery. She was not qualified for surgery of any kind and certainly did not have the tools or necessary equipment to perform one.

In the distance, the voices of the children, singing as they walked to school, delightfully carried to her. She knew most had been up and en route since before her roosters had begun to crow.

At the moment, classes were conducted in a large open area on the far side of the yard where poles had been erected with a canvas tarp stretched over them and tied down. This allowed some shelter from the sun. A single free-standing chalk board served as the only piece of educational equipment, aside from the two teachers. Perhaps, twenty children, aged six to fourteen appeared most mornings, with smiles on their faces and tin coffee cans with rope or twine handles carrying their lunches in their hands. Without books, paper, or pencils, most lessons were by rote.

Chapter 3

While he had detailed directions to the mission, in several places the road was little more than narrow tracks in the dirt, indistinguishable from lines cut by raging waters during the wet season and pathways worn by animals and villagers alike. It was clear most of the traffic in this area was created by foot, rather than any kind of vehicle. Trusting his inner compass and making note of the turns he had taken, in case he needed to backtrack, he finally made his way to the outpost in the, as yet, unnamed village.

There was an array of two dozen or more structures, each comprising little more than one or two rooms, and all comprised of hand formed mud brick. A few had thatched roofs, but the majority sported the ubiquitous corrugated metal. He had often wondered how and where the peoples across this continent were able to obtain it. They used it for everything from creating entire buildings, cladding buses, and lining showers, both indoors and out. He had even seen people cut hoes and shovels from it, adding tree branches as handles. Deep in the bush, he found men using it as a grill over open fires to on which to cook.

He smiled. The ingenuity of the peoples on this continent never ceased to amaze him.

He came to Africa because he had lost a sense of who he was. He had been afraid he had lost his humanity and he was ill prepared to return to his family and former life, certain they would soon discover he was merely an imposter, a shell of his former self.

In Germany, his brother Zeke had come to see him. A veteran himself, he came the closest to understanding the demons of the deeds, which hounded him, but even Zeke had not been called to the tasks he had. However, his older brother had a good idea the holes left in his soul, which needed filling before he could hope to return home. It was at his brother's coaxing he had decided to take a year or three; however long it took, to regain his sense of self again.

Africa had given him time to heal.

Time on the continent was a separate dimension than time elsewhere, particularly in the states.

There was the dry season and the wet season. The dry season typically ran from November to April in most parts of the continent. The wet season was any time it was not the dry season, but it was also bifurcated into two seasons: the major rainy season from April through June and the short rainy season from October to December, which just happened to run into the dry season. Of course, West Africa was different from most other parts of the continent. He learned from the locals the dry season was actually any time it was not raining.

When construction depended on mud bricks and mud bricks took twenty-one days in the hot, dry sun to cure before they could be used, dry season was the optimal time to build.

Western thought processes dictated most of the bricks needed for construction would be manufactured during the dry season.

However, African sensibility directed bricks were made as they were needed and when and if the weather and other responsibilities allowed. In a nutshell, there was no stockpiling of bricks during optimal brick-making conditions.

While initially frustrating, infuriatingly so, he had come to appreciate the ebb and flow of African time. He had no choice. It was simply the way of things. He learned things happened in due course and not a moment early.

He found the peoples of the continent with whom he had interacted shared a near fatalistic approach to things. There was peace in the moment. If it rained, there was appreciation for what the rain provided, rather than resentment of what the rain precluded, such as the curing of bricks. Flooding was accepted as an opportunity to replenish the earth with nutrient-rich sediment to fortify next season's crops. Everything had its season and things happened in due time, not to be rushed or perverted into something it was simply not meant to be.

Challenge and hardship were opportunities to reveal one's true character, and there were an abundance of opportunities with 42 of the continent's 54 nations considered impoverished.

It was Africa where he was able to recognize and jettison the preconceived notions of who he thought he had to be, which allowed him to discover, not only who he was, but who he was meant to be.

His soul and his life laid bare by literally waiting for mud to dry.

Chapter 4

By mid-morning, she heard the familiar whine and pop of Buck's ancient Range Rover in the distance. It had been several weeks since his last visit. She set the kettle to boil in anticipation.

The water was ready to pour as he drove up.

She greeted him from the door of the clinic. "Good Morning, Buck!"

He grinned at her from his ride. At least sixty, she knew he had been in country for forty years and guessed the vehicle had been with him at least that long. The top and doors had long since been removed, along with the front windshield. It looked as though he had driven under an exceptionally low bridge and had everything above the hood sliced right off; however, it ran and brought much needed supplies with fair regularity.

Alighting from the truck, he pulled the cap from his head, slapped the dust off it on his thigh, and gave her a sweeping bow, "Top of the day to you, Vic!"

"Tea first?" She inquired.

He grabbed a box from the passenger seat and carried it over to her before responding quietly, "Just a few special things first, my dear."

Taking the box inside, he quickly followed with two more.

She reheated the kettle a bit before pouring a mug for each of them.

When he returned a final time, he handed her a rough flax bag. Opening it, she found several items she had requested some time ago. "Oh, Buck," she breathed gratefully.

"Yes, it took a while, but there are a few things for you."

She took them straight to her room to enjoy later and came

back with an envelope, which she passed to him across the small table.

"Thank you very much!" She smiled.

Tucking it away in one of the many pockets of his cargo pants, he winked as he took a sip.

"Jasmine tea, my favorite."

"I do save the best for you."

"I see our builder has yet to arrive?"

"I thought he was not due for another two weeks."

Buck shrugged, "Western time or African time?"

She knew time was a relative concept on the continent. Yesterday could mean twenty-four hours ago or a lifetime ago. Tomorrow seldom meant the following day, and two weeks, well, two weeks was anything but tomorrow.

No sooner did she take a sip of her own tea, did the distant rumble of a motor bike alert them to a newcomer.

A known entity, neither Buck, nor his geriatric truck had stirred any curiosity, but the sound of a completely different engine roaring ever closer, piqued everyone's interest, including the school children. Their teachers unable to restrain them, they ran around the side of the building to peek.

Within minutes, the unknown man and his gas-powered horse pulled alongside the old Range Rover. He wore a black helmet with full face shield. From the long-sleeved canvas shirt neatly tucked into his khaki trousers, the hems of which were, in turn, smartly tucked into his laced boots, everything about him screamed virile western man, at least to her.

Killing the engine, he engaged the kick stand before standing and effortlessly swinging his right leg over the bike. His back was to her as he removed the helmet and placed it on the seat. As he turned, he pulled a pair of sunglasses from his breast pocket and covered his eyes.

He was tall and lean with thick and wavy dirty blond hair. Both his hair and full beard appeared freshly and neatly trimmed.

Despite the facial hair, she could plainly see he had a strong chin. Nothing masked the breadth of his shoulders, slim waist, or long muscular legs. A sucker for blue eyes, she silently hoped they were as dark and brown as hers.

She heard Buck finish his tea behind her and place his mug in the sink before skirting past her in the threshold to greet the man.

"How do you do, Sir? Buck Tralvaney at your service."

They shook hands, as the man's deep and low voice responded, "Samuel Buchanan."

She listened to Buck inquire as to his journey and saw the man nod. The dark glasses protected his eyes from the sun, but also obscured them. She was not certain, but she suspected his eyes were trained on her, rather than her companion.

Samuel nodded absently in response to the litany of questions posed by the man in front of him, his focus squarely on the woman behind him. Slight of build with short black hair, creamy smooth skin, full lips, and beautiful eyes, she took his breath away.

Stepping past the man, he advanced toward the woman, and removed his sunglasses to reveal deep blue eyes. Extending his hand with a smile and bowing slightly, he took a chance, noting her almond-shaped eyes and jade bangle on her left arm, "Nǐ hǎo." He greeted her in Mandarin.

Her eyes grew ever slightly wider before an enchanting smile overtook her face. She shook his hand firmly and responded in the softest, sweetest Southern accent he had ever heard. "Victoria Zhao, I am pleased to meet you."

"Samuel Buchanan, Ma'am, and the pleasure is definitely all mine."

∞∞∞

Made in the USA
Monee, IL
26 July 2021